"I'm not leaving tonight."

Abby whipped around to face Campbell. "You can't stay here."

"I can and I will. I'll sl̶... have enough room."

"It's not that."

"Then what is it?"

"It's not decent."

"What's not decent? I'm a friend of the family." The tension he'd been carrying relaxed in the face of her protest. "Besides, what do you think we'll be doing for the next week in Paris?"

"Working."

"Sharing a home."

"That's a setup. This is real."

At her use of the word *real,* a different sort of tension returned, desperate for release.

"You think so?" Before she could reply, he moved close to her, his hands on her hips as he pulled her into his arms. By the way she tumbled into him, clearly he'd caught her off guard.

Never one to miss an opportunity, Campbell leaned in and took.

House of Steele: Danger is their legacy. Love is their destiny.

Dear Reader,

I'm thrilled to introduce you to the world of the Steele siblings. Liam, Campbell, Kensington and Rowan established their company—The House of Steele—as a resource for wealthy clients the world over. As they fondly think of their offering—they can find anything, fix anything...or break anything.

In *The Paris Assignment,* sexy computer geek Campbell Steele is paired with beautiful CEO Abigail McBane. Abby's dealing with a problem deeply rooted in her communications company and as she heads to Paris for her annual board meetings, knows she needs help dealing with the nameless, faceless threat who has infiltrated her technology and has the ability to ruin all she's built.

What she believes to be solely a professional problem quickly spills over to her private life as she and Campbell discover her assailant has a very personal motive for doing her harm, even as he's targeted her company's upcoming launch of three new satellites into orbit.

The Paris Assignment is my first book for Harlequin and it's absolutely a dream come true for me. I've read the Harlequin Romantic Suspense line for years and count the books from the line among many of my absolute favorite reads. I can only hope *The Paris Assignment* adds to the rich legacy of Harlequin Romantic Suspense stories and finds its way into your hearts.

Best,

Addison Fox

The Paris Assignment

Addison Fox

HARLEQUIN®ROMANTIC SUSPENSE

Recycling programs
for this product may
not exist in your area.

ISBN-13: 978-0-373-27832-9

THE PARIS ASSIGNMENT

Copyright © 2013 by Frances Karkosak

Printed in U.S.A.

www.Harlequin.com

Books by Addison Fox

Harlequin Romantic Suspense

The Paris Assignment #1762

*House of Steele

ADDISON FOX

is a Philadelphia girl transplanted to Dallas, Texas. Although her similarities to Grace Kelly stop at sharing the same place of birth, she's often dreamed of marrying a prince and living along the Mediterranean.

In the meantime, she's more than happy penning romance novels about two strong-willed and exciting people who deserve their happy ever after—after she makes them work so hard for it, of course. When she's not writing, she can be found spending time with family and friends, reading or enjoying a glass of wine.

Find out more about Addison or contact her at her website—www.addisonfox.com—or catch up with her on Facebook (addisonfoxauthor) and Twitter (@addisonfox).

For Eric
The brother I always wanted.

Chapter 1

"We're not taking this job."

Campbell Steele stared at the travel itinerary in his sister's outstretched hand and wondered—not for the first time—how a self-proclaimed computer geek like himself had morphed into an undercover operative. He liked a good adventure as much as the next guy, but nearly eighteen months straight on the road with an array of jobs that boggled the imagination with human depravity was getting old.

Real old.

The success of House of Steele had surpassed every expectation he and his siblings had when they established the firm three years before and the latest assignment—a babysitting job for a rich heiress—wasn't high on his list of priorities. "I've made my feelings more than clear."

"And you know my feelings on work. We take it when it comes."

He made a valiant attempt to stare his sister down and failed miserably. "You look like Grandmother when you get all uppity like that." As an insult it was horrifically low, but the narrowing of Kensington's gaze had the desired effect.

"Here are your tickets. You'll meet Abigail McBane here in New York and then fly with her to Paris tomorrow evening."

"Because some disgruntled employee keeps sending her nasty emails? There's nothing in this for us, Kenzi. Her security folks should be able to uncover something as routine as this."

"There's plenty in this and Abby doesn't want this going through her corporate folks. That's why she contacted us."

"At least be honest with me. You're doing this as a favor for a friend, not because it makes good business sense. I could be helping Liam on that job in London or Rowan figure out her Chicago museum problem. Both need some serious electronics work."

"I've got them covered. Now." Kensington pointed toward the TV mounted on the far wall of her office as a series of photos came up. "McBane Communications had a seven-minute security breach two days ago when their entire satellite system was unreachable from their central command. None of her experts could get remotely into the system while it was happening. Nor could Abby and her electronic skills are rock-solid."

Campbell took in the images that flashed on the screen before coming to rest on Abigail McBane. She stood in front of a large backdrop, obviously speaking to an audience, her slender frame clad in a fitted business suit and sky-high heels. A lush fall of dark hair fell down her back while wide-set chocolate-brown eyes lit up her expressive face.

The entire package screamed professional and competent, yet innately feminine and he couldn't quite pull his gaze away fast enough.

"She's a beautiful woman."

Since Kensington always saw too much, Campbell deliberately turned away from the screen. "What else?"

"Did I mention her top security team can't find the breach?"

"Inside job?" The question came out, despite his best intentions to stay uninterested.

"Not on the surface. That's what's not jibing for her."

Campbell moved closer to the TV, the images pulling him like a lodestone. The damned Steele curiosity, he knew, even as he turned back to look at his sister. "They've got military-grade security. How else would someone get in? It's got to be an inside job."

Kensington's gaze was laser-sharp, the frank assessment behind her cobalt-blue eyes direct and unyielding. "Maybe yes, maybe no. We both know not everyone can be stopped with a firewall, even ones supposedly as impenetrable as McBane's. Or the government's," Kensington added for emphasis.

Campbell ignored the not-so-thinly-veiled jab at his youthful—and idiot-fueled—choices. "Seven minutes?"

"Yep."

"And her systems people have checked the code?"

"Forward and backward and there's no trace of tampering, viruses or remote entrance."

"She's got a ghost." Campbell knew the level of skills required for a job of this magnitude belonged to a handful of people. He ran through his mental list, discarding names as he went.

"Which is why she needs another ghost. One not employed by the company."

"There are traces. Somewhere, there's evidence in the system of where someone tampered with it. You can't divert that much equipment without leaving a mark."

"Exactly, Campbell. This isn't just me wanting to take this job for a friend." He saw the subtle pleading in his sister's eyes and wondered why she hadn't just started there in the first place.

He might enjoy riling her up and giving Kensington a hard time, but there was no one's opinion he respected more. "Fair enough."

"You're the only one who can find this problem."

He might not be the only one, but he knew damn well he was one of the few who had the skills to match a foe with this degree of systems knowledge.

He also knew Kensington's considerable instincts had hit on something.

So why was he still so reluctant to take the job?

He couldn't fully blame it on lack of sleep or a back-breaking schedule that invigorated even as it pushed him to his limits and beyond. Nor could he blame it on the lingering unease that never failed to tighten his chest when he thought about the threat that had methodically stalked and baited Sarah.

So what was it?

A security breach, conducted through electronic means and across a company with the size and scope of McBane's, was squarely in his wheelhouse.

Kensington pointed toward the travel itinerary in his hand. He saw the briefest flash of sympathy light up her eyes before it vanished as if it had never been. "Get your game face on. You need to be there in an hour. Forty-five minutes if you want a good seat."

Campbell glanced at his watch and quickly calculated the crosstown traffic between their offices and the Midtown high rise owned by McBane Communications. "It's just a press conference. I'll stand in the back. There's no rush to get there."

"I couldn't care less where you plant your petulant ass. Just get going. Find the bad guy and keep an eye on Abby in the process. Do what we do best."

Abby McBane watched her key staff members file out of her office, a well of suspicion hovering in their wake.

Was one of them responsible?

One of these individuals—all of whom she'd known for years. People she'd worked with. Shared holidays with. Traveled and ate with.

They'd all participated actively in their pre-press conference prep session and none seemed different. If anything, Abby knew, she was the one who seemed off, scrutinizing each and every one of them as she attempted to discern a traitor.

She glanced at her inbox and fought to maintain a spirit of hope that had been steadfastly missing the past few weeks. Only time would tell.

With a small sigh—one of the few she'd allow herself today—she turned back toward her email. A quick scan of her messages had her gaze alighting on a familiar name.

Kensington Steele. College roommate and the first person who made her realize she had more to offer the world than a smiling face and her family pedigree.

Abby clicked on the message, not surprised with the news.

He'll be there.

Of course he would be. Kensington always got her

man, from a series of hot and interesting boyfriends to capturing a surprising number of criminals to getting her reportedly stubborn brothers to do her bidding.

Her friend could kick the ass of the male of their species and have each and every one of them begging for more.

Why'd you stop taking lessons, Abby girl?

Deleting the message and tamping firmly down on those whispers of self-doubt, Abby grabbed her tablet and flipped through her slides for the press conference. The words floated through her mind as she pictured the various inflection points, the moments she'd pause and where she'd push through the dense information.

Her computer dinged like the final-round bell in a prize fight, signaling it was time for the meeting. She stood and smoothed her skirt, the tablet in hand and her stilettos sinking into the plush carpet as she crossed to the door.

Time to face the music.

Even if she had no freaking idea who was playing the tune.

Do what we do best.

Kensington's words still echoed in his ear as Campbell took a seat in the large auditorium that would house Abigail McBane's press conference. Despite his protests to his sister, he'd arrived early and taken a seat near the front, his long legs stretched out in front of him as he took in the room.

The turnout was considerable, a mix of press and Wall Street analyst types all anxious to hear the next big thing in communications technology.

While he'd moderately enjoyed baiting Kenzi, he'd done his homework, just as he did for every job they took on. McBane Communications was a global leader in satellite and communications technology. The daughter of the founder, Abigail McBane was reported to be cool under pressure and a highly competent executive.

Which meant she must be seriously running scared if she'd go outside her own security team—individuals who'd been vetted and background-checked—to come to Kensington for help.

A light hush fell over the room as Abby and her team crossed the stage to the podium. He mentally catalogued the line of executives that walked with her—men and women clad in highly conservative business attire—before taking in the woman everyone had come to see.

Abigail McBane.

That same fall of dark hair he'd noticed while in Kensington's office looked even lusher in person and high cheekbones framed her face with distinction. The V of her jacket revealed a smooth neckline displaying a simple strand of pearls. She was elegant and efficient, beautiful *and* businesslike.

And when she took a spot behind the podium, Campbell briefly registered a moment of sadness that the spectacular legs on display under the severe cut of her skirt were now hidden.

Just as well, he admonished himself. Between his unexpected resentment over the job and the quick lick of attraction that rode the back of his neck, he needed to get his head in the game.

He glanced down at the slim tablet on his lap, flipping through a few screens of data that matched the opening of Abby's speech. When he'd checked in, the corporate drone who'd greeted him had offered a folder of data or a secure site to download the presentation. Intrigued at the depth of preparation, he'd taken the electronic version and used the download code as his entrée into the McBane portal to do some nosing around.

Pleased when several layers of security prevented him from digging further, he admitted their surface protocol was as impressive as he'd expected.

"Which is why our new series of satellites, scheduled to enter orbit in the next quarter, will enable the next layer of consumer technology." Campbell allowed his attention to drift back toward the stage. Abby deftly moved the presentation through several slides, addressing the room with a presence that was as impressive as it was sharp.

He watched heads nod around him and caught the heated excitement of two people next to him as Abby wrapped up the presentation with the implications for the telecommunications industry. Hands flew up and questions buzzed from the floor as she moved into Q and A.

Again, he marveled at her smooth answers as question after question flew her way. From her impressions on the implications to wireless providers to an explanation of how each satellite would orbit Earth, there was nothing she couldn't answer. No topic she couldn't speak to with ease.

It was hot as hell, this incredible package of brains and beauty. Campbell felt his attention narrowing on the woman at the podium until a question from the back of the room pulled him from his thoughts.

"Ms. McBane. There are rumors you had a recent security breach of your satellites. Could you explain what that was about?"

The flash of anger in her eyes was brief—he'd have missed it if he weren't watching her so closely—but it was there all the same. "We have regular maintenance on all of our systems on a daily basis. It's routine to manage and repair any and all attempted breaches on our security, as anyone in our industry is well aware of. Hackers don't sleep."

"Yes, but there's a difference between offense and defense. Did you not recently deal defensively with a security breach of McBane Communications?"

Campbell turned in his seat to the smug reporter in the back of the room asking the question. Whispers and murmurs echoed through the room at the man's persistence.

"We have reviewed all of our existing security protocols and found no breaches into or out of our systems."

Campbell knew the response was technically true—the mysterious seven minutes hadn't yet been tied to any formal breach, per Kenzi's intel—but the damage had already been done. Hands were up and people were clamoring with questions, but she drew the presentation to a close.

"Your packets contain all of today's meeting materials. Thank you for joining us." Abby left the stage in reverse order of her arrival, the various members of her team following in single file.

Campbell didn't miss the hard set of her shoulders or the steady clip of her heels as she walked out of sight.

"Damn, damn, damn." Abby dropped her head in her hands as she stared at her laptop screen. Her head of PR had already emailed her with the name of the reporter who'd asked the question about McBane security, confirming what she already knew.

Dan Porterfield was a nuisance, but he was damn good at his job.

So who the hell had told him about the seven minutes? The information was on lockdown until they could figure out what had happened and the few members of her team who did know held positions of trust in her organization.

Could the one responsible have leaked the information?

And what the hell was she really dealing with?

Her phone rang and she snatched it up as her admin's name registered on the display. "Your three o'clock is here to see you. A Mr. Campbell Steele?"

Kensington's brother.

"Thanks, Stef. You can send him in."

With one last look at her computer screen, Abby tapped out a brief set of instructions that the party line to Dan or anyone else who asked was the same. There was no breach and there were no problems with their firewalls. "McBane Communications maintains the highest standards and layers of industry-leading technology," she muttered to herself as she finished typing the email.

Even if the sentiment didn't sit all that well with her— she *was* worried enough to call in an outside firm—they technically hadn't found anything newsworthy.

The door opened and Stef gestured the man through, before closing the door with a light click. Abby crossed the office toward him and took in a sharper-than-normal intake of breath as she stared up into a pair of blazing blue eyes.

"Mr. Steele?"

A smile that was too sweet to be fully cocky lit up the hard planes of his jaw. He extended a hand and she caught the briefest glimpse of long fingers and a broad palm before his hand clasped hers. "Campbell. Please."

Heat lit up her nerve endings, the sensation completely at odds with the purpose of his visit. She'd seen photos of him before, but nothing two-dimensional could have prepared her for this reaction. "Abby McBane. It's so good of you to come. Would you like anything? Coffee? Water?"

"Water's fine."

She retrieved a bottle for each of them before gesturing him toward the bank of couches on the far side of her office.

The urge to take the seat behind her desk and put some distance between them was strong, but the very fact she wanted to do that had her choosing the opposite.

The brief walk also gave her an opportunity to examine Kensington's brother. She'd met the oldest, Liam, once before, but never Campbell and she marveled at the distinct differences between the two men. While no one would miss the resemblance as brothers, Liam had a suave charm that was heady when fully turned on. Campbell had a more subtle attractiveness.

His frame was leaner and if she hadn't felt the strong grip of his hand she might have been tempted to call him skinny.

The memory of that masculine grip had her amending that assessment to lean and rangy as they took a seat on the couch. She watched him shrug out of his jacket and had to acknowledge he was deceptively larger than her first impression, his broad shoulders filling out his button-down shirt.

Oblivious to her assessment, he leaned forward, his hands clasped between his knees. Abby didn't miss the way his dress shirt stretched to accommodate his movement.

Nope, nothing skinny about him.

"My sister filled me in on your circumstances, but I'd like to hear it from your perspective. Especially since it was obvious the question during the press conference caught you off guard."

Abby took a deep breath. "I handled Porterfield's question."

"Yes, you did. Doesn't change the fact that he asked it."

"No. No, it doesn't."

"So why am I here? From your perspective."

"McBane Communications has several satellites in various stages of deployment, development and design. Per today's press conference, our latest designs are nearing the end of production and will be operational in less than ninety days."

"Anyone who wants to stop that from happening?"

The decidedly sensual thoughts she'd not been able to shake when looking at him faded at the problems facing her company. "I've got a select group of competitors and my competition is stiffer than most. The race for the latest modernizations has implications across the telecom industry."

"You think it's another provider?"

She shook her head. "The signature...isn't identifiable."

"Signature?" Interest blazed in the depths of his gaze and she felt herself drawn forward at his focus. Most—even members of her own team—tended toward a glazed look when she got going in the inner workings of her business, but Campbell seemed fully engaged.

Tamping the rush of interest that barreled through her own veins, she tried to focus on the point at hand. "Most major providers have a series of protocols in place. Checks and balances in their systems that make it incredibly hard to do anything undetectable. The sheer invisibility of whatever this was—"

"A breach."

She winced at that, more than willing to drop her

poker face. "I'm not ready to concede to that word. But to the original question, another telecom provider just doesn't ring true for me."

Abby watched as a series of emotions played across his face. Underlying all of it was that ready curiosity and sheer inquisitiveness that was intriguing. "So not a competitor. Anyone else who'd like to see you fail?"

She couldn't hold back the small laugh. "I'm sure there are several."

"Yes, but any of them who has a real reason to do you harm?"

The casual, almost sweet air she'd originally perceived was gone, replaced by a hard man without a trace of humor on his face. The lightning-quick change was as surprising as its source and she sat back and tried to parse out her whirling thoughts.

She knew Kensington Steele—had known her for over a decade—and had met much of the woman's eclectic family. Her Scottish-Irish grandmother and dyed-in-the-wool British grandfather knew how to leave a delightful—and altogether unique—impression and their smart, interesting and savvy grandchildren followed suit.

But she'd never met Campbell.

There had been whispers of trouble. Nothing that went public, but Kensington had hinted that her brother was too smart for his own good.

Was that the root of his computer abilities? And his very quick leap to overt threats to her and her business?

Add on the fact that he was the one assigned to her problem—a problem that originated in the rarified universe of computer security—and she couldn't help but wonder if Campbell Steele was the equivalent of fighting fire with fire.

* * *

Campbell didn't miss the assessing glances of the oh-so-intriguing Ms. Abigail McBane. He'd sensed a sharp, discerning businesswoman throughout her presentation at the press conference, but the woman seated opposite him was an intriguing mix of qualities.

Shrewd, yet perfectly willing to lay a few cards on the table. Smart, in a way that was approachable instead of stuffy and irritating. And very, very beautiful.

He'd been a student of many things through the years, game theory riding high on his list of interests. The choices someone made through a negotiation—and the implications of those choices—had always fascinated him. The average person thought of a negotiation as something simply to win, but the truly adept negotiators—the ones who most often got what they wanted—understood that it took some measure of give and take to net out in an acceptable place.

Abby was honest with her analysis and had also been more than willing to share it with him. So what was her bigger game?

And who was the nameless, faceless threat?

"I can't imagine anyone wants to hurt my business. Or me," she voiced the afterthought, in direct opposition to her drawn brows and slight frown.

"Yet you're sitting on a significant problem in your technology infrastructure. A problem—" he leaned forward for emphasis "—that has possible personal overtones."

"Why do you say that?"

"Why else are you looking for a resource outside your company to fix it? You clearly don't trust the people who work for you and have access to that technology."

The dark depths of her eyes clouded over with a noticeable layer of fear and Campbell inwardly cursed himself for his hasty words.

Damn it.

His brother, Liam, was the smooth one, not him. Why the hell had Kensington sent him into this job in the first place?

Despite his best intentions, Campbell knew his own personality swung more often to blunt instrument than suave operator. And now he'd gone and scared their client, five minutes into their first conversation.

"My sister often accuses me of being so narrowly focused on my goals, my manners suffer. I think this is one of those times." Campbell sat back, settling into the plush leather of the couch. "Why don't we start at the beginning and you tell me in your own words what you think is happening and why you felt the need to call us."

Campbell saw her visibly relax and he felt his own stomach muscles unclench a bit. Damn, but Kensington was right.

As usual.

His rush to solve a problem usually meant a polite facade and any lick of charm he might possess were nowhere in evidence. And if he peeled back the layers of the woman opposite him, it was clear she was more scared than she was letting on.

"Do you mean Kensington or your other sister, Rowan?"

Campbell couldn't hold back the grin. "Both of them, really. But I was actually referring to Kenzi. She's accused me of being the proverbial bull in the china shop on more than one occasion."

Abby—and that was the name he was fast coming to think of her by—cocked her head. "Oh, I don't know. You seem to be a man who simply likes to get things done. There's something innately practical and efficient about that."

"So now I'm a vacuum cleaner?"

A light flush crept up her neck. "I didn't mean it that way."

He shrugged. "I've been called worse."

"Well, I count practicality and efficiency as virtues to be celebrated, so please consider it a compliment." She took a deep breath, the light fall of her blouse fluttering around her breasts. "No matter how poorly given."

"Why don't we call it even and start over again." He leaned forward and extended a hand. "I'm Campbell Steele. It's nice to meet you."

She flashed a quick grin before extending her hand. "Abigail McBane. And likewise."

The feel of her hand in his registered somewhere in the middle of his chest with a hard swift punch as her palm rested against his.

Her deep dark eyes grew wide for the briefest moment before he let her hand go and Abby exhaled on a heavy breath before she sat back. "Okay. The beginning. As you no doubt know, modern business depends on the integrity of the services we provide."

"As does modern government, modern education and pretty much every other industry you can name in the technology-laden world we live in."

"Exactly." She nodded. "So to the point I made in the press conference, we maintain a very strict set of procedures for ongoing checks of our systems."

"Are the mysterious seven minutes the only breach?"

"Not exactly."

"You've had other problems here at McBane?"

A light flush crept up her neck. "Not exactly."

"Abby. What's going on?"

"I've had several attacks on my home system."

Whatever Campbell expected her to say, that answer wasn't it. "Your home? As in personal threats."

"Nothing as overt as a threat. Just problems. Inconsistencies. And a whole lot of attacks on my firewalls. I maintain government-level security on my home systems."

"How long has this been happening?"

"A few weeks. A month, maybe."

"Well, what is it? A few weeks or a month?"

"The first thing I noticed was about five weeks ago."

He shook his head, unable to believe it had taken her so long to do anything. "Why'd you wait so long to call us?"

The slight flush of embarrassment flipped to irritation in the blink of an eye. "I know how to manage my own affairs. I called your firm for another opinion. Kensington indicated you could look at our systems."

"That's my first priority but my sister led me to believe you need more than another opinion. I've got tickets to fly with you to Paris tomorrow."

"Yes, well, that was a bit premature."

Campbell stood and paced the office, the sudden wave of panic in his limbs forcing him to walk. He wasn't easily panicked, but he was well aware something that had escalated to her home was a different sort of threat.

It was personal.

The city spread out before his gaze at the window. He turned around, determined to make his point. And despite his earlier protests to his sister, suddenly very determined to get Abby to take on House of Steele to deal with her faceless threat.

"I don't think there's anything premature about it,

Abby." He crossed back to her, ready to sit and attempt to make his case when she stood, meeting him eye to eye.

Or as close as she could get to eye to eye.

Even with heels, her tall frame didn't match his own six foot two.

"I'm assessing your capabilities."

"Like hell you are." Campbell knew he had a competitive streak to rival an Olympic athlete's, but her words had him seeing red. Add on the image of her scared and in danger from some psycho and his emotions were far more raw than he'd have expected. "I can run circles around any problem you have. And for the record—" he leaned forward, unable to keep the disgust from his tone "—I'm not here to try out."

Chapter 2

Abby had heard the term "baiting the bear in his den" before—had even experienced it from time to time in difficult negotiations—but the tension that radiated from Campbell gave new meaning to the old adage.

With the focus she'd honed through years of boardroom negotiation, she pressed on and avoided thinking about how interesting it was to stare up into his eyes. "As I told Kensington, I've no doubt you're good, but the team I have in place includes some of the brightest minds in the world."

"And what if the problem is coming from within your organization? From one of those bright minds?"

"I'm well aware that's a possibility, but it still doesn't mean you're the solution to my problem."

She saw the light of battle leap into his eyes. "I don't think you've got a better option."

"There are always options."

"Actually, darling, I think you're out of them."

The "darling" had her snapping her mouth closed before she pressed on with the first words that popped into her mind. "I thought you were the mild-mannered one."

Although the sentiment wasn't all that polite, Abby was surprised by the hard bark of laughter that followed his raised eyebrows. "You've met my brother, I take it?"

"A few times."

"Liam's honed the dark and brooding routine to a perfect fit."

Abby thought about the large, imposing man who held a James Bond sort of sexiness to his demeanor and couldn't quite shake the impression that Campbell had been sorely underestimated if they gave his brother more credit. "You're no slouch. I've been in business long enough to know mild-mannered can be a rather effective strategy."

His smile was back but it bore the distinct notes of family baggage and sibling rivalry. "I'm well aware I have to work a bit harder."

As an only child, she was endlessly fascinated by family dynamics and the ways siblings related to and communicated with each other. Support and resentment, love and frustration and always—*always*—a fierce sense of devotion.

If she weren't mistaken, Campbell's responses about Liam held a lifetime of feelings toward his brother, from genuine affection to a dose of competition with a small dash of big brother hero worship on the side.

She dropped back into her seat, satisfied when he followed suit. Perhaps the clouds of battle had blown over.

With a firm voice, she tried once again to make her point. She'd always found that calm voice soothed a rowdy business meeting or a loud press conference, but, strangely enough, it hadn't been all that effective in soothing her nerves of late.

"My take away from my conversation with Kensington was that you'd come over here and evaluate my situation."

"Consider yourself evaluated."

His words—were they intentional?—had her fumbling briefly to stay on track. Perhaps she'd been too hasty in thinking the man lagged behind his brother. Where their approaches may be different, both men had a ready sort of charm that made a woman well aware she was being watched.

"Kensington leaped to the plane tickets?"

"Yes."

"I'm not sure why."

"I'd trust her instincts."

Abby tried a new tactic, willing the man to see reason. "Look. I've known your sister a long time. She's just being overprotective of an old friend."

"Since she has the irritating habit of never being wrong, I'd get on board with those instincts."

"Mine aren't too shabby, either." The quiet voice inside that had been questioning those instincts rose up to argue, dancing through the back of her mind on swift feet.

Why was she resisting the help?

Especially when it came from someone who was capable of understanding her business at its most basic level.

"I'm sure they're not. Which is why I can already see you relenting and agreeing to bring me on this project."

Abby held back the sigh, unwilling to give up any more ground than necessary, even as she admitted he was in the right. "Okay. Let's assume I'm in agreement with your capabilities. How do you propose to deal with this…situation? Kensington said she'd leave specifics up to you."

"I spent some time assessing your systems."

She glanced at the slim, high-tech tablet in his hands, a match for her own. "When?"

"During the press conference. Your firewalls are good."

"You tried to hack into my system during the press conference?"

"Yes."

His expression was so bland—so devoid of any bit of remorse—she had to take a quick breath. "Why the hell did you do that?"

"Why not? I'm here to find problems, aren't I?"

"Yes, but…" She felt herself sputtering to a halt. "You shouldn't do that."

"Do you think your competition is resting?"

"No."

"So I wanted to see what we're up against." He lifted the tablet with a slight wave. "Your security is good."

"Oh, thank you."

He tapped the screen of his device without looking up. "I heard those delightful overtones of sarcasm and snark."

"I meant you to."

He handed her the tablet and Abby was struck by the heat of his body that still warmed the metal frame. The brief moment of intimacy ran a line of shivers down her spine and she tried to shake it off.

"Look there." He leaned closer and pointed to a series of images on the screen, the same heat she felt warming the device now in imminent proximity to her body.

She pushed thoughts of heat and broad shoulders from her mind and nodded at the layers of commands and computer code that were as familiar to her as reading English. "The system's secure."

"Which means your seven-minute man got in a different way."

She sat back and gave the screen of the tablet one last glance before she met his gaze. "Why do you think it's a man?"

"A vague sense. And it doesn't mean I'm ruling anyone out at this point."

"Anything beyond that?"

"There aren't a lot of people who can pull something like this off. And while there have been some very successful female hackers, women generally aren't drawn to hacking like men are."

"Women have better things to do with their time?"

"Something like that. Add in a driving sense of anarchy and men have a strange affinity to the field."

"You seem to know a lot about it."

The ready smile and easygoing nature vanished. "I've had my career ups and downs."

Campbell had spent very little time thinking about past sins, but they weighed around his neck under the intensity of Abby's gaze.

He knew women talked and it would be stupid of him not to think Kensington hadn't shared some of his past exploits with her good friend. But even his sister didn't know the full depths of his past choices.

Only Grandfather had a real sense of what he'd done.

"I know there's a short list of individuals who have this type of skill. Does that mean I can rule out my staff?"

"Afraid not. In addition to creating a mess, anarchists have a rather sizeable affinity for mercenary jobs."

He saw her agile mind click through the implications of a mercenary-for-hire and the hope that her trusted colleagues weren't involved faded from her eyes. "So it just got more complicated. Not only are we looking for a responsible party, but we're also looking for the money."

"Yep."

"Well, Mr. Steele. It looks like I stand convinced. Consider yourself hired."

"Campbell."

She nodded. "Campbell."

"I understand your annual board meetings are in Paris this week. Any chance I can convince you to postpone them?"

"I'm not canceling them."

"Postpone, not cancel. Just for a few weeks until we have a sense of what you're really dealing with."

"I won't run in fear and I won't change my plans. We've got serious business to discuss."

Whatever fear he'd sensed in her gaze vanished at the implications she should pull back on her business. Campbell turned it over in his mind, again fascinated by just how sexy she was with this intriguing mix of beauty, brains and drive.

He'd always been attracted to strong women, having been raised around a group of females who could more than hold their own. He didn't care for weak people—regardless of gender—but he'd never understood men who found strong women a threat.

Campbell had always believed a smart woman was more than worth his time and interest.

Besides, what fun was life without a little challenge?

"Since you won't postpone them, it looks like you've got a travel buddy. It's a good thing I've already got my tickets."

"That's not necessary. You can do the job from here. Computer issues aren't location-specific."

"You don't want me along?"

"I don't want to put you out."

"A trip to the City of Lights is hardly being put out. Besides, the technology might not be location-specific, but your problem is centered with an individual. I'm not just digging into your computers, I'm digging into your team."

"Campbell. These people aren't just colleagues. They're friends. I've known them for years. You can't come in and start poking around. All of them are senior experts in their field and they'll suss out an investigation in a heartbeat. If—and that's a big if—one of them is responsible, he or she will be in the wind before you can blink."

"Not if I beat them at their own game."

He saw it the moment the words hit their mark, those lush brown eyes narrowing under the sleek arch of her eyebrows. "What are you suggesting?"

"The best hacks are a result of a whole lot of pre-planning."

"Social engineering the con. I'm familiar with it, Campbell. The mark is identified and a whole host of information is secured in advance before a single piece of technology is breached, like phishing scams for passwords."

Once again, Campbell had to admire her agile mind and deep grasp of her business. He'd worked with some of the best and brightest and few had such an immediate and intuitive understanding of the things he rambled off when setting up an investigation.

Pulling his thoughts back to the problem at hand and off of Abby McBane's perceptive gaze, he continued.

"Let's assume that's happened. Our hacker has manipulated a password or a key piece of data out of someone."

"Who? My staff knows they can't share that information. Even if they were attempting to be malicious, their actions within this building are monitored. Anything they do with a piece of technology equipment from this company is monitored."

"Just because someone's monitored doesn't mean your senior team had to give up the information. A lower-level person could have inadvertently allowed the break-in. That's what we have to find."

"I've got over twenty thousand employees. I realize we could likely narrow down a group of suspects, but the breach could be anywhere."

"Which is why we're going to social engineer a little con of our own."

Confusion and curiosity combined in equal mix across Abby's face. "And what do you propose?"

He wasn't sure where the idea came from, but the moment the words were out, Campbell knew it was the exact right course of action. "You're looking at your brand-new boyfriend."

"No way. Absolutely not."

"Come on, it's the perfect cover."

"It's so *not* the perfect cover." Abby stood to pace, unable to sit still any longer.

"Come on, Abby. As a cover, it's ideal. People will grant a dewy-eyed couple, wrapped up in a fresh, brand-spanking-new haze of passion quite a bit of leeway."

She came to a halt at his words. "We're not brand-new *or* spanking."

A light flush crept up her neck at the obvious gaffe,

especially as a decidedly naughty twinkle lit up Campbell's gorgeous blue gaze. "You know what I meant."

"I think I do but maybe you can give me a few pointers."

Abby crossed to her desk, eager to escape the sudden shot of sexual tension that gripped the room. Although her initial reaction to his idea was less than positive, his scheme actually had quite a bit of merit. Presenting a social front to her team would give Campbell the leeway to investigate behind a legitimate cover. Add on the idea of having an ally with her for the week of meetings in Paris—both with the board as well as with her key European management team—and she couldn't quite shake the sense of relief that she wouldn't be facing it all alone.

"Do you really think this will work?"

Campbell stood and crossed the room. Try as she might, she couldn't keep her gaze from following the long lines of his body or the competence that sat on his shoulders. "It's the cover we need to find who's doing this to you. And it will give me access in a way no one will dispute."

A light knock on the door broke the moment and Abby turned to see Stef opening the door and poking her head into the room. "I'm sorry to interrupt but you've got one more meeting this afternoon and your dress came for the benefit." Stef held a garment bag high.

"Thanks. Mr. Steele is actually joining me for the benefit this evening. If you could give him the details."

Her stalwart assistant simply nodded, as if Abby brought last-minute dates to every event. "I'll have the details for you when you leave. I'll just need your address, Mr. Steele, and we'll get the car service rerouted to pick you up."

Whatever surprise Campbell might have had was

masked behind that ever-present smile that managed to be an intriguing mix of endearing and sexy as Stef turned on her heel and walked out.

As soon as the door closed, he added one raised eyebrow to the mix. "Your date this evening? I assume this means you're fully on board?"

"Yes, I am."

"Then I've only got one question."

"What's that?"

Campbell moved up and took her hand in his. The moment his fingers brushed over her wrist her stomach cratered as heat flooded her entire body. "How did we meet, darling?"

Abby struggled to keep a hold on her emotions three hours later as her limo glided down Fifth Avenue toward Campbell's home in the West Village. Her stomach had continued its weird gymnastics routine since that brief moment in her office when he'd held her hand and try as she might, she couldn't get her emotions in check.

What was it about the man? He was attractive, certainly. And she was a healthy, single red-blooded woman who could appreciate a man with a strong intellect and a ready self-assurance that was confident without being overbearing.

But it was something else.

Like a good old-fashioned dose of sexual attraction, her inner voice piped up as she stared out the window. With the unfailing honesty she was known for—especially when it came from within—she acknowledged the sentiment. And then went to work debunking whatever insanity had gripped her since he walked into her office.

Campbell Steele was an enticing package. Altogether

too enticing, she quickly admonished herself. And, as of this afternoon when she'd signed off on the contract Kensington had sent over, he was also an employee.

"So get a freaking grip," she whispered to herself and turned toward the window in an effort to quell the feel of her hand enclosed in his.

The lights of Washington Square Park and the George Washington Arch filled up the early fall dusk as her driver took a right onto Waverly. The neighborhood was known for its effortless blend of old townhomes and bo-hemian apartments and she held no small measure of surprise when the car pulled up along one of the town-homes that ringed Washington Square Park.

She'd have pegged Campbell for the bohemian apart-ment, for sure.

Of course, the debonair man swathed in a custom-fit tuxedo standing on the front steps went a long way toward assuaging that thought. The nerves that had ac-companied her trip downtown took off on another flight through her stomach, but this time they were paired with a dose of anticipation as he beat the driver to the car door.

Campbell slid his long frame into the limo, the fad-ing evidence of a shower curling his slightly damp hair at his nape as he shifted toward her on the bench seat. The driver had the door closed and the light winked off overhead as Campbell's leg brushed against hers.

"You look beautiful."

That anticipation morphed another determined step toward infatuation as she allowed her gaze to settle on his mouth. "And you look very handsome. Not the bo-hemian I'd taken you for."

His lips quirked into a slow smile. "What?"

"When the driver mentioned we were headed to the

West Village, I pegged you as the resident of a bohemian studio for sure."

Where she expected a quick retort, instead a far more sober note tinged his face with the slightest edges of sadness as the smile faded. "It was my parents' first home. My mother's sister kept it until she retired to Florida and I moved in a few years ago."

Of course.

"I'm sure it's absolutely lovely."

Abby forced herself to keep the sympathy at a minimum, but knew instinctively she'd hit a raw nerve. Charles and Katherine Steele had been killed in a car accident a few years before she and Kensington became college roommates. Although she'd visited some of the family's other homes, the brownstone on the Upper East Side that now served as House of Steele's headquarters had been the most frequent destination. Even so, she knew their wealth had extended to other homes.

Other memories.

"What's that look for?"

She saw the question in his gaze before adding a question of her own. "I'm trying to understand how it is we've never met. I've known your sister for twelve years."

"I had quite a few years where I didn't spend much time at home."

"What changed?"

"A lot of things." He shrugged, the motion casual, but she knew there was much more behind his words. "I grew up, mostly."

"It happens to the best of us."

"I suppose it does." The shadows faded from his eyes, replaced with another vivid, killer smile. "You bring up a good point, though, which reminds me you never answered my question earlier. About how we met."

"I'll follow your lead."

"Nope. We need to be in sync on this, especially if we're asked separately."

The point was a legitimate one and she threw out the first thing that came to mind. "Walking in the park."

"Too cliché."

"Cliché?"

"This is New York. A lot of people meet in the park."

"Which would make it a logical way to meet."

He shook his head. "Nope. It's too efficient. You strike me as the type who pops in her earbuds, does her run and pays no attention to anything, or anyone, around you. Something else."

The urge to argue was strong, but she had to give him credit for being spot-on. "How'd you know I was a runner?"

"Those legs." His gaze roamed lightly over her body and she sucked in a breath at the electricity that hummed underneath her skin at the perusal.

"Hmm. All right. How about at a business meeting?"

"Nope."

"Why not?"

"Then people will ask what I do, leading to another lie."

Abby had to give him credit. What started out as a simple exercise was rapidly morphing into a more serious discussion where walking in unprepared could give them away. "What do you do, then? You know. If I'm asked."

"I'm in software. If anyone pushes any harder, say fractal wave patterns and it's usually more than enough to shut them up."

"You do realize fractal wave patterns are a legitimate, documented phenomenon in the financial industry. What are you going to do if you get a banker asking the question?"

"Ramble."

She had to laugh at that. "You do this often?"

"Often enough to know that people really don't want to know the ins and outs of a computer geek's mind."

"All right. Let's just say we met on an internet dating site and be done with it."

"I don't need to get a girl through my computer."

She shook her head at his sexist—and outdated—comment. "First, it's a perfectly respectable way to meet someone. Second, you do live your life attached to a computer. It would make sense."

"No."

"Fine. You've got a better idea?"

"We met through my sister. A simple family connection. It's not exactly a secret you went to Radcliffe. So did Kensington. It's a perfect cover and it has the added bonus of being one hundred percent true."

"If this was your goal all along, why not just say it?"

"Wasn't it far more fun to debate it? Add to it that you're far less nervous than you were when I got in the car and I'd say it was well worth the time."

And there it was.

That simple knowledge that he wasn't to be underestimated, under any circumstances.

He saw far too much and thought too much.

And most of all, he *saw* her. From the workings of her mind to her exercise routine, he observed, dissected and analyzed. It was unnerving.

Not to mention more than a little exhilarating.

"So what is this event this evening?"

Abby welcomed the change in topic as the lights of

Lincoln Center came into view outside the car windows. "The opera."

A dawning look of horror covered Campbell's face. "Any chance I can convince you to turn the car around just throw money at the event instead?"

"I've already thrown money at the event. This is the result."

"So they already got what they wanted. Let's bail. We can get a few hot dogs at Gray's Papaya and go to the movies instead."

"What is wrong with you? It's a few hours and a few arias. It's not that big a deal."

"Who's this evening's diva?"

"Carlotta Luchino. Why?"

"Don't say I didn't warn you."

Whatever questions Abby had at his not-so-subtle rejection of the opera vanished in the whirlwind of the evening. The requisite ode to culture only involved about three pieces of music and the swanky after-party kicked into high gear.

Campbell and Abby mingled with the evening's attendees, drinking post-performance cocktails and dodging requests for additional donations. He kept his hand steady on her back and played the attentive lover as he watched the room for any sign of the suspicious or out of place.

As covers went, he could hardly complain. He was sharing the evening with a beautiful woman. What troubled him was his inability to keep his mind on the task at hand.

Instead, his thoughts filled with her.

Abby, her long legs stretched out in the limo and visible through the thigh-high slit in her dress, so close to the tips of his fingers.

Abby, her lush mouth drawn up into a smile as she talked to the CEO of a key telecom company.

Abby, stripped from the long column of her gold-sequined gown, naked and willing in his arms.

Although he hadn't technically observed that last one, the image was crystal clear in his mind's eye all the same.

Conversation swirled around him, voices high and happy in the glow of expensive liquor when his gaze alighted on a man about ten yards away. Although the man stood in a group, his gaze was steady on Abby.

The intrusion was immediate.

"Champagne, sweetie?" Campbell leaned down to press a kiss to her cheek, whispering in her ear, "Who's the man at your three o'clock?"

Her eyes widened but it was the only evidence she was alarmed. Instead, she shot him a gentle smile and nodded. "Yes, I'd love some."

Campbell waved a waiter over and used the motion to cover her as she turned to look at the stranger. When the champagne arrived, she gave him a slight head shake as she reached for a fresh glass.

"I think I see an old college buddy. Would you excuse me for a moment?"

The CEO and his wife were well into the champagne and sent him off with jovial smiles as Abby resumed a story about her last analyst meeting. As the husky, cultured tones of her voice faded behind him, Campbell moved around the perimeter of the room, blending with the guests as he assessed the potential threat.

While he knew every man with a pulse had given

Abby a once-over since they'd arrived, the man's continued focus had Campbell's hackles up.

Which was the only excuse he had for missing the cloud of perfume and the voice accented with the heavy notes of Italy as two long arms snaked around his waist. "Campbell, darling. You're here yet you don't come find me."

A heavy pout pushed Carlotta Luchino's rich red lips into a tight line before she leaned forward and pressed them to his cheek. "You wound me, darling."

"Carlotta." Campbell fought to keep his gaze on his quarry but the opera diva's hands were too busy with holding his face still.

"I've called you."

"More than once."

"And now you've come to see me. Tonight. Clearly you have just been playing games with me."

"No games, Carlotta. I promise." He set his champagne glass onto a small tray with a heavy thud and was grateful the stem didn't break. With quick moves, he reached for the hands that cupped his neck and face, not surprised at the tight, determined grip.

"Yes, games. Always games with you. You think I didn't know how you wanted me? How you longed for me?"

Campbell fought the urge to roll his eyes as he tried to shift their bodies. Although he wasn't a short man by any means, her tall frame was augmented by five-inch designer heels and a dark cloud of hair atop her head. The combination of all three conspired to obscure his vision of the possible threat to Abby.

What couldn't be obscured was the cool, collected voice that resonated over his shoulder.

"Darling. Aren't you going to introduce us?"

Chapter 3

Abby fought the urge to clench her fists and wondered how she ended up agreeing with Campbell Steele's harebrained scheme to be fake lovers. What had seemed like a good idea at the time suddenly felt petty and childish in light of the barracuda wrapped around him.

As Campbell worked to remove himself from the diva's arms, Abby amended the mental reference to octopus. She was also more than a little surprised to feel a spear of jealousy tunneling its way through the center of her heart. Since the emotion was as unwelcome as it was unexpected, she pasted on a smile as she turned toward Campbell and the opera singer.

"Abby. Let me introduce you to the evening's entertainment, Carlotta Luchino."

Campbell wasn't kidding on the entertainment, but Abby forced every ounce of good breeding into her voice as she extended her hand to the singer. "It's lovely to meet you, Ms. Luchino. Your performance this evening was beautiful."

The woman preened slightly under the compliment and did release her grip on Campbell as he made quick introductions. Abby could practically see the question on the singer's expressive face as the woman's eyes narrowed. "You own McBane Communications?"

When Abby confirmed she was both owner and CEO, the transformation was nearly instantaneous. A broad smile covered the diva's face and she barely gave Campbell another glance.

Whatever else she was, Carlotta Luchino was a businesswoman and she knew the success of the evening depended on the generosity of its patrons. The hand she'd left on Campbell's arm fell as she smiled broadly and gestured to the room at large. "You are enjoying the evening, no?"

"Absolutely."

The lie tripped off her tongue as Campbell's freedom from the woman's clutches gave him the opportunity to resume his perusal of the guests. Although she hadn't paid any attention to her surroundings until Campbell had pointed out the man, it was all she could do to stay still and not go after him herself and find out what he wanted from her.

And why he was watching her.

When Campbell's scan of the room turned up nothing—evidenced by a slight shake of his head—he reached for her hand. "Carlotta, while it was lovely to see you again, I'm afraid we're going to need to get going."

Carlotta sighed, but Abby didn't miss the narrow-eyed gaze the woman had already bestowed on an aging widower standing at the edge of a nearby conversation circle.

"That was interesting."

"To say the least." Campbell tugged on the collar of his shirt and it brought a quick smile to Abby's face. While she knew it wasn't all that broad-minded of her, she couldn't quite shake the small stab of glee that he'd spent those last few minutes with Carlotta as uncomfortable as she.

And then he went still, his discomfort vanishing as if it had never been.

"What is it?"

"Your friend is back."

Abby fought the urge to turn around and instead, reached for Campbell's arm and forced an adoring tone into her voice. "Walk me toward the door? I'm in need of some fresh air."

He clasped his hand over hers where it rested on his forearm and she followed his guidance as they walked through the throng of partygoers. Her heels were high, but she couldn't quite see over the people milling around and she'd do far better to simply allow Campbell to lead her where they needed to go.

"Do you see him?"

"Yep. He's near the far side of the theater and heading for the stairs."

She felt the impatience in his large body and pressed a hand to his lower back. "Go. Don't let me hold you up."

"Stay here among all these people. You'll be a lot safer here."

"What if this guy's capable of real harm?"

"An even better reason you should stay. In fact, why don't you find security and suggest they head for the parking garages. I'm pretty sure that's where he's going."

The urge to argue was strong; the urge to follow him even stronger.

And stay or follow, it was more than a little unnerving to find herself left behind as he took off through the crowd.

She gave herself the briefest moment to watch him depart, his height ensuring she could see his head as he threaded his way through the crowd.

How the heck did I end up with a bodyguard?

The thought gonged long and loud in her mind as she moved in the opposite direction of Campbell and toward a couple of security guards she'd seen earlier.

The bodyguard thought continued to press at her as she navigated the jovial crowd.

She'd hired a computer expert, not a bodyguard. And now Campbell had placed himself in potential danger on her behalf.

She picked up her pace, moving to the perimeter of the crowd to find the guards.

"So here you are."

A flood of adrenaline rushed her system as Abby looked up into the face of the man who had been pointed out to her. With her only thought the safety she felt in Campbell's presence, she took off down a nearby well of stairs and her last memories of Campbell's retreating body.

"Wait!"

The heavy adrenaline rapidly morphed into sheer panic as Abby worked to keep her high heels steady on the stairs. She felt the man boring down behind her and let out a small scream when he reached out to touch her shoulder.

She had to get away.

Had to get to Campbell and safety.

She saw the gray-tinged lights of the parking garage spread out before her, the glass entry doors that separated the performance building from the parking lot propped open at the base.

The thought crossed her mind that Campbell may have changed course, but that fear vanished as she heard him scream her name.

"Abby!"

Scrabbling footsteps echoed behind her as the man pursuing her realized she had backup. He whirled on his heel, the heavy sensation of his body bearing down on hers vanishing immediately.

From her periphery, she saw Campbell change gears, moving from his path to intercept the man who'd followed her.

And then she could only stare as it all happened in a blur of motion.

Campbell's long strides had him easily reaching the man, who he collared and slammed into the nearest car, all in one coordinated move. He kept the man pinned to the car and a silent thrill rode her as she observed Campbell's predatory grace.

"What do you want with her?" The mild-mannered man who'd accompanied her to the opera had vanished, and in its place was a man who obviously understood violence.

"Nothing."

"Wrong answer." Campbell pressed harder against the man. "What do you want with her?"

"Nothing, man. Nothing."

"Who are you working for?"

Abby was torn between watching the exchange and running for help. Although Campbell appeared to have the upper hand, she was afraid to leave him alone. The sound of shouts and heavy footfalls ensured she didn't need to make that decision as two security guards barreled through the glass doors.

"Sir! Stand back."

The entire scene ran like something out of a bad movie as Abby watched the two men separate Campbell and the stranger, then drag both of them some distance from the cars.

"I've got credentials, if you'll just let me get them from my pockets." Campbell grit out the words as his gaze stayed locked on the man he'd had pinned.

The guard holding Campbell waited for a nod from his partner before agreeing. "Can she get it for you?"

"Abby?" Campbell's gaze met hers. "My inside front pocket."

Tension gripped all of them in tight fists and she made quick work of the job, reaching inside his open tuxedo jacket. As he promised, there was a small leather folder there and she pulled it out and opened it for the guard.

The guard released his grip and she watched, fascinated, as Campbell extended his arms in front of him to keep the man at ease. "You're in security?"

"Yes."

"You want to tell me what's going on?" The guard handed the badge back while his partner kept a firm hold on the other man.

Campbell provided a quick recap of events both during the cocktail hour and what led them into the garage.

"The man followed you, ma'am?"

"Yes."

The guy screamed that she was a liar, but it was only while he was screaming that Abby truly caught sight of where his gaze had landed.

On the diamond necklace that encircled her throat.

Understanding flooded her in a rush. "You're a thief."

"I am not."

"That's what this is about."

The accusation had little effect on the man's mood, but it was enough to shift the conversation with the guards to their favor as well as the two additional guards who came down after receiving radio calls.

Abby watched in bewildered fascination as Campbell worked the new guards, reconfirming his license and what had happened.

And she was even more shocked and amazed when, after providing their contact information only, they were both given permission to leave.

"How'd you do that?"

"The license helped." Campbell's hand returned to her lower back and he led them toward the waiting line of cars. "I also let the guard know you were a highly respected businesswoman under my protection. They'll follow up with you."

Campbell waved in the direction of the limo line and she saw a quick flash of lights from their driver. "Come on. Let's wait for him over here."

"Do you think they'll get anything out of him?"

"Where'd you get the idea he was a thief?"

Abby thought back to that brief flash of insight. It wasn't anything she could fully describe or explain, but she'd known the moment the man's gaze had settled on her neck that his intentions were about the jewelry.

She'd spent long years reading people and she couldn't shake the bone-deep certainty that had been his motive.

"There was an avarice in his eyes I can't quite explain. I'm sure once they run him it'll become more than obvious he was casing the event to set up a few jobs."

The car pulled around and their driver hopped out and got them settled. Campbell took his seat opposite her and she sunk against the padded seats, unable to stop the events of the evening from flashing through her mind.

"I'm sure the police will follow up, but I'll also run that guy through a facial-recognition program. If he's got any sort of a record, or even a whisper of suspicion around him, he'll pop."

"Good." Abby tried to shake off the lingering feelings of vulnerability that were as unwelcome as they were uncomfortable.

"And just to cover ground I know you'll be asked again. You've never seen him before?"

"No, I haven't. Which is more than I can say for you and the Sophia Loren wannabe back there."

Her own words surprised her but they had their desired effect as they shifted Campbell's focus. His grin was back, whip-quick and more than a little dashing. "You didn't believe me when I told you I didn't like opera."

"I assumed you didn't care for the music."

"Among other things," he muttered as he reached for his bow tie.

Abby held her tongue, the image of those slender arms and luscious curves wrapped around Campbell still haunting her mind's eye. Not only was the reaction beyond inappropriate—he owed her no explanations—it was damned infuriating to feel like the cuckolded lover.

Even if the lover part was imaginary.

"How about a drink? I want to discuss tonight as well as our plans for tomorrow."

She flirted briefly with turning down the invitation, but discarded the idea. They didn't have much time before leaving for Paris and there was still much to go over. Besides, her adrenaline was still so sky-high she knew she was unlikely to fall asleep anytime soon. "Where would you like to go?"

"The Four Winds is on the way to your home. It's dark, it's private and it's a classic with those big wide windows overlooking Central Park. Let's head there." After a quick set of instructions to their driver, Campbell dragged the tie from his throat, wrapping it up and dropping it into his suit pocket. A small patch of skin was visible at the open neck of his shirt and Abby felt her temperature spike another few degrees.

Their destination decided, Abby tried to mentally regroup. She *had* to get a grip on these ridiculous feelings. She and Campbell were going to be spending a lot of time together in close proximity and ogling her newly acquired business associate wasn't going to help her keep her mind on the game. Already tonight, she'd been more than surprised when he'd pointed out the steady gaze of the tuxedo-clad stranger.

She hadn't even noticed the man.

"What was your take on this evening?" She saw the bright lights of the Time Warner Center as their driver took the turn at Columbus Circle and she knew they weren't far from their destination.

"Aside from our criminal du jour, it was a relatively harmless evening. Lots of well-dressed people having stuffy, boring conversations."

"That's what you thought about tonight?"

"Sure. Didn't you?"

A laugh welled up at his frank assessment. "Well, yeah, but aren't we supposed to pretend we had a good time, drinking in the atmosphere and reveling in the talk of important matters?"

"What for? It was a bunch of privileged people standing around talking about privileged things."

She couldn't hold back her curiosity at the entirely unexpected shift in the conversation. "Unless I'm mistaken, that townhome we picked you up at smacks of privilege and wealth."

He shrugged, the lines of his shoulders stiff and uncomfortable as his gaze drifted toward the window. "It just seems like there's more to life."

"Is that why you do this?"

He turned back from the window. "Do what? The business?" When she nodded, he added, "Sure, to a point. It keeps me active and productive and it seems to be working if the profits we're turning are any indication."

"Did you ever expect your services would be in such high demand?"

A quick light sparked in Campbell's eyes and Abby didn't miss the clear notes of excitement there. "Nothing prepared us for the reaction we've had. We knew our parents' friends had the need for quiet inquiries into certain matters or help managing an enemy bent on destroying them, but we were unprepared for the response we've received."

"So you help the very lifestyle you disdain?"

"It's not disdain—"

Intrigued, Abby sat quietly, waiting for him to say more. She sensed something underneath his words she couldn't quite identify and for some reason it was suddenly very important to her to understand what drove him.

His words were quiet when he finally spoke again. "I want more out of my life than watching my stock portfolio all day."

"Your parents raised you and your siblings with a work ethic. There's nothing wrong with that. There's also nothing wrong with enjoying the fruits of your labor, however you choose."

"This from a woman regularly known to work ninety-hour weeks. Tell me, Abby—" he leaned toward her across the expanse of the limo, his voice husky "—how often are you enjoying the fruits of your labors?"

She could hardly argue with the assessment, even if it suddenly struck her as a rather cold view of her life. "I enjoy a full life."

"Outside the boardroom?"

She laughed, the sound surprising her with its hollow echo. "I lead a privileged life. I'm hardly in a position to complain."

Their driver pulled to a stop and Abby sensed their conversation was at an end. "Speaking of privilege, what you do does have a few perks."

"Perks?"

"You weren't exactly fending off the advances of a world-renowned diva, now were you?"

She purposely looked away from Campbell's widened eyes as the driver held her door open. Abby took the man's proffered hand and stepped from the car, satisfied that—for the moment—she'd had the last word.

Campbell walked behind Abby through the ornate entryway to one of his favorite bars, his gaze returning again and again to the long cascade of her hair falling rich and lush over her back. The woman was a sight and he couldn't quite shake off the small kernel of enjoyment that Carlotta had gotten to her.

He also thanked his lucky stars the diva hadn't ruined his cover.

Carlotta had a rather sizeable chip on her shoulder at her ill-fated seduction attempts and this evening could have gone sideways faster than a computer virus in a mainframe if she hadn't recognized the financial value in sucking up to Abby.

He could only offer praise to the few brain cells he possessed that he'd never taken the diva up on her more than generous offer—one given while stark-naked—the previous fall. She was an assignment—the victim of a high-end ring of identity thieves—and he didn't mix business with pleasure.

So why was he struggling to keep that in the forefront of his thoughts as he spent time with Abby?

And what the hell was he thinking coming on to her in the limo? He had no idea how she chose to live her life and insinuating otherwise was seriously out of line. Despite the knowledge he needed to stop this ridiculous curiosity about his newest client, he couldn't deny how the woman intrigued him.

Nor could he deny the overwhelming urge to wipe away the sadness he saw in the depths of her lush brown gaze.

He was neither a fanciful man, nor a poetic one, so the fact *that* thought even crossed his mind was proof positive he was far more gone than he'd realized.

The hostess led them through the bar to a prime seat in front of the oversize windows. The south entrance of the park sat open before them and he could see several horses with their riders waiting to ply their trade.

With deliberate movements, he slung an arm around Abby's shoulders once they were settled on a small high-backed settee before the window.

"There's no one here," she hissed as she looked up at him.

"What's the matter? Not enjoying my company?"

"That's not what I meant. The event is over and we're

not on display any longer. You said the evening didn't seem out of the ordinary."

His impressions earlier in the day as well as observing her throughout the evening were one of a woman used to being in control. Add on her comments in the car when he tried to probe deeper and he knew she wasn't used to giving up one precious bit of that power.

Whether it was his own stubborn, subversive nature that his family regularly cursed him for or the fact that the woman tantalized him like no other he wasn't sure, but he couldn't resist baiting her.

"Just because the evening didn't *seem* out of the ordinary didn't mean there wasn't anyone watching. Nor does it mean we don't need practice for our trip to Paris."

"Practice?"

"Of course. People have to believe we're really together. If a few drinks together can't loosen us up, there's no way we're going to convince a room full of people who've known you for years that we're an item."

"They'll just think we're not a very affectionate couple."

The pert retort gave him the exact opening he needed. With deliberate slowness, Campbell leaned in, pressing his lips toward her ear. "Like anyone would believe you could be cold and indifferent in a relationship."

"There's cold and indifferent and then there's wildly inappropriate. I wouldn't be inappropriate at a business function."

Her spine was arrow-straight and her face was a mask of that indifference he'd accused her of and suddenly, despite the fact she was a client, he simply couldn't resist seeing where she was willing to take things. With deliberate slowness, he ran a finger down the length of her forearm, the soft feel of her skin beckoning him. "Shame."

"Wh-what's a shame?" Her voice was breathless as he trailed his finger once more over that delicate skin, turning her hand over so the expanse of her wrist was bare to him.

"It's a shame that you wouldn't allow even the tiniest bit of passion to make its way into your business meeting."

"The boardroom's not the time or place."

"I suppose you're right." With a quick shift, he put some space between them as their waitress came over to take their drink orders. He gestured Abby to go first, then ordered his standard whiskey and soda.

And settled back to see what move Ms. Abigail McBane decided to make next.

"Don't think I'm not on to your game."

Campbell's gaze was diverted as he scanned the room but his words held no hesitancy. "I've no doubt you are."

Yet again, Abby felt herself caught off balance as he fully acknowledged what had roared to life between them. "Oh."

He finished his perusal and turned the full power of that vivid blue gaze on her. "We're attracted to each other. It's a wee bit inconvenient, but some of the best things in life are."

She watched his face in the subdued lighting of the bar, curious at the mix of ennui and matter-of-fact sincerity in his tone. "You're rather practical."

"There's that word again. I just prefer to think of myself as honest." He reached for a pretzel nestled in a small silver bowl on the small cocktail table between them and popped it in his mouth. "There's a difference."

"Honest? You know all about the inner workings of computer fraud and high-level hacking. Isn't that a bit like saying the fox should have access to the henhouse?"

"It all depends?"

"On what?"

He leaned in once more and Abby couldn't fight the delighted shiver that raced down her spine at the warmth emanating from his body. "Whether or not you open the door."

A discreet cough from their waitress caught Abby's attention and she watched as the woman set down a glass of cabernet. Abstractly, she wondered if the wine matched the flush trying to work its way across her face.

Why was she so upside down over this man? She'd attended meetings with the President of the United States, damn it. She could do this.

Even more important, she *had* to do this.

This strange attraction might have thrown her for a loop, but she'd be damned if she were going to behave like she was a slave to her body. This was a business arrangement and it was time to start treating it like one. She waited until their waitress left them before pushing their conversation back onto safer ground. "I'm on the committee for the opera charity. I can probably get a list of attendees tonight if you think you could do something with that."

He took a sip of his drink before setting it down. "Good. That'll save time and I'll run it against a few of the databases I'm pulling from your systems. I set a few other things up to run overnight and I can look at the data in the morning."

"You were busy this afternoon."

He shrugged. "A few simple programs to begin organizing your staff lists. I'll take it up a few notches after we get to Paris and get set up at your offices there."

"I can get you access to the Paris office but I won't be able to join you. I'm holding the meetings at my home."

Her words hit a mark she wasn't even aiming for as he put down his glass without even taking a sip. "You can't be serious."

"Of course I am. I use this week of meetings to entertain and I always do it from my home. It's more personal that way."

"Abby. You're dealing with a security breach that may have originated with your staff. You can't put yourself at risk like that." All hint of teasing and innuendo was gone as he stared at her with that stark blue gaze.

"Nothing's going to happen in my home. And no one stays there. They're brought in from a nearby hotel."

"Doesn't change the fact they're there for hours on end. Do you have any idea how easy it will be for someone to slip away for a few minutes and get a sense of the house?"

Abby had been diligent about tamping down her own sense of paranoia, unwilling to allow the out-of-control feelings to invade her annual meeting plans and in a few brief moments, Campbell had managed to bring them welling right back up to the surface. Forcing a sense of bravado into her tone she didn't really feel she pushed back. "It can't be that bad. I'll add some additional security detail."

"So you have some? At the house now?"

"I have a state-of-the-art alarm system, installed a year ago, and maintained with monthly software upgrades."

He was already reaching for his phone when she stilled his arm. "What are you doing?"

"Getting someone in there now. You can't just rely on the technology, especially if the person we're dealing with has the skills we suspect."

"There's nothing to be done for it tonight, Campbell."

"It's five in the morning in Paris and the best don't sleep anyway. I want a team in there immediately and I want the house swept for devices and bugs before you arrive tomorrow."

"It's a good system. Custom designed." She couldn't resist adding that last bit, more than a little embarrassed to have her ability to protect herself found lacking.

His eyebrows rose at that as he reached for his whiskey once more. After a hearty sip, he turned toward her. "I'm not trying to scare you, Abby. Believe me, that's the last thing I want to do, but I don't understand why you aren't taking this seriously. You were concerned enough to call my sister to secure our help. Add on you can't account for a significant problem in your security protocols."

"I am taking this seriously." She snapped out the words. "I've been through this before and it was nothing. I'm not going to look like I'm crying wolf and running around like a helpless little woman. I won't do that again."

His already sharp gaze grew even more pointed. "What the hell is that supposed to mean?"

"Nothing. It was a long time ago."

"Then why'd you say it?"

She took a deep breath, willing her raging emotions to cool. Why had she even mentioned it? She wasn't helpless. She was a strong, resourceful woman and she knew how to take care of herself.

So why the hell couldn't she find her balance?

"I don't want to live in fear. That's not a way to live."

"No, it's not. But ignoring the problem isn't going to make it go away. And ignoring the true root of your feelings isn't helping, either." When she remained silent, he pressed on. "So what happened?"

"I had an incident about a year after college—almost seven years ago, I guess. I was assigned to our London office and one of my coworkers took an inappropriate shine to me."

Campbell nodded, the hard set of his jaw tight as he listened to her story.

"It was little things at first. A few emails. Mutual trips in the elevator as I was leaving. Then it got worse with a visit to my flat."

"What did you do about it?"

"Gently rebuked his interest at first. Then more forcefully when he wouldn't take the hint."

Although time had faded the memories, Abby was surprised by how quickly she could pull it all back. "I escalated it up when it became evident he wouldn't stop and Human Resources took care of him. European employment laws are different than the U.S. but the owners' daughter gets a bit of extra special attention. It was all a moot point in the end."

"Why's that?"

"He was found dead about two weeks after the human resources department arranged for his departure."

"Did you investigate it?"

"Of course. Nothing turned up and the cause of death was ruled a heart attack."

"How old was the guy?"

"About thirty."

"And you didn't find a heart attack suspicious?"

"It was ruled a condition from birth. One of those strange circumstances of nature."

Campbell's intense focus—complemented by a heavy dose of skepticism at the story of the man's death—had her rethinking the incident in light of her current situation.

Was it possible there was a connection, even a distant one?

"And you've never dealt with anything else?"

"You mean other than the routine, vitriolic letters that come into the McBane press office, suggesting I'm the spawn of Satan for running a company that sends satellites up into orbit?"

"Something like that."

"Then no. Nothing has happened since London." She hesitated, the need for reassurance warring with the concern that she was just being silly. "Do you think there's a chance they could be connected?"

"I think I'm glad you told me about it so we can rule out any connection." Campbell reached for her hand, his voice thick with the shades of his whiskey. "I'm not going to let anything happen to you, Abby. You do believe me?"

"Yes."

His fingers returned to the sensitive skin of her wrist and he rubbed gently against the small space with the pad of his thumb. Desire wrapped around her with sly tendrils, soft fingers of need that beckoned her toward him. The urge to simply lean forward and kiss him—to find out if the strength she sensed in him would follow through to his ability to draw a response from her—had her nearly acting on the impulse.

In the split second between desire and action, the bar exploded in confusion. The heavy, unmistakable sound of a gunshot echoed through her ear as the window opposite them exploded into a million pieces.

Chapter 4

Shouts erupted through the bar as Campbell threw himself over Abby's body. The soft velvet of the settee rubbed his cheek as he waited on that tender precipice between immediate action and a rational hesitance to see if there'd be another shot.

"Let me up." She struggled underneath him, pushing at his shoulders as she used the silk of her dress to slide off the settee.

"Abby. Wait a minute."

"Come on." Her voice was distracted as she fumbled with her small clutch, dragging a dark clump of something squishy from its depths.

"What's that?"

"More comfortable shoes." She bit out the words as she switched out the sky-high heels on her feet for something that looked like ballet slippers. "Come on."

With moves a sprinter would admire, she leaped

through the broken window and was already weaving herself across traffic as she raced toward the park.

"Abby!" His voice echoed in his ears, still sensitized to the heavy gunshot, but she never turned as she raced past one of the horse-drawn carriages that rimmed Central Park.

The driver had his buggy whip extended, pointing toward a darkened path into the park as Campbell flew past him. "He went that way. And so did she!" the guy added for good measure.

Even if his hearing wasn't functioning optimally, Campbell couldn't have missed the body language if he'd tried.

Although she had the advantage of surprise and a good fifteen seconds on him, he gained on her with little effort, his six-foot-two-inch frame—most of which was legs—eating up the ground.

Without stopping, Campbell bypassed her and used his lead to follow a distant figure who darted in and out of the shadows up ahead.

The late hour ensured they didn't meet too many people, but the gunman had time on his side. Every few yards, Campbell could have sworn he heard the pounding of feet, but the sounds were rapidly absorbed by the abundance of trees surrounding the path.

New Yorkers loved their park for its capacity to drown out the sounds of the city but it was that same ability that finally had Campbell ending the foot race.

"Is he gone?" Abby's breathless voice assaulted him from behind as she drew up to his side.

"Yeah." Frustration and anger built in his chest before it burst forth at a handy target. "What the hell were you thinking?"

"What?"

Adrenaline added its powerful punch to the mix and he hauled her up against his side, the urge to protect overpowering the barely veiled urge to shake some sense into her. "Running off like that. After some bastard who'd just fired a damn gun on you."

"I told you. I'm not a victim."

"You're damn well going to be if you go chasing off after armed men."

The absolute lack of apology in her upturned face had a renewed wave of irritation flooding his veins before it was replaced with the fleeting thought that the woman was a formidable opponent.

And altogether too sexy for her own good.

Awareness sparked in the dark depths of her eyes as she stepped back, the sudden shift between them heady and immediate.

His gaze dropped to the rest of her body. The silly slippers—and who carried slippers in their purse?—still covered her feet, capping off a pair of spectacular legs.

"Where'd you get that sort of jump? And how does a CEO get legs like those? I suppose I didn't miss the mark earlier when I called you a runner?"

"Three miles a day since I was fifteen. Five on Saturday and Sunday." Pride steeped her tone, but something else hovered underneath it. Was it a light sheen of regret? No, he quickly amended as he hit on the answer. That tone held the distinct notes of sadness.

"Well, it clearly does a body good. I knew your legs were spectacular, but watching them eat up the ground was an altogether invigorating experience."

"Thanks. I think."

"Oh, no, thank you." He reached for her hand to pull her back along the same path they'd raced over in pursuit of their quarry. "So why does all that running make you sad?"

The slim shoulders underneath his arm stiffened but she continued moving forward without the slightest hitch in her step. "Running gives you endorphins. You can't be sad with endorphins."

"Could have fooled me." He glanced down at her profile where she stared straight ahead, the park lamps lighting the outline of her face.

Police lights were visible in the distance—no doubt already parked in front of the bar securing statements from witnesses—and Campbell wanted to avoid them altogether. "Were you all that fond of those stilts you wore tonight?"

"My shoes? Of course I'm fond of them. They were part of this year's fall collection from my favorite designer and tonight was the first time I wore them."

He let out a long-suffering sigh. "Deliver me from women and their shoes."

"You asked."

"I need you to give them up to the cause."

"What cause? Those are really fabulous shoes."

"Fleeing the scene of the crime. Let's avoid the bar and exit out of the park onto Fifth in front of the Plaza."

Her gaze alighted on the flashing lights and he heard the ready agreement in her town. "Those shoes are a small price to pay for avoiding suspicion and wasting several hours neither of us has. Besides, we'll let them be a reward for some poor woman who doesn't get to escape our fate and has to sit and answer questions for the next three hours."

"That's my good little CEO. Altruistic yet crafty. It's an admirable combination."

Her smile was bright under the streetlamps as she stared up at him. "You ain't seen nothing yet."

Whatever impression she'd had of Campbell Steele at three o'clock that afternoon had been turned on its ear more times than she could count in the ensuing eight hours. From the earnest and somewhat playful computer geek to society rogue and seducer to predator after its prey, Campbell had shown an endless array of facets.

Abby suspected it was what made him so good at his job. She also suspected it was part of a bigger personality trait.

The effortless ability to fit into any situation all the while leaving nothing of himself behind.

Although she'd never met him before today, she knew the rest of Kensington's family. Liam was the oldest, Kensington and Rowan the two younger girls and Campbell took the spot above them. An older brother and younger brother, all at the same time.

It was an interesting position, she mused, to have both familial leadership while never being the true top dog. If her observations through the years were correct, the Steele siblings were each other's fiercest champions and most wicked adversaries.

And they all had a bond that went well beyond mere family ties when they'd all borne the horrible price of losing their parents at a young age. Whatever the Steele siblings might have been, the death of their parents had the strange consequence of pulling them close while driving an inconsolable wedge of resentment that split them into four equal parts.

They each had a mysterious ability to stand out all while morphing into whatever image the viewer wanted to make of them and Abby suspected it was a skill they'd first honed with each other.

She'd certainly seen Kenzi do it time and again at school. The shy debutante their freshman year at Radcliffe. The daring bad girl who knew how to secure cigarettes and liquor every weekend. The sexual temptress who drove the boys crazy with interest.

All were her yet, Abby had always thought, none were her.

And it seemed as if her brother had the same trait in spades.

"Why do you think I'm sad?"

"I read people, Abby. And I know how to look beneath the surface. It's what I do."

A heavy laugh leaped to her lips, unbidden. "It's widely believed I have no depths at all. Many an article have suggested it's the loss of my mother at a very early age, the loss of my father early in my tenure at the company and 'my sharp mind coupled with a tireless drive to succeed' that have made me a cool, aloof, somewhat soulless leader who doesn't suffer fools."

"Why suffer fools?"

She wrapped her shawl around her shoulders, surprised the thin cashmere had made the rough-and-tumble journey. She'd had the material fisted in her hands with the clutch and it was amusing to realize she still held both. "Exactly."

"But I don't think it's those fools who make you sad when you run."

He settled his hand on her back, the heat of his fingers warming her in the evening breeze of early fall. Although the thin shawl had cut the breeze, Campbell's hand brought the true warmth.

"It's my mother. She's why I'm sad when I run."

He moved his hand in simple, even strokes along her spine, the light touch conveying any number of thoughts without words.

Support.

Understanding.

Comfort.

"She died when I was little. I barely even remember her, truth be told. But several years after her death my father was remarried for a few years."

"Stepmonster?"

"Pretty much. Add on, she was my stepmonster for those delightful years between thirteen and seventeen and you have a recipe for disaster."

"Only four years?"

"She and my father couldn't stand each other much past that."

He nodded but avoided the usual platitudes she'd grown used to hearing about the perils of a "trophy wife." "So what happened?"

"I'd put on weight going through puberty and was a bit chunky by fifteen. At that time I'd also developed quite the vocabulary and was openly defiant to said stepmonster and what I believed was her love of my father's bank account."

Abby mulled over the right words, suddenly feeling as clumsy as she did that terrible, awkward summer.

"I also had an unrequited love that took up every ounce of my time, energy and a mountain of tears sobbing that his feelings weren't the same."

"Love and loss in the American high school. I had a few of those myself."

"You? Campbell Steele of the legendary Steele family? Grandchild of one of Britain's most famous parliamentarians and a regular attendee of garden parties at Buckingham Palace?"

He snorted at that. "Like I'd have told anyone I attended garden parties. Besides, I was a beanpole for all four years of high school. Why else would I like computers so much?"

"Ah, yes. It's almost Dickensian in its simplicity. Our greatest sorrow leads to our deepest joy."

"Something like that. Of course, this beanpole became rather popular junior year when he hacked into the school's computers and changed a grade for a poor beleaguered cheerleader."

"You did not."

"I most certainly did. It was my first glorious foray into hacking and, to be fair, her D in chemistry wasn't deserved. But this story isn't about me. Back to that unrequited love."

"Gina and I had been fighting pretty much every day at that point. And I was invited to a party where said unrequited love was sure to be in attendance. She bought me an outfit for the event. Something that was intentionally unflattering and I didn't realize it until I got there."

"You didn't put it on ahead of time?"

Even now, more than a decade and a half later, Abby remembered that moment. The sheer panic of being caught off guard. And the absolute pain of being found lacking. "It was a slumber party for the girls and we were getting our nails and hair done during the day. So she packed my bag and I wore jeans and a T-shirt for the prep."

"And it was only when you got to the party that you realized the outfit didn't fit."

"Exactly. We fought about it later and she point-blank admitted to doing it. Said I needed to learn a lesson."

"Hardly." The word dripped with anger, matching the stiff set of his body. "You were a child and that wasn't a lesson anyone needs to learn."

"On her best days, Gina was never going to make stepmother of the year, but that one was particularly bad, even for her. So the next morning, I walked to the park and started running. I've never looked back."

Abby knew she'd lucked out. Gina's intentions had been cruel, but she could have ended up with an eating disorder. Instead, she'd simply learned to channel her pain and anger into something more productive, allowing her body to grow stronger as the distance between her and her father grew larger.

"So why are you still sad?"

"I started running with the intention of losing weight and that part came rather quickly."

"But?"

"The lost pounds were only a side benefit. No matter how many miles I run, I always come back to the same set of problems."

"They don't go away, no matter how far we run. They just hang around until we deal with them."

The comprehension in his gaze caught her up short and again, she saw a real understanding in those blue depths. While she knew she wasn't the only one who'd dealt with grief in her life—and diligently fought the urge in her quiet moments of solitude to give in to feelings of gloom or self-pity—Abby also knew few people were without both parents in their early thirties.

Yet here they both were, in the same position.

It was a strange bond, but it was one all the same.

And no matter how she fought the moments of self-pity, she also knew she lived with the very real circumstance that she didn't have a parent to fall back on.

A listening ear who was absolutely and completely on her side.

The press was fond of calling her a soulless leader, but she knew better.

When she walked into a boardroom, she was alone. When she traveled, she was alone. And when she went home at night, she was alone.

So why couldn't she shake the feeling, staring into Campbell Steele's eyes, that she wasn't quite so alone anymore?

The gunman moved through a darkened path in Central Park, the smell of fall in the air on the late-September evening as the distant whir of police sirens pulsed in the distance. The job had been an easy one—he was meant to cause confusion, but no real harm.

The chase was as unexpected as it was exhilarating.

As jobs went, he'd taken this for the pay, but knew full well the purposeful lack of action was a disappointing detail he'd have to accept.

The fact the hellcat gave chase was almost too delicious for words. Add on the unexpected new boyfriend and nothing about this job had gone quite like he'd planned.

He *loved* when that happened. It kept him on his toes. Kept him sharp.

Kept him prime.

The new boyfriend was also convenient.

Here he'd spent the day waiting for the perfect time to approach Abigail McBane's house, her office all but impenetrable, and instead her new boyfriend dragged her straight out into the open. In front of a wall of windows, no less.

Hot damn.

The gunman moved deeper into the park, on paths that were nearly empty save for an occasional jogger or bicyclist passing by in the cool evening breeze. Satisfied he wouldn't be overheard—and that his racing pulse had slowed enough for him to maintain the stoic calm he prided himself on—he pulled his phone from his pocket and dialed the number he'd been given.

"Yes?"

The cold voice never failed to give him a jolt, which spoke volumes. He'd spent his professional career working with individuals who made it their business to hurt others yet this man unsettled him more than he wanted to admit. "The job was completed to your satisfaction."

"You staked out her home as we discussed?"

"No."

"Why not?"

"It was a game-time decision. I followed her from work as we discussed, but she had an event this evening, along with her new boyfriend. He was an unexpected wrinkle, but I handled it."

"New boyfriend?" The somber tone grew harder. Sharper. "I assume you left both of them untouched. The instructions were to create fear only."

"You've got plenty of that." The gunman ignored the swell of pride and held himself in check, saying nothing further. It wouldn't do to explain the footrace. Nor was it a meaningful discussion point to let on the tall boyfriend had gotten a bit too close for comfort a few times.

"Excellent."

The gunman continued to wait through the long pause on the other end of the phone. He always allowed his clients to speak first; he simply awaited their instructions.

"We'll move on to phase two. And if you ultimately

need to deal with the boyfriend, as well, you will be compensated for the additional effort."

A rush of adrenaline spiked through his system, that glorious high the reason he stayed in the game. "Thank you."

"Good night."

Campbell slid into the cab line at the Plaza, his arm still pressed low against Abby's back.

"We need the car."

"We need a cab. We'll call the car separately and send him home." He stood calmly and allowed the doorman to open their cab door, slipping him a quick tip before climbing in after Abby. As she gave the directions to the Upper East Side block nearest her home, he looked back at a pair of red-and-blue lights that went speeding by.

Yep. They'd avoided a whole lot of questions.

"It's always some damn thing in this town. Something happened down the block. You know what it was?" The cabbie immediately broke into conversation after getting their destination and Campbell laid a hand over Abby's, giving it a light squeeze.

"Not sure, are we, honey?" She turned toward him, her face tilted up and a broad smile spread across her face. "We were just heading out of the lobby. Heard a bunch of people mentioning all the commotion."

The cabbie gave a philosophical shrug as he reached for the radio knob. "Sure it'll be all anyone can listen to soon enough. Always something going on in this town."

"That's for damn sure." Campbell pasted on a good-natured smile as he caught Abby's determined gaze, directed toward a bold notice posted in the front of the cab. The driver had audio and video surveillance equipment built into his dash.

"I can promise you it won't be the most exciting part of our evening, sweetie." Abby snuggled into him as she placed a hand on his cheek to pull him close.

He *knew* it was an act—knew it to the depths of his toes—but other parts a bit farther north weren't quite in on the joke. Campbell pressed his lips to her ear, intoxicated by the woman in his arms. Her slender body fit to his and for the briefest moment, in those last seconds while their gazes locked, Campbell felt something shift. It spun in the small space between them, surrounding them in a quiet cocoon that shut out the rest of the world.

Her hand tightened at his waist as she grabbed a fistful of his shirt and he fought to keep his head. To anyone who might watch the surveillance tape, all they'd see was a happy couple, snuggling together in the back of the cab.

To his overheated body and increasingly confused mind, the ride was an exercise in delicious torture. He pressed his lips against her temple, desperate to keep his wits about him. "Nice catch."

She nodded, but her words maintained their act. "Mmm. That was a fun night."

He went along with the assessment, snuggling her closer. "I couldn't agree more, darling."

They drove the rest of the way to her home like that, heads bent like two tired lovers, wrapped up in each other at the end of a long evening. In his mind, Campbell tried to make a checklist of all he needed to do, but he got tripped up every time she moved.

The steady exhale of her breath as she sighed made him think of balmy summer breezes over naked flesh.

The thin whisper of silk against her breast brushed against his forearm, increasing his discomfort even as he refused to move an inch and risk losing the delicious contact.

And when her fingers flexed once more against his hip bone Campbell was nearly ready to give up the charade and drag her into a long, luxurious—and altogether too real—kiss.

Desperate, Campbell tried once again to return to his checklist, the alarming reality of their near miss in the bar pushing through the sexual haze of his thoughts. His first call would be to deal with the crappy security on her home in Paris, followed by a few discreet inquiries to a detective he knew at the NYPD. He wanted to keep attention off of Abby and their hasty departure and he had one person who might work with him on that front.

By now, the NYPD had likely begun reviewing surveillance video from the bar. Their departure through the window would likely raise some suspicions and he'd like to head it off at the pass if he could.

The cabbie pulled to a stop at the end of Abby's block and Campbell threw some money at the man. What he didn't bank on was the overwhelming sense of dread that filled him as he and Abby stood on the deserted street corner, wide out in the open as the cabbie sped off in search of his next fare.

"Campbell?"

He paused from his perusal of the street and the flash of vulnerability that lit up his nerve endings with an entirely different sort of awareness than he'd just experienced in the cab. "This isn't safe."

"Come on, it'll be fine. I'm just midway down the block." Yet again, she seemed to underestimate the possible danger that waited for her in a moment of careless neglect.

"Here. At least put this on. It's dark and will cover the bright color of your shawl."

He shrugged out of his tuxedo jacket and slipped it around her shoulders before pulling her close.

"It's a pashmina."

Her words came out on a breathless rush as she stared up at him. Hot, liquid need flared from the center of his chest like fire. "A what?"

"A pashmina, not a shawl."

He shook his head as they began to move. "Does it matter?"

"Probably not. Look. Just three more doors and we're there."

His gaze roamed the shadows as he did his best to shield her from view. The noises of the city—the horns and honks and general activity he took for granted—faded away as the blood pounded in his ears. Step by agonizing step they moved before she nodded toward the large brownstone that rose up five stories from the street. "We're here. Just up these steps."

With years of familiarity, she had the door unlocked and was through the entrance, already reaching for the blinking panel on the wall.

Campbell pressed the heavy door behind him as she tapped in several numbers on the keypad and let out a breath he didn't even realize he was holding. "Ten-digit code?"

"Yep. It's hell on the staff, but it makes sense."

"More than you can imagine."

A light beep indicated the alarm was disarmed before she rekeyed the instructions to arm it. "I'll turn it off when you leave."

"I'm not leaving tonight."

Abby whipped back around to face him from where she set her clutch on a small hallway table. "You can't stay here."

"I can and I will." He glanced up at the two-story foyer, an ornate crystal chandelier filling the space over-head, and couldn't hold back the grin. "I'll sleep on the couch if you don't have enough room."

"It's not that."

"Then what is it?"

She waved an arm, the long sleeve of his jacket flap-ping around her wrist as it engulfed her hand. "It's not decent."

"What's not decent? I'm a friend of the family." The tension he'd carried for the past half hour relaxed in the face of her protest and the solid door at his back. "Be-sides, what do you think we'll be doing for the next week in Paris?"

"Working."

"Sharing a home."

"That's a setup. This is real."

At her use of the word real, a different sort of ten-sion returned, coiled in the pit of his stomach, desper-ate for release.

"You think so?" Before she could reply, he moved to-ward her, his hands on her hips as he pulled her against him. His tug on her was gentle, but he clearly caught her off guard by the way she tumbled into him.

Never one to miss an opportunity, Campbell leaned in and took.

Abby gripped Campbell's large shoulders, the thin hallway table against her back as he pressed his body to hers. She wanted to protest—*knew* she should—but the feel of his large form against hers was too lovely to resist.

So she settled into the kiss and gave as good as she got.

His lips were firm against hers and she opened her

mouth as his tongue slid in to tangle with hers. The kiss was so blatant—so carnal—she felt her grip on his neck tighten as she tried to pull him closer against her body. The heavy tuxedo jacket she still wore felt too heavy, the material hot and scratchy as the urge to strip to nothing but flesh consumed her along with his mouth.

How can I feel this way?

Thoughts—deliberate yet fleeting—drifted through her mind as the moment spun out between them.

And with it, the very real understanding that she wanted this man.

Desperately.

It was that knowledge that had her pulling away, pressing against his shoulders as she slid from his embrace.

"Abby?"

Despite their brief acquaintance, she'd seen many facets of Campbell Steele, but nothing prepared her for the raw, naked need that rode his features into harsh, craggy lines. The vivid blue of his eyes had darkened in the heat of passion and thick cords roped his neck as he stared at her.

Feminine power filled her at the proof she'd drawn such a response and the urge to walk right back into his arms and see where the moment took her—took both of them—was nearly her undoing.

A flash of light lit up the hallway through the foyer windows and pulled her attention from his face. His gaze followed hers to the door as they both realized it was only a car driving down the street, but the brief interruption was enough to break the moment.

She pointed toward the stairs. "Let me go up and make sure a guest room's ready for you. You're welcome to help yourself to anything in the kitchen, just there down the hall. The finger food at the benefit wouldn't tide over a toddler. I'll come back down and join you in a bit."

He opened his mouth, then closed it again, before he simply nodded. "Thanks."

Abby slipped his jacket off and handed it to him, then gathered up her clutch and shawl. She fought the urge to turn back and look at him, fear lighting her heels and pushing her onward up the stairs.

If she looked at him, the need to go back into his arms might be too overpowering to resist a second time.

Lucas Brown reviewed the agenda for Abigail Mc-Bane's upcoming board meeting as the early morning London rain pattered outside his study windows. A sense of satisfaction welled in his veins and he reached for the aged Scotch at his elbow, allowing himself a second glass in celebration.

He was a man of refined tastes. Tastes he also knew how to manage, control and keep in check.

Sloppy men got drunk and careless men let their urges get the better of them.

He was neither.

Like that asshole he'd hired years ago to harass Abby in the London office. The man had taken his instructions to heart, becoming obsessed with the woman he was only meant to scare and Lucas had been forced to eliminate him.

From that moment on, he'd resolved to deal with Abby on his own. He could hire muscle, like the thug in New York, but the real work was his to handle. So he'd begun his campaign, planning and plotting, working tirelessly toward his goal.

And the past month had been the beginning of his reward.

The seven-minute lockdown on her system had gone according to plan, the information he'd painstakingly accumulated over the years all falling into place as he dug into the McBane systems, a ghost in the trillions upon trillions of bytes of data.

For seven glorious minutes, he'd played God with eighteen satellites orbiting the Earth and no one could find him.

As Lucas finished the last sip of the rich whiskey, he stared at the rain beating against the windows as the gray of early morning broke over London.

Today he'd take the next step.

Abby slipped from her dress and tried to hang it on its padded hanger, not all that surprised when her hands shook. That kiss had scrambled more than a few brain cells, but it was the shaky need that still coursed through her system that had her dropping to the small stool she kept in her closet.

The man did things to her. That was all there was to it. If she could look at it objectively—a straight case of sexual attraction—she'd be fine.

She would be fine.

She *had* to be fine.

"Get a grip, girl." The whispered admonishment did little except make her feel stupid for talking to herself in the middle of her closet.

Her gaze caught on a pair of yoga pants and discarded T-shirt on her shelf reserved for workout clothes and she snatched at them like they were a life preserver and she were drowning. Baggy and semi-unflattering, the clothes would offer some protection from the man.

Or so she hoped.

Flipping off the lights in her bedroom, she walked down the hall toward her office. Campbell had joked he was a family friend. Well, she'd let him fend for himself in the kitchen as she caught up on a bit of work. She'd fought the urge to check her emails during the event but too much was going on to fully ignore the office and the lure of her sleek, silver laptop beckoned.

Less than a minute later, Abby groaned at the long string of unread emails, proving she'd pay for her post-work absence. With practice born of long years of message management, she triaged the emails into the most urgent, either due to sender or topic and sorted the rest for when she could get to them.

"You want half? You barely ate anything at the benefit."

The deep voice penetrated the work haze she'd descended into and Abby looked up and blinked. The sight of Campbell standing in her doorway, his shirttails untucked and that sexy patch of skin visible at the V open at his throat, had her stomach clenching in another burst of attraction before it switched gears and focused on the half a sandwich he held up.

Her stomach let out a long, low growl in agreement. "I'm so hungry I'm not even embarrassed by that resounding shout of agreement."

"Here." He crossed the room and set the ham and cheese down, her half wrapped in a napkin.

"Thanks."

He swallowed a bite of his own half, then gestured toward her desk with his dinner. "What are you working on?"

"The bane of every professional's existence. Email."

"Can I look at a few things while you're eating?"

"What things?"

"I told you I set up those databases to run while we were gone."

She nodded, curious to observe him now that he seemed to be back in work mode. The change was intriguing, the sexy would-be lover gone in the face of a highly focused technology expert.

The thought was as fascinating as it was disappointing.

Especially when she realized she missed that sexy heat that had lingered in his gaze downstairs.

"Here." Campbell came around to her side of the desk and was already sliding the laptop in his direction. With mind-boggling speed, he tapped into her system infrastructure and had a series of scripts running on the page before she'd swallowed another bite.

"How'd you do that so fast?"

"Years and years of practice."

"Try again. I'm more than proficient in our systems and I could never move through the commands with that degree of speed. What gives?"

"I told you. Practice." He reached for the last bite of his sandwich he'd settled next to the laptop and popped it into his mouth before walking to the small framed photograph she kept on a shelf behind her desk. "Is this your mother?"

Abby focused on the lines of code racing over the face of her computer, unwilling to turn around. "Yes."

"She was very beautiful. You look like her."

"So I've been told."

"I'm sorry. It's difficult to lose a parent."

She rarely spoke of her mother so the fact she'd had to confront the subject twice in one night had her closing in on herself. Abby knew it—and knew Campbell, of all people, spoke from experience—but she wasn't able to calm down or channel a different reaction.

"I've had a long time to get used to it." The words were unnecessarily harsh and Abby knew she'd meant them to be. She also knew she was already sorry for the brusque tone and even edgier response. Before she could manage an apology, his gaze caught on the screen and his focus shifted once again.

"What is it?"

"You see that?" He tapped a few quick commands then scrolled back to the point he wanted to highlight. "Right here. See the gap?"

She saw it immediately and dragged the laptop a bit closer. "How'd you find that so quickly?"

"I've got a few tricks up my sleeve."

"No, really, Campbell. I understand this stuff. Clearly I don't live it and breathe it like you do, but I understand it. What'd you do?"

"I reprogrammed an old honeypot to see if I'd get any nibbles."

"And?"

"He bit."

Campbell pulled the computer back toward him, suddenly itchy for the multiple screens in his office. He made a mental note to add a few to his remit list for the setup in Paris, then went back to the task at hand.

Abby leaned over the computer, her arm brushing his as she left her dinner forgotten on the other side of the desk. "I know my team has an entire honeynet in place as part of the security infrastructure, but it's clear you've done something differently."

"The design is simple and hardly sophisticated. I replicated a few basic program functions he'd have to work around to come in undetected. I'll put something more extensive in place tomorrow but this gives me something to go on."

"A fingerprint for our ghost?" She moved closer, the thin cotton of her T-shirt soft against his forearm. Her movements were unconscious, but his body reacted immediately.

And how the hell was baggy cotton suddenly the sexiest damn thing in the universe?

"Not yet." The words came out on a harsh bark and he pulled himself back, the insane urge to drag her against his body and continue what they'd started in the foyer flashing through his mind like a blinking sign.

Softening his tone, he forced the sexy images from his mind and pointed once more to the computer. "But this information should get us closer."

She stood up, the heat of her body vanishing as she crossed around the desk and took a seat opposite him. "Nice work, Mr. Steele."

"I haven't caught him yet. Or her," he amended quickly, still unsure of what they were up against.

"How is it someone hasn't snapped you up yet? I know what your skills are worth. There are companies that would pay big to have you on their side."

The image of working for a large corporation had always given him an itch between the shoulder blades. "There's not enough money in the world to tie me to a corporate job."

Her eyebrows rose as she pointed toward the laptop. "Isn't this, by definition, a corporate job?"

"This is a job with a defined beginning, middle and end. Then I move on to the next thing. No strings attached."

No strings attached.

It was his philosophy and it had served him well for his thirty-two years. Campbell saw no reason to shift gears now.

"You don't like roots?"

"I've got roots in the form of two meddlesome sisters, a hands-off brother and a pair of well-meaning grandparents who are perfectly happy to see me when I'm in town and not nag at me when I'm not."

"And you're happy with that?"

"As a clam."

"I never understood that."

Whether it was her lack of accusation—most women would have been on his no-strings comment faster than a lightning strike—or the curiosity that stamped itself in her tone, he didn't know.

Maybe it was just a vague sense when she'd spoken about her mother that they were kindred spirits, but her comment had him talking when he'd usually default to saying nothing.

"They're my family and they've always been more than enough." *They had to be.*

"I meant the clam."

"What clam?"

"The happy one. How does anyone know that? They're not exactly high on the evolutionary chain. They certainly don't show emotion."

"This is an odd conversation."

"Very." She picked up the sandwich once again. "This'll go better with a glass of wine."

"Doesn't everything?"

"Usually. Grab the laptop and we'll head back down to the kitchen. We need to figure out our game plan for the next few days."

"I thought you'd never ask."

Chapter 5

As her great-grandmother's grandfather clock chimed four in the morning, Abby dropped her head onto the kitchen table. She'd had only one glass of the rich Cabernet—a feat of restraint she now applauded herself for—and tried to focus on the diagram Campbell held in his hands.

"So where's the study?"

"There is no study on that floor. The hallway's longer than your diagram and there's a sitting room at the end of the hall."

"How far away is the study?"

"Two floors up."

"And where are you holding the meetings?"

"In the dining room on the first floor."

Campbell groaned as he scribbled a few notes on a legal pad she'd hunted up shortly after midnight. They'd been going over the layout to the Paris house for hours, mapping out meeting strategy and all the potential ways they could trap their ghost in the flesh.

"Why are you so worried about the study?"

He reached for his coffee mug as he tapped on the crudely drawn map. "It's the most likely place you'd keep information which would mean it's the most likely place he'll look. But, I need to set up the security team in there. We want to set a trap for our ghost, a physical one, but we don't need one inadvertently set for us."

"And you really think it's one of the attendees for the week?"

Abby knew it was possible—had resigned herself to that fact even before she'd contacted Kensington about the job—but it continued to rub her the wrong way. She *knew* these people. Knew each and every person who would be in her home in the coming days.

How it was even imaginable any of them had made threats, violated the integrity of McBane's systems and very possibly shot at her and Campbell tonight and she didn't know.

Yet even as she questioned it, when she added up each of those factors it wasn't only possible, it was highly probable.

"Abby. I know this is hard but you've got to give me a little bit more."

"Fine. What else do you want to know?"

"The server and uplink to the office you keep in the Paris location. Who put that in?"

She sighed and reached for her own cup of coffee but gave him as thorough an answer as she could. "Two of my key tech guys installed it, following my set of specifications. I've got a matched set here if you'd like to take a look."

She saw the interest spark in his eyes and gave up the

thought that she might be lucky enough to snag an hour or two of sleep. "Do you trust them?"

"I did. Now I don't know who to trust."

"Were you there for the install?"

"Most of it. I had them do it over a weekend and I'm also there when upgrades to the system are installed if they require outside techs. No one gets into any of my homes without my say-so."

"Smart. Okay. I'll look into their backgrounds but let's assume for the moment your home system's clean. Does anyone else in the company know the extent of what you've got at home beyond the team that help you put it together?"

"There's no reason to think anyone does, but up until a few weeks ago, there wasn't a reason to think anyone cared all that much." She held up a hand. "And before you think I'm minimizing this, my home system is a replica of the command details at the office. I don't have any personal authority over the satellites. Just because my name's on the building doesn't change the security protocols I follow, as well."

"So give them to me."

"Four people, including me, have full access to the nerve center that is McBane Communications. We have eighteen satellites in orbit and another six set to launch over the next three years. No one has sole access—every major command into the system requires at least two of us to initiate."

"Can that be changed?"

"Not without a hell of a lot of us knowing about it. There's a secondary layer another eight people have classified access to. They can't formally override any systems—even in tandem with each other—but they need to be able to access all the software, manage maintenance and upload new iterations of software. We also have a team that interfaces with those who lease space from us."

"Those were the names you gave me this afternoon?"

She traced the handle of her mug, the images of each and every one of those trusted colleagues flashing through her mind on a loop. "Yes. They're the best place to start."

The overwhelming desire to rant and rail that none of them could be responsible—that none would betray her that way—was strong but Abby held back. The story she'd shared with Campbell earlier about her stepmother was only half the story.

That resounding sense of betrayal had irrevocably changed her and it hadn't taken a whole lot of self-analysis to realize her entire adult life had been built around a small, trusted team of people she'd carefully vetted, in both her professional and personal lives. Very few people were part of her inner circle, by her own choice.

Her gaze drifted toward Campbell. His sister had been part of that inner circle since college. Despite going months without talking to each other—their daily lives hectic enough that even living in the same city had never ensured regular visits—they were close. Abby knew to the depths of her being that Kensington Steele had her back.

Was that what made it so easy to trust Campbell? Or was it something else?

He scribbled a few notes on the pad of paper, his concentration absolute, and she couldn't help but be fascinated by his focus. Since their meeting that afternoon, he'd immersed himself in her problem, and with an attention to detail she'd rarely seen in another person.

The sharp buzz of the doorbell startled them both and pulled her from her observations.

"You regularly get callers at four in the morning?"

"Never any good ones." An image of the night her father died flew to her mind on swift wings. His unexpected death skiing in Vermont had brought a late-night visit from the police. Even now, she could recall the immediate mixture of shock and disbelief as a kind-faced officer stood outside her door with his partner and told her why they'd come.

Before she could get up, Campbell was out of his seat and heading for the hallway. "Stay here."

"I need to key the alarm."

"Fine, but stay here until I see who it is."

The heavy, hammering beats of her heart kicked up a notch at the idea he might be facing an unexpected visitor on the other side of the door. A door framed in decorative glass that would give someone bent on doing harm an easy shot. Unwilling to allow him to face a possible threat alone, she followed him down the hall.

"Are you physically incapable of taking direction?" She didn't miss the anger that boiled underneath his words before his hand flung out and pulled her behind him.

His actions were so immediate—and so protective— a strange sense of wonder filled her at his touch.

"I didn't hire you to be my damn bodyguard."

"Consider it an extra service. On the house." His hand tightened and she drew in a hard breath as his long fingers connected with her waist.

"Who is it?"

"Campbell. It's Kensington."

"Just a sec." Campbell sighed hard before he turned around. "She can't use the phone?"

"She must have found something if she's here."

"Go ahead and key in the code then get back behind me."

"Campbell. It's your sister!"

"Doesn't matter. Come on." The alarm beeped off and Campbell pulled her behind him once again before opening the door. She wanted to push her way past him—this was her house and her friend, after all—but something held her back.

For the first time in her life, she didn't have to face the other side alone.

Campbell kept the increasing urge to argue in check, but he was hanging on by a thin thread. What the hell was Kensington doing over here? And at four in the morning, to boot. He'd already pressed her on why she couldn't have used the phone, but her pointed stare and flick of the wrist hadn't been an answer so much as a dismissal.

Now the three of them were back around Abby's kitchen table, full mugs of coffee fueling each of them.

"You want to save the attitude this time and tell me why you rushed over here instead of using the phone?"

"I wanted to make sure you were both all right."

Abby's hands tightened on her mug, her features drawn. "You shouldn't have put yourself in danger. What if someone's watching the house?"

"I'm fine. Besides, T-Bone brought me."

"There's someone out there?" Those drawn features changed immediately to concern as she leaped out of her chair. "He needs to come in."

Campbell reached for her hand and held tight until she stood still and looked at him. "T-Bone's more than capable of sitting in the car. A car with bulletproof glass, I might add."

Some of the fight went out of her shoulders as she dropped back into her seat. "T-Bone?"

"He's worked for the Steele family for a long time. Rowan named him when she was a kid because he looks like a slab of meat. I can't believe you've never met him."

"T-Bone prefers staying in the background." Kensington brushed it off. "And he hasn't needed to do a lot of the day-to-day for a long time."

"So why's he here now?"

Kensington took a sip of her coffee and Campbell didn't miss the piercing stare across the top of the mug. He'd spent his life with the common-enough remark that the Steele siblings all had the same eyes, but he'd always felt Kensington's were the most penetrating.

Add on the same skill as their mother and grandmother—the ability to see beneath the surface of most any situation—and Campbell had the sneaking suspicion his sister knew he had the hots for one of her oldest and dearest friends.

"I'm also here because I have to tell you something."

Campbell fought the mixed urge to throttle his sister for dragging out whatever it was she had to say and appreciating the fact she took the time to ease Abby into whatever news she'd come to share. "What's going on?"

"I started the security order for Abby's Paris house and came across a bit of disconcerting news."

"What'd you find?" Whatever well-merited concern Abby had for T-Bone transformed instantly into a cool, competent businesswoman used to situation briefings.

"The homes on both sides of yours in Paris have been broken into in the past year."

"There's no way, Kensington. I realize we don't exactly run a neighborhood watch, but I'd have heard about it. Two in one year?"

"You likely wouldn't have heard about these." Kensington shook her head. "Aside from the fact those with the most desirable address in Paris prefer to keep things like this to themselves, nothing was stolen and both were hushed up by their respective security companies, neither of which is the same as yours. It's only when I gave your address and said Avenue Foch that I got a hit with our team."

"Which was? Come on, spill it, Kenzi."

Campbell suspected Kensington held back the urge to stick out her tongue—barely—before she gave them the high points. "The security team said there were two mysterious hits in the neighborhood that were over a year apart. No one thought anything of the first, other than that it was either an interrupted event or a trial run for something bigger. They've kept a close eye and that was that. It was only when the second happened, two doors down, that the interest grew more speculative as to what might be going on."

"Two break-ins. On opposite sides of my home?"

"Yes." Kensington nodded.

"And nothing taken from either address?"

"Nothing at all, even after a thorough search by both owners."

"Any guesses on motive?" Campbell pressed the question, but he suspected he already knew the answer.

"Absolutely none."

"I know." Abby's quiet voice punctuated the moment and for the first time since they'd met that afternoon, he saw the true depth of the strain this was taking on her. "The motive was me."

"Yes, that's what I believe."

* * *

Abby drew her legs up under her and made room for Kensington on the overstuffed couch in her sitting room. They'd left Campbell down the hall in the guest room and took a few minutes to catch up in the small alcove off of Abby's bedroom.

"I appreciate the personalized service but you really can get back home. It's almost morning and you must be exhausted. Besides, T-Bone's downstairs waiting."

"It's what he does best, which is strange and comforting all at the same time."

Since it was useless to argue with Kensington once she made up her mind—a trait Abby could hardly fault her for as she was known for a similar bent—she offered up a quick apology instead. "I'm sorry this is turning out to be such a difficult project. I never expected this."

"It's our job, Abby. We'll figure it out." Kenzi paused for the briefest moment, the rare sign of hesitation evident in her gaze, before she pushed forward. "Is my brother behaving himself?"

Abby couldn't hold back the light snort. "That was quick."

"I see the way he looks at you."

"With the trademark Steele intensity."

A light swat hit her leg before Kenzi pushed forward. "No, that one's designed to intimidate and unnerve. I'm talking about the heat look. I'm hardly surprised—at all—but, well, actually I am in a way."

Intrigued at the hesitation—and more delighted than she cared to admit—Abby pressed for more. "What way is that?"

"He's a private man and that's as true with our family as it is with others."

Campbell's claims earlier that his family was more

than enough for him was an interesting contrast to Kensington's perspective. "I got the feeling that you all were pretty tight. You've all dealt with mutual loss and built a strong family unit, not to mention a business, out of that."

It was Kensington's turn to snort. "Like that would get my brother to open up to me about his love life. He's intensely private and lives inside his head. Always has. Add on the fact that Liam took on the role of crown prince of the dating scene pretty early and Campbell's quiet about who he's interested in."

"Especially since you're so discreet and all. Goodness, you and I were barely in this room for two minutes before you were grilling me."

Her friend didn't even have the decency to look the slightest bit chastised. "It's the girlfriend code of honor. Forged in the fires of a shared dorm room, bad dating choices and mutual hair-holding as we rode out the consequences of bad hangovers."

"Do you tell him about your love life?"

"Hell, no. Why would I want to do that?"

Abby shook her head, the sudden urge to laugh a welcome respite from the tension of the last several hours. "Isn't that a bit of the pot calling the kettle black?"

"Nope. It's being a smart woman who doesn't want my big brother nosing around in my life. But if we put that aside, all I'm really saying is that this same brother doesn't fall for women in front of me. So the fact that he showed real concern for you downstairs means something."

Although Kensington was one of her dearest friends— and one of her small inner circle she *was* willing to share things with—there was something about Campbell that held her back.

Whether it was her own inability to define her attraction to the man or the current professional situation she found herself in, Abby didn't know.

Either way, she just couldn't go there.

"He's a good man. But even if I did agree with you that something might be there, life is in the way right now."

"That's a cop-out if I ever heard one."

Abby planted on a broad smile, but didn't back down from their discussion. "Then don't listen."

Kensington laughed as she extended her arms for a hug. They might not see eye to eye, but Abby knew her friend always had her back.

Campbell finally convinced T-Bone to come into the house after Kensington went up with Abby. The big man filled the hallway with a hulking combination of sheer heft and dark menace that Campbell had always enjoyed being on the right side of.

"What are you dragging me in here for?"

"I want to know what you found out. Uncensored."

T-Bone sighed before pointing toward the stairs. "They out of earshot."

"Yes."

"Then here's what I know."

T-Bone gave him a quick recap that matched Kensington's before diving into the things left unsaid. Namely, the break-ins were nearly identical in execution and equally hard to understand.

As he watched the big man nod, Campbell felt the pieces click into place in his mind, like the tumblers of a slot machine that fell into a neat, even row. "You think something was left behind?"

"Yeah, I do."

"They sweep for bugs?"

"The security companies did. They didn't find anything and I'm not surprised. I don't think it's a bug."

"What do you think it is?"

"Whoever it is has figured out a way to get eyes inside Abby's house and into her equipment."

"Undetected?"

T-Bone shook his head. "You know as well as I do no one breaks in for fun. And they certainly don't do it twice. Those weren't random."

"How hard would it be to get me inside the houses?"

"How well do you speak French?"

Campbell let out a large bark. "About as well as I speak anything other than English."

"How could I forget? The only language you know is code."

"I know French." Abby's voice floated over them from the stairs. "Quite well, as a matter of fact."

T-Bone shifted his large frame to stare up at her. Campbell didn't miss the man's broad, calming smile and wondered abstractly why he never rated one of those.

Ever.

"Hello, Ms. McBane."

"Abby, please." She descended the stairs like a regal queen before coming to a stop in front of the big man and extending her hand. "You must be T-Bone."

"At your service."

"I overheard your conversation with Campbell. You think something was left in my neighbors' homes to spy on me?"

"I think they're spying on your technology."

"Well, then. What do I need to do?"

"How well do you know your neighbors?"

Chapter 6

Abby ignored the buzzing of her phone as she hunted up details on the Paris house. She kept a small leather notebook in her attaché case, full of all the minutia of her life. Those details filled the book, from family birthdays to her neighbors' names to various security and tax information.

She'd long laughed at herself for the attachment to a paper device, but there was something about the well-worn leather that comforted. Especially the pages in the front of the book that still held her mother's careful script.

She ran a light finger over the faded ink that outlined all the pertinent details on their New York home before flipping to the pages that detailed the house in Paris.

Monsieur and Madame Dufresne lived on one side of her and an aged widower, Monsieur Tremaine, on the other. Tremaine was a lovely old man who spent the majority of his time in the South of France. He was also the first house hit and likely was used for practice, his frequent absences making him an easier mark.

Abby shifted her muzzy thoughts to the Dufresnes. Etienne was a former diplomat and, if she recalled correctly, Celine was wife number three. Although she'd not formally met Celine, a vague image of Etienne roamed around her tired mind, finding no purchase as she tried diligently to conjure up a face. When nothing stuck, she reached for her coffee mug and turned to her computer.

"Ah, well, Abby-girl, you can sleep when you're dead," she muttered to herself as she tapped Etienne's and Celine's names into a search program. And as her gaze tracked the results, she allowed the hot rich coffee to slide down to her stomach, willing the brew to work its magic.

When it had become evident early this morning they weren't going to get any sleep, Abby had suggested to Campbell they shift gears and head to the office. Although a shower had gone a long way toward reviving her, the lack of sleep was definitely kicking in now that she'd been at her desk for the better part of an hour.

On a resigned yawn, she clicked on the first link and watched as an image of her next-door neighbors instantly downloaded to her screen. The portly man with the ruddy complexion looked pretty much as she'd remembered and a quick read-through of the text confirmed her suspicions.

The statuesque Celine was a relatively new acquisition.

The couple, dressed in formal wear, had her thoughts drifting to the evening before, along with a powerful image that hadn't quite faded from her mind.

Campbell Steele in a tuxedo.

Since the search program was still open, she went with instinct and typed his name into the open box.

The list of links associated with him numbered in the hundreds, which wasn't a huge surprised based on his lineage. Although Kensington had always played it down, the Steele family had a long and storied history, both in England and here in the States.

What she did find curious was that very little existed about the man *beyond* his family connections.

In the current day and age of social media, near-constant updates by friends and family and the press's fascination with anyone who possessed even the remotest bit of wealth, the lack of information was a surprise.

"You are a mystery, Mr. Steele."

Her gaze caught on a link to his parents' obituary and she clicked it, despite knowing the basics of their death. Fueling up on another hit of caffeine, she read the article. Even as someone who'd lost both of her parents, the story of the car crash that killed Charles and Katherine Steele on their twentieth wedding anniversary trip in the Welsh countryside never failed to leave her with a restless sort of sadness in her heart.

The question of why hovered briefly in her mind, even as she knew there were no answers for the vagaries of life.

As the why over Campbell's parents faded, two questions rose up to take its place in rapid succession.

Why was she so interested in him? And why was she fighting it so hard?

They were a couple of healthy, unattached adults. Although there was the slightly messy connection with Kensington, it wasn't insurmountable, especially if her friend's eager nosiness last night was any indication. A fling with Campbell would have very little—if any—impact on her friendship with Kenzi.

So why was she holding back?

The heavy knock on her door pulled her from her thoughts—and from answering the question.

"Stef. What's up?"

"You're in early this morning."

"No rest for the weary. And I know you'll be happy and relieved to be rid of me for a week."

Stef flashed a wide grin before offering up a quick wink and extending a heavy file folder. "I'm counting down the minutes."

Abby reached for the folder, groaning at its heft. "What's in here?"

"I know, I know. You're trying to get out of here and there are a million things to do. I've held back what can wait, but I need everything in there signed off on."

"What is it?"

"Several memorandums to the foreign offices, the proposed insurance plan changes for next year that require your final signature and a review on one of your patents."

"That can't wait?"

Stef shrugged. "You're the one who's brilliant enough to even need to file a patent on your ideas. Do you think it can wait? You're the boss."

"No." Abby shook her head as she dropped the folder on her desk, the heavy thud going a long way toward adding to the bone-weary exhaustion she felt. "I'd best get to it, then."

"Can I at least get you a refill on the coffee?"

"Only if you want me to get down on both knees, sing your praises and possibly propose."

Stef's grin only widened as she reached for the near-empty mug. "That's my guy's job. And if this past weekend's any indication, I think he's getting close."

Whatever fatigue she felt vanished at the happy news. Jumping up from her chair, Abby crossed around her desk to pull Stef into a tight hug. The woman's body was momentarily stiff and Abby had the strange sensation she might have overstepped before her assistant wrapped her up in a return hug.

"Sorry." Stef waved the mug as they pulled away. "I didn't want to break the mug."

"No, no, I'm the impulsive one." Abby waved it off, well aware she wasn't known for her personal interaction with her team. "This is wonderful news. You need to call me the moment he proposes."

"I can't do that while you're in Paris. You'll be busy."

"Of course you can. All the details will give me something to smile about as I'm sitting through one meeting after the next."

"Probably thinking up new ideas to patent." Stef's tease was just that—and it was shared in the tone of someone who knew her well—but Abby fought the strange sense of hopelessness that welled up at the woman's words.

Her assistant's description wasn't far off the mark. She *was* a patent-filing thinker who always had a million projects on her plate. She'd always been invigorated by working and living at that pace, so what had changed?

A quick glance at Stef and she saw almost a mirror image of her thoughts, the woman's face drawn and slightly wan.

"Everything okay?"

"Oh, yeah. Lot on my mind." Stef lifted the mug before pointing over her shoulder with her free hand. "Let me just get you a refill."

"Sure thing."

Abby watched Stef's slim, almost frail, frame cross the room before she exited to the welcome area outside the office. Could it be she was working the woman too hard? She'd thought over the past few months it might make sense to add a second assistant. One who oversaw the more personal aspects of her life, freeing Stef to focus on the day-to-day urgency of the business.

A glance at the thick file and Abby resolved to get on that when she got back.

"In fact," she whispered to herself, "no time like the present. Email Human Resources right now while you're thinking about it."

Her gaze alighted on the article about Campbell's parents and she shut out of the browser window, also shutting down whatever vein of curiosity had opened up this morning.

Whatever fanciful notions she might have about Campbell Steele needed to stop. What man would be all that interested in spending his time with a brainy workaholic who never sat still long enough to be in one city, let alone one country?

Nope, it just wouldn't work.

They might consider a fling, but even that was probably a less-than-smart idea. She'd crafted a very full—and rather lonely—life for herself and this coming week was yet another raging example of that. Strange, mysterious threats or not, she had a major series of meetings and twenty people to entertain for a week.

After she hit Send on the email to Human Resources, Abby opened the file Stef had left behind.

She'd best get to it.

Campbell sifted through another layer of code as he kept up a steady conversation with T-Bone. Well, conversation might be a stretch, he admitted to himself, even if they were speaking intermittently on their mobile phones.

They had a strange sort of half language that consisted of a lot of swearing, fragmented sentences and another layer of swearing.

And they understood each other perfectly.

"I don't believe this. How the hell did he do this?" T-Bone added a whistle to his frustration. "There's no fingerprint on this."

"He's definitely a ghost and from the looks of it he's been sneaking around for a while."

"How's he getting in?"

"Damned if I know." Campbell ran a hand through his hair, tugging on the longish ends he knew his grandmother would give him a hard time about next time she saw him. He mentally added "haircut" to his to-do list and knew it would vanish in mere moments.

Best intentions and all…

"I'll be dipped—" T-Bone's voice faded off as Campbell hit a few commands. "He's been all over the system."

"If I wasn't so hell-bent to figure out who it was, I'd have to admire the guy's style. He's got some skills."

"You're not kidding."

"You know who it might be."

T-Bone let out another low whistle. "First thought was Juno but he's been out of the game for a little over a year."

"No one ever really gets out."

"We did."

"We just play for a different side, T. I'd say we're about as in as you can get."

A gruff laugh rumbled through the phone. "Well, rumor is, Juno's really out. Got a wife and a kid and went legit."

At the words *wife* and *kids,* Campbell was unable to resist the image of Abby in his arms. Their night before had left him with a steady dose of erotic images that refused to leave.

The tense moments at the bar, both of them fully aware of each other.

That tender interlude in the cab, wrapped up in each other in a "show" that felt far too real for comfort.

The press of her slender body against his in the hallway of her home as their mouths fused.

Hell, he could still feel the imprint of her body at every point they touched.

Would a wife and kids make him legit? Tame him, as it were? He'd always scoffed at the idea of ever wanting to get out, but what if there was an exterior motive to do so?

Could a person change you if you loved each other enough?

There were elements of the idea that were as appealing as they were appalling.

Wasn't the person who loved and cared about you supposed to love you as you were?

Yet, if your choices weren't the best for the relationship, didn't you owe it to the one you loved in return to make changes for them?

Endless questions without answers.

Which was why he'd avoided relationships like the plague. A few dates. A good time. That was more than enough.

Especially since House of Steele had taken off beyond their wildest dreams.

When he and Liam, Kensington and Rowan had formed the company three years ago, they'd used it as a way to create something lasting while leveraging each of their innate skills. He was their e-man, Kenzi covered the running of the business, Ro knew art and antiques like the back of her hand and Liam...

Well, Liam did as he pleased and somehow always came out on top.

Literally *and* figuratively.

For a long time, that had bothered Campbell more than he'd wanted to admit. He loved his brother and knew they had each other's backs, but everything had always come easy to Liam and it had taken more than a few years to understand that didn't mean the man was happy or even remotely content with his life.

It had taken a few more years after that to accept that his brother's choices had nothing to do with his own. And now, despite more than a few rocky years, he and Liam were in a good place.

A highly productive one, as well, if the projected profit statement Kensington had shared with all of them last week was any indication. They might be a motley crew—albeit with a touch of polish that got them in and out of the world's most elegant environments—but with House of Steele thcy'd built something that worked.

"I still think the neighbors are the key." T-Bone's words interrupted his musings and Campbell pushed aside thoughts of his family.

"Abby's hunting up their details this morning. She doesn't know them all that well."

"Not a surprise. Homes on Paris's most exclusive street don't exactly scream block party."

Campbell couldn't hold back the bark of laughter at the image that one evoked. "No barbecues and bocce?"

"Hardly."

"Guess I need to make sure I pack a tie."

* * *

Abby was still signing paperwork an hour later when Campbell gamboled into her office, two large paper cups in hand and a slim laptop tucked under his arm.

"I come bearing caffeine."

"Do you have any answers to go with that coffee?"

"No answers, but T-Bone and I have ruled out a few suspects." He set the paper cup on her desk before taking the chair opposite hers. "Any luck figuring out who your neighbors are?"

She watched him fold his large form into the steel-framed chair and wondered again why she was fighting her attraction so hard. The man was far too attractive for his own good. Dark hair fell over his forehead and the black T-shirt that stretched over his shoulders had kicked off an appreciative hum under her skin.

Kensington had run to Campbell's house and picked up his clothes this morning, neither of them willing to leave her in the house by herself. Abby had thought the move silly at the time, yet despite her internal scoffing, she'd appreciated the company.

And she certainly couldn't argue with the clothing Kenzi had selected and stuffed into a well-worn leather duffel.

With a sip of the rich latte to center herself, Abby passed him a few notes. "The second house hit is our best bet."

"Etienne and Celine?"

"Yep. Former diplomat and wife number three. They travel a lot but make the Paris house their main residence."

"Were they in town when the break-in happened?"

"Funny enough, they were on their first anniversary trip, in a private residence in Jean Cap Ferrat."

"Convenient."

"Too convenient, don't you think?"

Campbell offered up a simple "Hmm" as he took a sip of his coffee.

His image wavered slightly before her eyes and Abby pinched the bridge of her nose. Even without the added concerns about security, safety and the company's overall well-being, this was always a difficult week on her schedule.

"You okay?"

"Just tired."

"It's only ten and you've been here for four hours already. Let's go out and get some fresh air."

"Campbell, I can't."

The penetrating blue stare that greeted her protest brooked no arguments. "Half hour. You can spare a half hour."

She'd gotten about halfway through Stef's folder and lifted the remaining stack of papers. "This suggests otherwise."

"It can wait, too. Come on."

The urge to agree—to simply escape for a few moments—was too lovely to resist. "Half hour."

"Scout's honor." He made some convoluted gesture with his fingers that didn't look like any Boy Scout promise but she was up and around her desk, anyway, suddenly desperate for the break.

"You'll need a coat." He snagged the thin raincoat she'd left on her office couch and held it open for her. The brush of his fingertips across her shoulder blades had a delicious warmth drifting under her skin and her traitorous thoughts once again pushed the idea of a fling to the forefront of her mind.

Where her thoughts while doing paperwork had been

hazy and full of a weariness she couldn't get a handle on, two minutes in Campbell's company had her waking up, her body humming to life. The sensation was as exhilarating as it was sexy and the same thought that had hit her several times over the last day punched up once more.

It was nice not to be alone.

A quick glance from the corner of her eye confirmed his gaze on her and Abby fought the urge to blush.

When was the last time she was so interested in a guy? And why did that scare her even as it invigorated?

They passed Stef in the outer area of the executive suite. Abby was struck once again by the woman's slim shoulders as Stef bent over a mahogany credenza and she was glad she'd made the outreach to Human Resources to secure additional help. "We're running out, Stef. No more than about a half hour."

"Can we get you anything? Coffee or some breakfast?" Campbell's words were warm and genuine and Abby was momentarily bemused by his thoughtfulness. Where many would have walked past her assistant without so much as a glance, Campbell had done the opposite.

"No, no. I'm good. Thanks." Stef waved them off with a quick smile.

"I've got my phone." Abby patted her coat pocket.

"Of course you do." Her assistant gave her a quick wink before she slid back behind her desk. "Get out for a few minutes."

Campbell waited until the elevator doors slid closed behind them before he spoke again. "How long has she been with you?"

"About three years."

"She knows you."

"Too well." Abby smiled, the years they'd worked together floating through her mind on a loop. "Unfortunately, I realized this morning that it's time to accept I've overworked the poor woman. I'm finally giving in and adding another assistant to the team. Between the business stuff and the personal details Stef keeps up with, it's too much. And she's about to get engaged so I'm going to lose about three-quarters of her brain to that, anyway."

"So she knows you exceptionally well and knows all your comings and goings. Does that ever worry you?"

"Stef? Oh, goodness, no. She's my right hand. And many days, my left as well as both my feet."

"She has carte blanche to come and go as she pleases."

Warning bells clanged like a fire alarm as his questions poked through the warm buzz she'd departed her office with. "What are you suggesting?"

"That she has unprecedented access to you. Does that frame up any thoughts about her that might make you reconsider her loyalty?"

The elevator came to a halt on the lobby floor and Abby laid a hand on his arm. "Let's wait and talk about this outside."

She was grateful for the brief silence as they moved through the lobby of the large building that bore her name. Steve, one of her key security managers, nodded his head as she came up level with the gleaming chrome doors that were the centerpiece of the lobby. He set the revolving panels rotating for her as she walked up. "Morning, Ms. McBane."

"Morning, Steve. Thanks." The insane urge to look him up and down and grill him about his loyalty, his computer skills and his satisfaction in working for the company lodged in her throat.

And damn Campbell for that.

She'd worked with these people for years and now she was looking at each of them as if they were criminals.

The moment they'd cleared the block, she whirled on Campbell. "How dare you do this to me?"

"What have I done?" His tone was calm but she saw sparks in the bright blue of his eyes along with a heavy dose of speculation.

"You've made me wonder about the people I work with. The people I care about."

"You have to wonder, Abby. Whoever is doing this to you not only has some sort of motive you're unaware of, but they're close to you."

A faceless sea of New Yorkers thronged around the two of them. Why was it easier to think of the threat being one of them—nameless, faceless strangers—instead of one of her own?

As soon as she asked herself the question, she knew the answer with a resounding certainty that couldn't be denied.

Because if it was one of her own, it was yet another point in the betrayal column that was her life.

Her mother—while unintentional—had left her when she was far too young.

Her father had made the unfathomable mistake of taking a wife who was neither warm and caring nor all that interested in mothering another woman's child.

And now this?

Work was the one place she was safe. The one place she could come and escape from the deeply unsatisfactory elements of her personal life.

And now she had to accept that even that cocoon had holes. Rather sizeable ones, in fact.

"Let's go in here." Campbell pulled her into a thronging diner that would guarantee even further anonymity as they talked.

"This is going to take longer than a half hour."

"Nonsense." Campbell held up two fingers to the waitress. "These places know how to get people in and out. And it's fairly empty and the griddle is no doubt hot."

"Fruit doesn't take that long." She shrugged as the hostess walked them toward the back of the diner.

Campbell waited until she was settled, her menu folded in front of her. "You need pancakes or French toast. I'd go with the French toast. It feels oddly appropriate based on tonight's trip."

"Fruit's fine."

The calm facade he'd carried since they were in her office faded and in its place was the distinct hum of a steady burn of anger. "You're killing yourself slowly. You barely had anything at the benefit. I forced that half a sandwich on you last night. You've had nothing but coffee this morning. Eat something and make it stick."

"I'm a healthy eater."

"No, you're a noneater. There's a difference."

"I'm photographed everywhere I go. There's nothing wrong with staying trim."

"No, there isn't. But there is something wrong with starving yourself."

"I'm busy, Campbell. I do eat." She played with the edge of her menu, the image of a heaping plate of warm egg-battered bread taking root. "Really, I do. It's just a stressful few days and I'm not a good eater when I'm stressed."

The anger banked in his eyes as their waitress stepped up to the table, a pot of coffee in hand. "Then I'm glad I dragged you here."

"What can I get you?" The woman multitasked, pouring their coffees while she nodded through the order.

Campbell selected that heaping plate Abby had

imagined—the French toast special with a side of bacon and hash browns.

"I'll have the same." Abby handed over her menu and watched the woman hustle off. "Happy?"

"I'll reserve judgment until you've finished eating it."

He poured a generous shot of sugar in his coffee. "You're as bad as my sister. I swear, if given the chance she'd live on tea and gum."

"Kenzi's not that bad."

"She's damn close."

"Why are you so upset about this?"

"There's nothing wrong with a little meat on your bones. In fact, it's rather attractive."

"Oh." Abby snapped her mouth closed, whatever she'd expected him to say clearly not in evidence.

"Add on you're working too hard."

"Not going there since you've not slept since I met you."

"Aren't we a pair?" He grinned over the rim of his cup. "I can't exactly fault you for that one."

"So why'd you ask me about Stef?"

"No reason."

"Nope. Not buying that. Something set your antenna quivering. Deny it and you're only going to take the mad I've already got simmering and make it worse."

"I just observed how close she is to you. I saw it yesterday and the thought registered then, but it went off a bit louder this morning. She's always there."

"She's my assistant. That's what I pay her for. To always be there."

"Which means she's got a lot of access, both to you and to McBane. She can go anywhere in the company and there's no one who'd think twice about it."

A small quiver of awareness settled along her shoulder blades. "Are you trying to scare me?"

"No, I'm asking you to look at all the angles and think through the possibilities."

"She's been at the company for years and has never given me any reason to think she's anything but loyal."

"Loyalties can change."

"I'm not going to argue with you about this. Stef is my inner, inner circle. I've known her for a long time and I'm not worried. So why don't you tell me what you've been working on?"

She saw the fight leap up before he tamped it down. "I'm not giving up on this."

"Neither am I."

Campbell was prevented from saying anything by the arrival of their waitress and a tray heaping with breakfast. He waited until their waitress was out of earshot before he gave a rundown of his morning.

"T-Bone's helping me run through the programs I set up. Reading lines of code, that sort of thing."

"Any more hits to your honeypot?"

The hard line of his jaw firmed before he nodded. "Several, as a matter of fact."

A wave of panic washed through her system, turning the bit of hash browns into ash in her mouth. "What are we doing here, then? We need to get back. Every minute away is another minute lost."

"The damage has been done, Abby. T-Bone's got a few programs running to see if we can get any clues but he still thinks we need to get into your neighbors' homes and I agree with him."

"We'll do that first thing after we get to Paris."

"He and I feel strongly about something else."

The sweet taste of syrup that sang on her tongue faded in the sober look he shot her across the table.

"I'd like you to reconsider canceling the meetings this week."

Campbell had always thought of himself as a gambling man, but the stubborn, mulish look that settled itself over Abby's features was far worse than he anticipated.

"Absolutely not."

"Give me a good reason why you can't postpone them."

"You mean aside from the fact it's been on the calendar for a year and several high-profile individuals have their travel in place. Most of them are already en route."

"Meetings get canceled all the time."

"Not meetings that require a vote of the board. And not meetings that will decide several major decisions around investment, infrastructure and key global relationships."

Campbell understood the reticence to cancel instead of sticking to the plans, but he was growing increasingly uncomfortable with the lack of information he'd discovered so far. He didn't want to scare her, but he couldn't in good conscience let her think the trip was still a good idea.

He knew he was good at his job and he'd known going into this that whoever was hacking into an enterprise as massive as McBane wasn't some fly-by-night amateur.

But even he'd been surprised at the depths of skill the ghost had shown.

And the longer they went without answers, the more menacing this threat seemed. Add on the shooting at the bar and his gut wouldn't let up that Paris was some sort of final showdown.

"What if you're putting them in the line of fire, Abby? This isn't just about you."

"Of course it is." She set her fork down and Campbell didn't miss the subtle tightening of her lips as she marshaled her arguments. "Whatever all this is about, it's very personal. No matter how sick or twisted my ghost may be, there's nothing to be gained by targeting my board."

"You don't know that."

"I do know I'm not running scared. We've already added security. I'm perfectly willing to add even more. But I'm not canceling."

"Why won't you listen to reason?"

"And why can't you understand why I won't change my mind. I fight enough prejudice as a woman in my position. You think I'm going to exacerbate it by possibly crying wolf to my global board?"

Campbell fought to keep his voice low. "You've been threatened and shot at. Your company's technology has been infiltrated at several points. Your system was hacked into for seven minutes and you can't find the breach. That's not nothing, Abby."

"Business doesn't stop because we've got a problem. It can't. That's why I hired you, Campbell. Not to tell me how to run my business and not to ask me to change my plans. I hired House of Steele to find my problem and handle it and that's what I expect you to do."

The meal he'd dug into with gusto rolled over in his stomach and Campbell wondered—not for the first time—why the women in his life seemed to come in one category.

Stubborn and opinionated.

And when had he come to think of Abby as a woman in his life?

She was a job and she'd just made that point more than clear. Yet even as her unwillingness to change her mind chaffed, he couldn't fully fault her.

He'd been hired for a specific purpose and it wasn't her fault he'd not found her problem yet. Nor was he within his right to tell her to change her plans.

But damn it, something was *off.* It wasn't anything he could fully define, but that singular thought continued to beat through him in hard waves.

Right along with the fear that he couldn't keep her safe.

Chapter 7

For the second time in as many days, Abby struggled with both her words and her harsh attitude that had erupted in anger. She'd always prided herself on being a leader who accepted various points of view, synthesizing them into a responsible decision.

So why wasn't she able to get any perspective about this situation?

She knew Campbell was only acting on the information he had at hand. It was why she'd hired House of Steele and his services. She also knew the man didn't just understand technology, he understood the human behavior behind its use.

"You're awfully quiet, but I can hardly credit it to a carb hangover since you picked at your breakfast."

"I had a piece and a half of my French toast, smothered in butter and syrup and I ate all my bacon."

"Okay. So if it isn't a carb hangover, what has you so quiet?"

The city streets hummed around them as they walked the few blocks to the office. Even though there were people everywhere, the sheer volume of them ensured their conversation was a private one.

"You were a hacker before you became a good guy."

"I've always been a good guy."

"You know what I mean. The whole white-hat-black-hat thing." Abby knew the terms and knew the various classifications for those who thought the challenge of infiltrating a business or government entity was not only fun, but could offer rather enterprising benefits. "You were a black hat, weren't you?"

"What makes you say that?"

"Let's just say I put two and two together."

His eyebrows shot up but aside from that, his voice gave nothing away. "What, exactly, did you put together?"

"Your skills are extensive and you've got a good handle on the criminal underbelly of technology."

"Because it's my job."

"And Kensington mentioned a few times in college that you were in trouble for something or other."

Those eyebrows rose another notch. "Sold out by my sister?"

"No. She's loyal and she's a vault. I'm making the inference that 'in trouble for something or other' had something to do with technology. Especially since you knew how to change that cheerleader's grade."

They stopped at a crosswalk and his gaze drifted toward the Manhattan skyline. "Hoisted on my own petard."

"That's what you get for bragging about it."

He smiled as he turned back toward her. "And here I thought we were sharing childhood memories."

She knew he was avoiding an answer—or stalling to come up with one—but even in the evasion, she could still see that thin veneer of humor and easygoing nature she was fast coming to admire about him.

His still waters might run deep, but he knew how to navigate the waves with humor and a subtle aplomb that was appealing. He wasn't a man who needed to push his opinions on you.

Instead, he had a quiet confidence that was incredibly appealing. Add on a mischievous smile and she felt all her flimsy reasons for trying to resist him crumbling around her feet.

"Since you've been hoisted, are you going to come clean?"

"All right. Yes, I had a somewhat misspent youth. I was well on my way before my parents died and after… well, it only sped up the train."

"Why'd you stop going down that path?"

"My grandfather stepped in and gave me an ultimatum. If I didn't go straight he was going to turn me in himself."

The truth was so surprising—especially when she bumped it against her mental image of the very sweet and very gentlemanly Alexander Steele—she tripped as her heel caught in the sidewalk.

"Careful." His hand snaked out and grabbed her elbow. Even through the waterproof material of her raincoat, Abby felt the heat. "You okay?"

"Of course."

"Where was I? Oh, yes, my grandfather. He figured out what I was up to—"

"How?"

"I learned a long time ago not to question his methods. Suffice it to say, there's very little he's unaware of and what he might miss, my grandmother is right there to pick up the slack. It's actually a bit scary."

"They're sweet."

"Not quite the words that come to my mind first, but anyway. If you add on his various government connections he didn't have all that tough a time figuring out it was me."

"What tipped him off?"

"All that social engineering we discussed yesterday?" She nodded, encouraging him to continue. "That's still the best way to get into a con and I'd probed him about two or three government projects he was involved with. I then used that knowledge to my advantage."

"And like me, he figured out that two and two made four?"

"More like five or six—" he shot her a wide grin "—but you've got the gist of it."

"Why'd you clean up your act?"

"Three reasons."

When he didn't elaborate, Abby couldn't keep her curiosity at bay. "And they were?"

"I realized just how badly I'd disappointed him. The Steele family name has a long legacy of wealth, privilege and responsibility. My actions not only flew in the face of that, but it also put us all at risk."

"And?"

"What had started out as fun wasn't all that engaging any longer. Working on the actual project was a high but the after burn not so much. I never did it for the money, but rather so I could say I'd done it. And funny enough, when you're doing things you're not supposed to do, there's not a lot of people you can turn around and brag to."

"Which brings us to reason number three."

"T-Bone."

"Really? What'd he do, beat you up to get you to go straight?"

"He did me one better. He taught me how to use my skills to catch morons like me. He not only convinced me it was way more fun to be one of the white hats since we often have cooler gadgets, but he also proved to me that sooner or later, the good guys always get their man."

Their walk at an end, Campbell pushed at the revolving door to her building, gesturing for her to walk through. "So that's my story."

Abby said her hellos to the lobby staff as she and Campbell crossed to the elevators, his words ringing in her ears.

Did the good guys always win?

In her experience, that wasn't always the case. In fact, she'd often found the opposite in business. Those who were willing to be the most ruthless were often the most successful.

Even outside of the business world, she'd seen the ravages selfish individuals could cause, her stepmother sitting at the top of the heap.

She waited until they were once again alone in the elevator before pressing her thoughts. "I'm not sure you're right about the good guys."

"You don't agree?"

"Let's just say my experiences have clearly been different than yours."

"Come now, Abby." He reached for her hand and she took a sharp intake of breath at the contact. "You have to have had a few experiences that reinforce good choices."

"I have. I just don't think good always triumphs. I think there are a lot of bad people in this world who come out on top, over and over again."

His eyes narrowed at that, that heady blue of his eyes growing cloudy with concern. "Has life really been that hard for you?"

"Of course not." She tugged lightly on her hand but when he refused to let go, she just left it wrapped in his. "I lead a good life and I've got no complaints."

"Could have fooled me."

"It's true. I'm not some poor little rich girl and I'm not going to try to pretend I am. Life has its challenges for all of us. No one is immune. I was just making a broader observation that I don't think the bad guys always get caught."

"I guess we're going to agree to disagree on that one."

"What about the problem here? What if you don't find him? What if there is just a mysterious seven minutes we can't identify and it ultimately becomes some small blip, annotated in our logs and forgotten about after enough time passes?"

"You won't forget." His hand tightened on hers as his gaze bored into hers. "And you know the seven minutes is only the beginning, not the end."

"Which only reinforces my point."

He was prevented from answering by the pinging of the elevator as it opened on her floor. She glanced back over her shoulder, his intense gaze never wavering from hers.

"Good breakfast?" Stef looked up from where she typed out something on her computer.

"It was nice to get out." Abby tried for a smile after the sudden realization she was probably still frowning after her strange conversation with Campbell.

If she noticed the surly mood, Stef was unaffected as she pointed toward the edge of her desk. "Here's your mail. I haven't had a chance to go through it."

"Don't worry. I'll toss it in my bag and catch up on the flight."

"The car will be here at three to pick you both up."

Abby didn't miss Campbell's pointed stare that suggested Stef's comment only reinforced his earlier point. "Have you heard from the other board members?"

As Stef began rattling off various itineraries of the week's attendees, Campbell slipped out the exit with a brief excuse. The woman waited until Campbell was out of earshot before switching topics. "He's awfully easy on the eyes."

"He is that."

"And even better, you look like you enjoy each other's company."

Stef's words caught her up short as Abby picked up her mail. She'd been deliberately vague about why she was meeting with him and had put the meeting on her calendar herself. What had started out as a matter of discretion now worked to her advantage.

"The timing's not great."

"Love rarely is."

"Love?" Even though it was only pretend, Stef's use of the word was like a cold shower. "We should probably take it a day at a time."

"Oh, I don't know." Her assistant's eyes held a merry twinkle. "When you know you know."

"Is that how you feel about your guy?"

"Absolutely. He came into my life unexpectedly and was exactly what I didn't even know I needed."

"Poetic."

"Nah." Stef waved a hand. "I'm just happy."

Abby replayed the conversation in her mind as she walked back to her office. Although she knew there was no relationship with Campbell, she couldn't deny the attraction.

An altogether inconvenient attraction, her conscience whispered.

With a pile of work that still awaited her, Abby forced thoughts of the delectable Campbell Steele from her mind. It was time to get some work done.

The walk, food and fresh air had done her good. She was no longer tired, but she was a long way from finding her balance.

Lucas stepped into the waiting area at Charles de Gaulle and saw the driver who held a small placard with his name on it. He'd briefly toyed with having his driver drop him at the apartment he'd set up for what he was fast coming to think of as the final showdown, but knew the eagerness might cost him.

No need for that trip to show up in the driver's logs.

No, he'd continue as planned and head for his hotel. He'd waited this long. There was no reason to let his impatience get the better of him.

A quick scan of his personal email had confirmed all was moving along right on schedule.

PACKAGE CONFIRMED.

It sure was.

The mousy woman had been a calculated choice, but Lucas couldn't argue with how much of an asset she'd ended up being. Stef Nichols had been a wild card and he'd played his hand close as they got to know each other. For a woman who didn't care all that well for her outward appearance, she'd been surprisingly adept naked, which had made the experience more pleasurable than he'd originally anticipated.

She'd also been more than accommodating when he'd manfully sobbed to her about his mother and her poor, broken life. Dear old Mom's accidental pregnancy with him and the coldhearted McBane family who had done nothing for her. The repeated attempts through the years to meet and have a relationship with his father which had fallen on deaf ears.

The hard work he'd exhibited, pulling himself up by the bootstraps as he built his own reputation in the international business community.

Oh, yes, he'd worked Stef hard and she'd come through like a champ.

"Welcome to Paris, Mr. Brown. I've got the car waiting for you. I'll just get your bags."

Lucas barely paid the man any attention as he shifted his rolling suitcase into the man's care. "This is all."

"Then we can be on our way."

Anticipation leaped in his veins as the September air wrapped around him. He'd always enjoyed Paris and knew this would be the best trip he'd ever made to the City of Lights.

Once they were in motion, Lucas dialed the New York number that never went to voice mail.

"Hello, love."

He rolled his eyes at the platitude but kept the disdain from his words. The voice he'd worked long and hard to culture *just so* came out with a heavy layer of dark, seductive notes blended in. "Ah, my love. Words that never fail to make me feel better."

"How was your flight?"

"Short and quick. But most important, it has brought me to the last step."

"Everything's in place as you'd asked."

"Ah, my sweet. You understand me and it is the greatest gift a man could hope for." With the promise he'd dangled from the start, Lucas fed her more. "Next week. By next week we will be together and this will be behind us."

He didn't miss the sharp intake of breath on the other end of the phone, or the breathy tone of her voice. "I can't wait."

"All these years of waiting. All the endless hours of grief will be behind me as I begin my new life. As we begin our new life," he added for good measure at the end.

Although Stef had been more than willing to go along with his requests, he'd worked hard to paint an image of Abigail that was less than flattering.

Her irrational outbursts when they sat in meetings.

Her demands of his company that simply weren't possible.

And her inability to lead with the remotest sense of compassion.

It was lucky for him his half sister was known for her cool head and standoffish manner. He could only be grateful that tone and manner had extended to her dealings with her staff. While Stef had been hesitant at first to believe him, he had worn her down with examples while playing on her innate desperation for a happy ending.

"I do have an update for you. She seems to have become rather attached to a new man."

And there it was. The same bit of information he'd received when his associate had reported in early that morning.

"This is a new development, yes? Your frigid boss, she doesn't have much heat."

"Seems to have more than enough for this one."

Again, Lucas couldn't hold back the smile at the unexpected vehemence of his little wildcat.

Who'd have thought it?

"He's accompanying her to Paris."

"A distraction, then. Perhaps her mood will be improved over her last visit?"

The lie tripped off his tongue as he turned the new threat over in his mind. The boyfriend seemed like a strange addition at an odd time.

While he'd made up the so-called "incidents" that supported the image of a cold-blooded boss, Abby had made it easy. The woman was cool and aloof and entirely focused on her work.

So why now?

He wasn't going to let anyone stand in the way and knew his instructions had been more than clear to his hit man. The boyfriend wouldn't stand in the way and he needed to be dealt with.

It didn't change the fact that he might be a bigger nuisance than expected before all of Lucas's plans were finalized.

This was a new wrinkle he needed to account for.

"My love. I'm nearly to the hotel and I'm so tired. Can I call you tomorrow?"

"Of course."

Of course. Of course. Of course. Whatever soft feelings Lucas had allowed for her delivery of the package vanished. The woman was so eager to please it dripped from her. He'd be well rid of her.

He pretended his last few pleasantries, then disconnected the phone.

As his driver navigated the Champs-Élysées, Lucas turned the problem of the boyfriend over in his mind. A quick glance at his schedule confirmed tomorrow evening's events kicked off with a dinner at her home.

Images of the mansion on Avenue Foch floated through his mind. Lavish rooms. Lush amenities.

They should have been his.

Mentally forcing down the ever-present anger, he thought instead about the layout of the house and how he might make the best use of his time tomorrow evening. And as he let that thought move to the back of his mind to brew for a while, he tapped a few commands into his phone.

It was time to take a quick peek into McBane's computer systems and see if anyone noticed what he'd been up to.

The heavy rumble of engines kept company with her roiling thoughts as Abby stared out the window of the McBane corporate jet. As the plane took to the sky, the island of Manhattan winked like a glittering jewel below them. Although the view was one of her favorites, she took no comfort in the moment as the conversation with Stef continued to rattle around her thoughts.

Was there something to Campbell's assessment?

Or had he just added one more thing to her list to make her paranoid and nervous?

She looked over at Campbell, her intention to take a quick glance and see that he'd settled in and was comfortable. A set of earbuds were in his ears, playing a tune only for him, and his fingers flew over the keyboard of his laptop.

The opportunity to observe him without his knowledge was too good to pass up and she gave herself a minute to simply drink him in. He still wore the black T-shirt from earlier that day but he'd paired it with a sport coat. The look should have screamed bohemian businessman or natty college professor, but she saw neither.

All she did see was a man who seemed innately comfortable in his own skin. That thought had embedded itself earlier and now that it was there she couldn't let it go. It was part of his appeal and the more time they spent together the more she found herself drawn to that aspect of his personality, especially as it flew in the face of how she saw herself.

Competent and distant, unwilling to remove her armor.

Where competent and distant had described a brainy, motherless child throughout her youth, she'd added the rigid armor as she'd grown in her responsibilities at McBane. What had begun as a way to keep some distance between herself and the thousands and thousands of employees who depended on her to lead them had evolved into a mantle of protection she wore like a shield.

But it was that same attitude that also ensured an increasingly lonely existence she hadn't altogether realized she lived until faced with the opportunity to partner with an ally.

Campbell ran a hand over his stubbled jaw, a light curse on his lips before he began typing again in earnest, and she couldn't fight the spark of awareness that lit under her skin.

Whatever beanpole qualities he might have possessed as a kid were well and truly in the past. The large man who sat across the cabin had a quiet strength stamped in every line of his body, from the broad shoulders that hunched over the keyboard to the long legs that stretched out in front of him on the bench seat that ran the length of the jet.

And while the exterior package appealed, it was the other qualities she was coming to know that cemented her interest. His quick and ready smile. A sharp mind that never stilled. The ruthless work ethic that matched her own view of the world.

Oh, yes, he interested her, in every way possible.

"You okay?" His words interrupted her musings before he added that devastating smile as he lifted his eyes from the computer.

"Of course."

"I can hear your thoughts from over here."

Campbell watched a light flush creep over Abby's neck and couldn't hold back the smile. He'd felt her scrutiny for the past few minutes and while he was intrigued at the attention, he'd finally grown uncomfortable with the close eye.

Even as it gave him hope she wasn't immune to the heat and interest that arced between them.

"I was just thinking."

"About?"

"Your work ethic."

Whatever response he'd hoped for, that one wasn't it. He knew it wasn't all that forward-thinking, but somewhere in the back of his mind he was disappointed the answer wasn't his body and James Bond–esque style.

It was his mind.

Always his mind.

"Why do you look so insulted? There's nothing wrong with a work ethic."

"Until it's the way someone describes you."

The gentle smile he'd come to associate with her—

it had a sort of Mona Lisa quality that enticed even as it kept him at a distance—spread at his words. "I truly didn't mean any insult. I think your work ethic is an appealing quality. Along with a sharp mind and a quick smile. And a really, really nice pair of shoulders."

"You like my shoulders?"

"I do."

He wondered what else she liked and nearly took them down that sexy path, but veered off at the last minute. Her light tone and manner was a refreshing change after their morning and he was loath to bring it to an end.

Even as his body screamed in selfish frustration and tried desperately to get him to switch tactics.

"You know my mother and grandmother always lamented the combination."

"Your shoulders?"

"No, the sharp mind and the quick smile."

"Ahh." She nodded. "They're excellent qualities."

"Until you're ten and making endless trouble."

"You? I'm shocked and dismayed."

"Of course, I then used said smile and considerable charm to get out of punishment." Campbell closed the lid of the laptop and set it next to him on the seat. "You know the London townhome?"

"Your grandparents' city home?"

"Yep." The image of a beautifully decorated Hyde Park townhome filled his mind. He loved that house.

Loved the memories they'd made as a family inside of it even more.

"Yes, I've been there."

"Did Kensington ever take you to the attic?"

"Why would she take me to the attic?"

"Go with me, then. There's a huge attic that covers the entire top floor of the house. While it could be incredibly useful space, it's the exact opposite since it houses generations of Steele family heirlooms."

Her gaze narrowed as excitement filled her voice. "Campbell. What sort of heirlooms? Have you gone through it? There could be some incredible treasures up there."

"Perhaps *heirlooms* was too hasty a word. Most would call it years of accumulated junk."

"Your father's family comes from a long line of English lords. There has to be good stuff up there."

"Hardly." Campbell fought the urge to snort, well aware of the absolute junk that sat in the attic. "My grandfather doesn't carry the title so he doesn't have the really good stuff. His father's brother's family got all that."

"I'd still like a crack at it."

"You're welcome to it."

"Fine, fine. Okay. What horrible evil did you rain down on the London attic?"

"I went through a snake phase."

"I hadn't realized London was a hotbed for snakes." The look of distaste that had spread across her face at his use of the word *snake* grew broader as she obviously thought through the implications. "And you've outgrown this phase, I assume?"

"Yes, you can find snakes in London, especially when you beg and plead for one as a pet. And no, once dear Blinky went on to the dearly departed afterlife I didn't replace him."

"That's good."

"Why?"

"Snakes belong in zoos. Or on other continents."

"They make great pets."

Abby waved her hands. "No. No, no, no. Just no."

"All right. I'll argue the merits of reptiles later. Back to the attic. I thought that it wasn't fair that Blinky had to sit in our old drafty house and I remembered we had a beautiful set of old clothes up in the attic."

"Like gowns and stuff?"

"Exactly."

"You wrapped your pet snake up in what was likely gowns from the 1800s?"

"Probably." Campbell couldn't hold back the laugh at her horror. "He wasn't a rodent. The dresses were as lovely after he got done with them as before."

Since Campbell could see he was losing his audience, he rushed through. "Suffice it to say, regardless of the temperature, a curious snake had no more interest sitting around wrapped in a ball gown than I would have. So he got loose."

"You just left him up there?"

"Sure. I figured he was warm enough and would stay put."

"But he didn't?"

"Nope. Crawled down out of the attic and worked his way through the various floors of the house until he ended up wrapped up in my grandparents' bed. Apparently their old quilt was way warmer than a bunch of cold silks up in the attic."

"And you got out of this with a smile?"

"Yep."

She shook her head. "Clearly this was what I missed not having brothers."

"Doesn't that make you sad?"

"It did until you left me with the thought I could have ended up with snakes in my bed. Thanks. I just feel a whole lot better about being an only child."

Campbell knew it was a dumb story—heck, he hadn't

thought about poor cold Blinky in years—but it was nice to see her smile again. And the image of his grandmother screaming from her room never failed to...

"The attic."

The words hovered on his lips as his mind flashed to the current problem with Abby's Paris home.

"What do you mean?"

"The attic is where it is."

"Where what is?"

Campbell got up from his spot and crossed to sit next to her. "Your neighbors. Whatever's in their house is in the attic."

"Why?"

"Why not? Nothing was reported stolen, right?"

"Sure, but..."

"No, think about it, Abby." He laid a hand on her arm, willing her to understand. "Think about it. It's a city home, right?"

"Sure."

"Big, arching eaves that encompass the attic, likely running across the entire top of the house?"

"Yes." As she nodded, he saw the understanding dawn slowly in her gaze. "And neither of my neighbors found anything missing after the break-ins."

"Because there was nothing to miss."

"There was something to leave behind."

Chapter 8

Campbell dropped his bags in the guest room Abby had chosen for him before crossing to the wide-framed window. The room was impressively large, with two windows that looked down on the street and a third that sat on the far side of the room, facing the house next door.

The security team he'd lined up had already spent the day in Abby's home. While half the team had focused on setting up the surveillance equipment he'd requested, another put together a discreet watch up and down Abby's street and yet another had searched the entire house for bugs.

As T-Bone had predicted, nothing was turned up in the sweep.

Campbell had already spent another hour with the security team upon their arrival and agreed to another briefing at eight. Which meant he had around two hours to get in some sleep.

So why the hell was he wide-awake?

He pulled out his computer and set it aside almost as quickly, followed by his tablet which he also set aside. While his electronics—usually an appendage on the best of days—kept him occupied, he couldn't get settled.

Couldn't concentrate.

Abby had shared plans of the house the night before in the kitchen and Campbell realized he hadn't gone to the study yet. If he remembered the renderings, the study should be up a floor and on the opposite end of the hall.

Since sleep seemed elusive, a visit to the study might help calm his thoughts. If he could get a solid image in his mind, maybe he could fall asleep and let his subconscious work on a plan for how to trap their ghost in there.

The remembered directions were pretty accurate and he found the study on his second try, after first entering another large guest room.

And walked in on Abby, seated behind a large desk, a small lamp illuminating her face.

"What are you doing up?"

Campbell crossed the room, the aged hardwoods under his bare feet quickly giving way to a thick rug. "I could ask you the same."

"I figured I'd be out before my head hit the pillow and surprise. Here I am, wide-awake."

"Must be that meal on the plane because I'm in the same boat."

"Maybe it's the brute squad you hired."

"The security team?" At the smudges that rimmed her eyes he crossed around the desk, pulling a chair with him. "Did someone say something to you?"

"Nothing specific, but I can't stop thinking about what they said. About what they've done inside my home."

"Abby." He laid a hand over hers, shocked when her

flesh was ice-cold. "Come on. It's their job to keep you safe."

"Safe, Campbell? Or scared out of my mind?"

He lifted her hand, bringing his other around to cup her palm, anxious to warm her. "They're trying to assess threats and identify the best way to keep you out of harm's way."

She shook her head and he felt tremors rock her body where they were connected.

And it wasn't nearly enough.

Standing, Campbell dragged her to her feet.

"What are you doing?"

He reached around her and lifted her, her slender frame light as he wrapped her up in his arms. A large couch dominated the center of the room and he dropped into it, keeping her tightly cradled against his body as he nestled them both into the couch. "Grab that blanket."

She pulled the heavy throw off the couch arm and he took it from her, spreading it over both of them. "You need to warm up."

"It's not that cold."

"Then why are you shivering?"

As if on cue, a hard shudder racked her body and he pulled her closer, using one hand to smooth the blanket more tightly around her body.

"There's someone in my life who wants to do me harm."

Another tremor went through her body and he tightened his grip, waiting for her to continue.

"Up until the briefing I'd put it out of my mind that it was really real, you know? And before you say I'm not taking it seriously, I *am* taking it seriously. But it's hard. I run a major corporation. I've had threats before and they have always been nothing."

"None of those have been personal."

"No." She shook her head, the crown of her head bumping lightly against his chin with the movement. "No, they haven't."

"I didn't hire the security team to scare you."

"I know."

Campbell shifted his head so he could look her in the eye. "Do you really? It seems as if you've looked at this threat as something distant from you because it's come in electronically."

"The events of the last few days have made it more and more evident that's just the opening gambit." Abby nestled more deeply into his arms and Campbell warred with the need to protect her and the increasing urgency of his attraction to her. "But it doesn't change the fact that I can't stop living my life. Nor does it mean I want to live in fear."

Campbell recognized the desperate truth underlying her words. Had seen it in his own sisters and their professional choices.

Hell, he'd seen it in himself.

A half life wasn't really living a life, no matter how you looked at it. When that knowledge was further informed by loss, as both he and Abby had suffered, you learned to realize just how precious time was.

How important it was to live fully.

So why did he continue to pull back from her? Why did they both continue to pull back?

"Do you fear loss?"

"What?" Campbell shifted again so that he could look into Abby's eyes. The soft light of the room danced in their dark depths and Campbell marveled at how her thoughts so closely mirrored his own.

"Loss? Because of losing your parents, do you fear it?"

"I suppose I do on some level, but I don't know if I feel it any more or less than anyone else. Fear of loss is a fairly standard human emotion."

While Campbell knew full well the death of his parents had shaped him and his siblings, he also knew it had been other events in his life that had put up the walls.

Losing his parents—while difficult—had been a part of the natural order of things.

"I lost a friend once."

"What happened?"

"You mean Kensington never told you?"

Abby's eyes narrowed. "Your sister is loyal to you and your family. We're friends, but it doesn't mean she's told me things that are private to your family."

He nodded at that and knew it wasn't fair to assume Kenzi wasn't discreet. Of all the qualities his sister possessed, her loyalty was one of the ones that most defined her.

"Sarah was a friend of mine. We'd known each other since we were small. Her family's estate was next to my grandparents' estate and we both used to spend our summers in the English countryside. Attend those garden parties you referenced yesterday."

He saw the faint smile hover over Abby's face. "Was she your girlfriend?"

"I wanted her to be my girlfriend but it never happened."

"Why not?"

"When we were kids it wasn't something that occurred to either of us. And as we got older I was too shy to do anything about it."

"And then, of course, you were busy impressing cheerleaders with your skills."

The gentle tease in her voice was somehow exactly

what he needed as he thought back to those dark days. He'd spent his early teenage years feeling awkward and whatever tender emotions he'd had for Sarah he'd pushed aside in his embarrassment over his gangly body and decided lack of social skills.

And instead, he'd delved deeper and deeper into the electronic world that offered him endless hours of comfort and acceptance.

"Those skills that so impressed the cheerleader when I was sixteen?"

"That would be the ones."

"Technology was my escape. It was like a big puzzle that I was always piecing together and I was good at it during a time when I felt like I wasn't good at anything."

"I'm not sure there's anyone who'd pay to go back to their teenage years. Except for the occasional prom queen and star jock and even then, I'd wager not very many of them."

"And that's more true for some of us than others."

"What happened to Sarah?"

"She was dealing with her own issues, including parents going through a divorce. She was vulnerable and a predator lured her online."

"Oh, no." Emotions he'd thought he'd long buried rushed to the fore of his mind as Abby shifted in his arms. He felt her move under the blanket before she reached out and gripped his hand. "What happened to her?"

"She made the decision to meet him and he ultimately took her life."

"Oh, Campbell. I'm so, so sorry."

His family had spared him the specifics, but with his computer skills it hadn't taken him long to discover what had happened to Sarah. And after he hacked into the police records, he'd seen her battered body.

Had read the reports of what had been done to her.

In that moment his life had changed, any shred of innocence he still possessed vanishing as if it had never existed.

"I decided I was going to find the man who did it to her. I had the skills and the tools so I moved forward on luring him out."

"Did you catch him for the police?"

"I caught him."

The words hovered between them and Campbell felt the imperceptible tightening of her body.

"You were only a child. On your way to becoming a man, but still fundamentally a child."

"It didn't feel like it at the time. And then when my parents died a few months later it didn't feel like it at all."

"A loss of innocence and too much responsibility way too soon." Abby lifted a hand and pressed it to his cheek. "And lessons no one should ever have to learn about someone they love."

The warmth of her palm—the opposite of the cold he'd felt when he'd first come into the room—heated his cheek as the bluish hues of early morning shone through the study windows.

"Another morning we're awake to see begin after a sleepless night."

"We're lucky, Campbell. We've got another day. Another chance. Something Sarah never got."

"I know."

She ran her hand down his cheek, over his neck to settle on his shoulder. "I'm sorry for your loss."

"Thank you."

For the moment, they simply sat like that, their gazes locked.

Campbell wanted to lean forward—to take the comfort so clearly offered in her eyes—but something held him back. Whether it was the fragile bubble of a moment that had wrapped itself around them or the simple fact that it seemed to tarnish Sarah's memory to do more, he didn't know.

Instead, he simply tightened his hold and pulled her against his chest as they watched the sun rise over the streets of Paris.

Abby laced up her sneakers and dug around the kitchen for the spare key she kept in a small catchall drawer. The security team Campbell had hired had already arrived and she'd spent the past hour briefing them on the layout of the house while getting a briefing in return of how they were going to protect each ingress and egress.

The very fact her home was referred to as having ingresses and egresses was enough to have her running for the hills.

Add on the news Campbell had shared in the study and she needed to clear her head.

Desperately.

I caught him.

Campbell's words were vague enough to leave her wondering exactly what he had done all those years ago and she was just concerned enough to not fully want to know the truth.

Although she'd gotten past it, the incident she'd faced years before in the London office had left its marks. Scarred her with the knowledge that she was vulnerable.

Campbell's friend had been vulnerable and no one was able to help her until it was too late.

The hard core she'd only sensed up until this point had become very real in those long lingering minutes they'd shared in the study and the man she'd originally thought of as lighthearted and easygoing was anything but. With the news of Sarah's death, she realized Campbell used the casual facets of his personality to keep a person from digging too deeply.

As if her thoughts of him conjured him up, Campbell plowed through the swinging door into the kitchen just as she moved into a few stretches to warm up her muscles. "What are you doing?"

"Going for a run."

"Come on, Abby. You can't just leave."

"I'm a runner, Campbell. I'm not giving up the one thing that keeps me calm."

"Use the treadmill."

"I want to go outside. And aside from the glorious benefits of fresh air, it'll give me a chance to unobtrusively take a look around the neighborhood."

She saw his speculative gaze and knew she'd at least made a small dent into his argument even as a frown rode his features in clear lines of annoyance. "It still isn't safe."

"Well, seeing as how I'm wrapped up in a bulletproof vest underneath my sweatshirt, I'm rather convinced it is."

"You can run in that?"

"Looks like I'm going to find out." Abby couldn't quite hold back the triumphant grin as he just stood and stared at her. "Are you actually speechless?"

"No."

"Then can we quit talking so I can get going?"

"Wait two minutes and I'll join you."

"Be my guest."

When he left, her gaze alighted on her work bag where she'd set it on one of the kitchen table chairs the night before. A glance at the open top had her remembering the mail she'd grabbed from Stef on her way out of town.

Abby pulled the stack of mail out, the majority of the letters hard, square envelopes that would be invitations to some event or another. And as she thought of all the RSVP'd regrets, she was once again pleased she'd made the call to add a second assistant to her team.

A small box sat on the top of the stack, attached to a fancy envelope, and Abby selected it first. Her curiosity was high as to its contents as she turned it over in her hands. The envelope was a rich creamy vellum, cool and smooth to the touch. She flipped it over once more, curious there wasn't any postmark, then assumed Stef had pulled it from a messenger's outer wrapping.

She pulled at the subtle wrappings, separating the box from the envelope. Following custom—even as she was dying to know what was in the box—she opened the envelope first.

SURPRISE

That single word was written in elegant script in the center of the card. She flipped it over, but there was nothing else to suggest a sender or even a maker of the beautiful paper.

With trembling fingers, she reached for the small box and tore off the wrappings. As she lifted the lid, the small kernel of fear that had wrapped itself around her rib cage with hard iron fists squeezed.

Hard.

A small card, in matched material to the larger stock

in the envelope, nestled in a hank of chestnut-colored hair, wrapped at the end with an elegant black bow.

The words on the card were unmistakable.

Elizabeth Abigail McBane.

Her mother.

The kitchen seemed to tilt as Abby sank to the floor, the thick wood of the cabinets the only support for her back.

It wasn't possible.

"Abby?"

She glanced up to see Campbell, clad in workout gear, as he barreled through the swinging door toward her. She felt his hands on her shoulders, willing her to look at him.

Felt his penetrating stare as he kept calling her name.

"Abby. What is it? Talk to me."

On a small mewl that didn't even sound quite human, she pointed to the box that had fallen from her hands.

Saw the hair and the card where both lay on the floor.

Remembered the image of her mother she kept in her mind's eye, the soft wave of chestnut hair that perpetually framed her face as familiar as it was distinctive.

Recognized the words that taunted even as they provided evidence of the box's contents.

And as Campbell picked up the locks of hair and the card, she felt the world go black around her.

Chapter 9

Campbell dropped the box and its contents once more as he reached for Abby. Even with the layers of bullet-proof vest, T-shirt and sweatshirt, her body was frail beneath his large hands.

"Abby. Can you hear me?"

She blinked a few times and another soft groan echoed from her lips before her head lolled back against her shoulder.

"Come on, Abby. Come back to me." He added a bit of gentle pressure to his sharp words before reaching behind her to give her head some support.

After one more rapid set of blinks, she opened her eyes and Campbell was rewarded with a deep stare from those chocolate depths. He saw the moment the reality of what she'd just discovered in the package registered as she leaped toward him, wrapping her arms around his waist. "Oh, Campbell."

Her forward movement was enough to push him off balance and he caught her as he fell backward from his crouched position. "Shh. It's okay."

He crooned the words as he kept a light pressure on her back, rubbing circles through the thick padding.

"Why is this happening?"

"I don't know." The truth of those words ate at him.

Who was doing this to her? And why couldn't he get a handle on the source of the problem?

He was good at his job, damn it. He knew technology. Yet this guy—and the fingerprint on the technology, coupled with this latest assault had him increasingly thinking her assailant was male—was practically invisible.

His gaze landed once more on the box. A very, very real gambit.

Tangible.

"Abby." He pulled on her arms so she was looking at him. "Where did the box come from?"

A light sheen of tears filled her eyes before spilling over onto her cheeks. "It was in my bag. Part of yesterday's mail."

"The mail Stef gave you before you left?"

"Yes." She rubbed at her eyes, realization dawning with the truth of his words. "Oh, no. No, Campbell. She didn't do this."

"We can't be sure."

"She didn't."

"Then we need to rule her out. Even if she's not doing it intentionally, she's likely a conduit of some sort."

"But she can't be."

"Come on, baby. Think about it." The endearment was out before he could snatch it back and as it fell off his lips, he didn't want to pull it back.

It felt good.

Comfortable.

"She's got complete access to you. She's not all that confident on her own. Someone could have used her to get to you."

"That's not fair." He saw the light of battle spark in her gaze and much preferred it to the shell-shocked victim he walked in on in a puddle on the kitchen floor. "So she's a little mousy. That doesn't mean she's sold me out."

"She's got a new boyfriend."

"So?"

"Have you met him?"

"No, and I wouldn't expect to."

"Not once, in all the time they've been dating. He never came to pick her up?"

She shook her head as she sat back, reaching for her long fall of hair to pull it up in a ponytail. "That's not the type of relationship we have."

"She's your assistant. She knows when you go to doctor's appointments, presumably. That doesn't lend itself to a certain sort of personal connection?"

A light blush suffused her cheeks and even while he wondered at it, he couldn't deny the color brought life back into her features.

"That's just not me. I'm not warm and buddy-buddy with people."

"You and Kensington could have fooled me."

"That's different. She's my friend, not my employee." She stood and began to pace the room. "I took the helm of McBane very early. I never wanted anyone to think less of me because of my age, so I cultivated a very cool exterior."

"Let no one in." Campbell got to his feet but stood in place as she paced.

"And don't give them a chance to second-guess me

because I don't come off as polished and professional. That extended to my personal staff. I've never been mean to Stef or to anyone. In fact, she's been well-rewarded for her service to McBane."

"But you're not friends."

"No." Abby shook her head. "No, we're not. And I'm not sure that speaks all that well of me."

Campbell watched, fascinated, as that veneer of control she maintained so well fell back into place while she used her mind to work through the problem.

Had he ever met anyone like her?

The small, traitorous voice that was quick to use Sarah as a comparison to any woman of his acquaintance stayed surprisingly silent as he stared at Abby.

The truth was, he hadn't.

And as he watched Abby battle her past choices he couldn't help but think her coworkers had missed out.

She was a beautiful woman, but that was only the external package. The woman inside was warm and compassionate, bright and thoughtful.

She was, in a word, *amazing*.

And he wanted her.

Whatever adrenaline-fueled response had him dragging her into his arms when he entered the kitchen and saw her crumpled there had shifted as the moments danced out between them. It transformed into a heavy need that settled in his core and wouldn't let go.

With deliberate movements, he walked toward her. Her pacing had slowed and she stared at him from her perch against the large island counter that dominated the center of the room. Where before he'd seen fear and a hopeless anxiety that speared him clean through, he now saw a vital awareness that seemed to light her up from the inside.

"Campbell." His name fell from her lips on a whisper as he settled one hand on either side of her, effectively caging her against the counter.

He couldn't hold back the small smile. "Abby."

"This probably isn't a good idea."

He nodded, considering, even as his body demanded he place his hands on her. Demanded he press his hard form against her core. Demanded he taste the unique blend of sumptuous flavors that were only her. "Probably not."

"None of it means I don't want you."

"Very good." He bent his head and nipped her lips. "Because I want you, too."

And then there were no more words as they both closed the space between them. He leaned in, fully capturing her mouth with his while she gripped his hips, pulling him more closely into her body.

The gentle pressure of her lips against his gave way as he slipped his tongue inside to mate with hers and felt the rush of need when she met his thrust with one of her own. The tender moments spread out between them as the kiss intensified. Campbell put every ounce of himself into the act, willing her to understand he'd protect her.

Desperate for her to know that he'd give his life to ensure she was safe.

The hands at his waist were restless before she placed them on his lower back and pulled him more determinedly against herself. He mimicked the sexy motion and drew her closer, reveling in the lithe lines of her slender form.

And as he got an armful of the heavy body armor, the moment broke, shattering into pieces.

What was he thinking?

She'd been threatened. She was scared. And she

needed his help and his full focus to deal with the face-less pursuer who was intent on doing her harm.

She needed his protection, not to be the object of his latest sexual fantasy.

"Campbell? What is it?"

"We shouldn't be doing this."

She placed a hand against his cheek. "We both want it."

"And that's the problem. You're wearing a vest for protection, for heaven's sake. We can't do this now. Can't lose focus."

The words had their desired effect as she dropped her hand. "Fine."

He'd nearly pulled away. Had almost dragged him-self from the warm, willing woman in his arms when the bleak chill in her eyes stilled him. Bending his head, he pressed his forehead to hers. "I need to focus on keep-ing you safe."

"You are keeping me safe."

The discarded box at his feet suggested otherwise. "Not safe enough."

With deliberate movements, he pulled away from her, then bent to pick up the box and the note. "I'm going to meet with the security team. I suspect they're going to want to talk to you about Stef."

She nodded as resignation painted her face in a subtle mask. "I suppose so."

If she was mad at him for stopping them from going any further, he could live with that.

Keeping her mad would keep her sharp.

And if the escalating threats were any indication, nei-ther of them could afford to fall off their game.

Abby had always loved the Paris house. While many chose Avenue Foch for its globally known swank factor, she'd selected the house for its proximity to her favorite park in Paris—the Bois de Boulogne. The beauty of the land was absolute, but it was its history that fascinated.

And it gave her immeasurable pleasure to think she ran the same paths people had traversed for centuries.

The image of her favorite path faded in her mind as she stared at the four walls of her study and walked the lead security guy—David was his name—through the events of the previous day and how the package came to be in her possession.

Yes, her assistant had included it on the heap of things Abby had shoved in her bag before departing for the airport.

No, she didn't think Stef could possibly be responsible.

Yes, she had the numbers for McBane's security team as well as the mail room. It would be easy enough to trace the delivery, if in fact, there had been one.

And then the hardest question of all.

Could it possibly be her mother's hair?

Despite his emotional distance in the kitchen, Campbell held her hand in his throughout all of David's questions. His touch reassured, even as she felt her world crumble around her.

"My mother was killed in an accident when I was five. I've never had any reason to think otherwise."

"What sort of accident?" David's question was expected, but even so Abby felt it like a gunshot.

"She was hit by a taxi in Manhattan. It was a rainy day, she tried to cross at a light and a cab driver came out of nowhere and hit her. The man suffered for years over the accident."

Abby knew because the man's wife had contacted her years ago to express her husband's lifelong grief. In all the years since it had happened, she had never thought there was anything more than the very sad news that we all had a finite number of days in our lives and her mother's had been up.

She'd long thought it was one of the things that had bonded her and Kensington so quickly when they'd met at school. The grief that something so sudden brings on leaves a deep, dark scar. But it had been through their shared experience that she and Kensington had forged a friendship that was rock-solid.

"I think it would be best to contact Abby's administrative assistant." Campbell looked at his watch. "It's about three in the morning. We can either send a cop over now or have her questioned in the morning."

"Please, please let it wait." Abby knew it was wishful thinking, but she still couldn't see Stef holding any responsibility for the things that had been happening. And if Stef were responsible…

Well, then it could wait a few hours, Abby resolved as she stood up.

"I've got twenty people arriving in the house in about eight hours. Caterers are due here before lunch and I've got a number of preparations I need to see to in the meantime."

Abby also thought of the visit she and Campbell wanted to make next door and knew she was rapidly running out of time.

"Of course, Ms. McBane." David nodded, then issued a series of instructions to his team.

"I'll also need you all to be a bit less obtrusive when the caterers are here. I don't wish for gossip to start or for my guests to believe there is anything wrong."

David looked as if he were about to argue, but a sharp,

pointed glance from Campbell had the man nodding instead. "Understood."

Satisfied he did understand, Abby made her excuses and left Campbell and David to continue working through strategy. She knew she still had to take the team through the guest list—a final precaution that matched photos with the names of her attendees so the security team had a ready understanding of who was who—but she resolved to do it later after she had a chance to settle her racing thoughts.

Climbing the stairs to her bedroom, she was anxious to shed the bulletproof vest. The already-restrictive vest had grown nearly overwhelming as she talked about threats, her mother's death and the increasing suspicion that hung over her trusted secretary's head.

And for the first time in nearly an hour, Abby breathed a sigh of relief when she loosened the stays of the protective garment. She shed the rest of her clothes and stepped into a hot shower, the steamy stall and the hot beads of water going a long way toward clearing her mind.

Reaching for the shampoo, she lathered up and began scrubbing her hair. The long strands sifted through her fingers, a vivid reminder of what she'd opened in the kitchen.

As she rinsed the soap from her hair, Abby's eyes flew open in shock and awareness.

The package she opened was full of shiny, sleek hair. Could something taken from a woman who died a quarter of a century ago have held up that well?

She knew hair lasted, but to look as if it had been cut and preserved neatly for that long?

She'd have to tell Campbell. Get his thoughts. But it seemed as if the package was more scare tactic than real message. As the shampoo slid from her head and neck to swirl down the drain, Abby could only hope so.

At the thought of Campbell, thoughts of her mother receded and she was surprised to find their early morning conversation take center stage. He'd suffered so much pain at such a young age, with the loss of his friend Sarah as well as his parents. The reality of that tugged at her and where she'd felt interest before she felt something even deeper.

Empathy.

And attraction, McBane. Don't forget that one.

And hoo-boy, did they have that in spades.

She could still conjure up the sense memory of his lips against hers, his body pressed intimately to her, hard angles against the softer curves of her figure.

He'd pulled back—pulled away—but she'd sensed his need. Knew her own matched his.

Did it make sense to continue denying it? Especially when they labored under the very real threat of danger from an unknown assailant?

She'd always thought the concept of falling for someone during a heightened period of danger seemed silly, but now that she was faced with the situation herself, she couldn't fully ignore how her attraction to him only continued to burn hotter and hotter.

She toweled off and found her comb, separating the long wet strands of her hair as she considered what might come next. And reached for her robe when she heard the knock on her bedroom door.

The thin silk didn't hide all that much, but it was a suitable cover as she crossed to the door.

And found Campbell standing on the other side.

"I'm sorry. I thought you were working."

"I will be, but figured I'd take a few moments to relax while I could squeeze them in."

"Wise choice."

She didn't miss how his gaze stayed firmly on her face. The sweet gesture arrowed to the center of her heart and lightened her dour mood considerably.

"You don't look quite so sad. As before."

"I've been through so many emotions in the last few days I'm not sure which one's the strongest." She opened the door wider and gestured him to a small sofa in a sitting room off her bedroom. "Come on in. I'm going to change and then we can figure out what we're going to do about the neighbors."

She didn't miss how his heated gaze roamed over her back as she moved into her bathroom, his reflection more than clear in the broad mirror that ran the full length of the wall.

Yes, she was sad. And overwhelmed by feelings she'd long thought buried, Abby thought as she closed the bathroom door.

But none of it could take away the sense of anticipation that filled her at the fact that he saw her as a woman.

Stef Nichols lay in her small studio apartment, splayed on the sofa bed she pulled out every night, and stared at the ceiling. Her conversation with Lucas played over and over in her mind as shadows played across the ceiling and the noises of Kew Gardens, Queens, echoed outside the walls.

He'd sounded so tired. So worn. And so very ready for all of it to be over.

It shot a spear of anger through her as she thought of the woman who'd put those feelings there. Who'd made him so sad and tired. So frustrated and disappointed at the continued lack of acceptance to any of his numerous outreaches.

Abby.

Stef hadn't believed Lucas at first—had been shocked and amazed and more than a little skeptical there was even a connection between her new lover and her boss—but he'd convinced her.

Oh, how he'd convinced her.

The emails he'd shown her. His mother's old journals. Even the tersely worded letter from Abby's father to Lucas's mother. All of them proved, without a doubt, that Lucas had been denied his birthright.

Stef lifted her left hand and gazed at her naked fourth finger in the ambient light from the streetlamps outside her window. The finger where he'd place a ring.

Soon.

So very soon.

A light sound—the barest scrape against the hardwood floors near her front door—had her sitting upright. She glanced toward her small galley kitchen, unable to see around the small bar that separated the galley from the front door. She swung her legs over the bed, but the light sound turned into a heavy thud as the form of a man appeared and fear cratered through her system.

A scream flooded her throat, but the man was on top of her before she could move, his hand over her mouth as he pressed her back into the thin sofa mattress.

How had he gotten in? Why was he here? What had she done?

She'd been awake. Daydreaming, yes, but awake. She'd never even heard him.

The intruder leaned down and pressed his lips against her ear. His hot breath sent the coldest of chills racing down her spine.

He was going to rape her. Or something even worse.

Willing her thudding pulse to calm, she fought to gather herself so the moment he moved—and he'd have to move if he wanted to remove her clothes and his own—she'd leap. Would knee him to within an inch of his life, then run.

Her landlord was downstairs. Neighbors she didn't know very well but who would help her. Someone would be there to help her.

They *had* to help her.

"Do you know why I'm here?" His voice scratched against her ear and she sensed the innate joy he took from the fear that flooded off her in sickening waves.

She tried to shake her head but he held her in place while she mumbled a denial against his hand.

"I'm going to tell you. I always think the people I kill have a right to know why I'm here."

Her eyes went wide at that, the simple answer smooth as velvet and colder than the Hudson in February.

"You trusted the wrong man, sweetheart."

The breath that was crushed from her by the heavy weight of his body fully evaporated at the man's words.

Lucas?

"I can see you know who I mean. Your boyfriend. Bet he told you something nice and sweet about how much he loved you. How great and wonderful you are and how you're the woman he's spent his whole life looking for."

Despite the roiling, greasy fear that glugged its way through her system, the truth of the man's words rang true. They were the voice of a stranger, come to prove to her for the last time why she'd never deserved love in the first place.

The executioner who'd ensure she knew each and every one of her sins before she paid for them.

"Your fancy London boyfriend is a liar and a thief. But—" the man's eyes grew philosophical as they bored into hers "—he pays well. And he ensures I get to do what I love more than anything else in this world."

Even without that confirmation, Stef knew. Knew he wasn't going to move. Knew he wasn't going to give her a chance to break free.

She saw it in his eyes—felt the determination in his touch—before he shifted for the final time, his hands at her neck.

Oh, yes, she knew he did what he loved—knew it with bone-deep certainty—as the world faded away to nothing.

Chapter 10

Campbell sat down on the small, refined couch Abby had directed him to and scrubbed his hand over his face. What the hell was he thinking, coming to her bedroom? He only intended to check on her and make sure she was all right. Instead, he'd been turned inside out and upside down by the mere sight of her in the thin robe that highlighted more than it hid.

The light sheen of moisture on her neck had nearly been his undoing, even as he tried diligently to keep his eyes above the V of her robe.

She was back in moments, but she could have been gone an hour and he'd likely not have noticed, his mind was so filled with her.

Campbell allowed himself a moment to simply take her in as she crossed the room toward him. She wore a baby-blue cashmere sweater that sculpted her body before falling just so to skim the tops of her thighs. The light color was set off by dark blue jeans that gave her legs a long coltish look and bare feet.

The look was sexy and a bit bohemian with the bare feet and her still-damp hair flipped back over her shoulder.

She dropped into the small wingback chair next to him. "We need to game plan for the visit to my neighbors."

"Abby. I'm not sure it's all that good an idea any longer."

"Why not?" She sat back, curiosity riding high on her face. "It made sense yesterday when T-Bone first suggested the problem was housed next door."

"That was before you got a threat that was far more personal than anything that's come before. He's escalating, Abby."

"And we're going to set up a trap to catch him and we need to use every weapon at our disposal in order to do that. You know as well as I do the likelihood of finding something next door is high."

Campbell knew she was right and he also knew she was the only one who had a chance of getting quick and immediate access into her neighbors' home. He could put the security team on it, but the amount of time it would take them to secure access to the home and then do a search, they might as well forget about it.

He glanced over at her, intrigued to see a rosy glow riding her cheekbones. "Was your shower too hot?"

"Hot enough, why?"

"You're glowing."

The briefest smile hovered in her eyes before she turned toward him, her gaze bright and eager. "I realized something when I slowed down and thought for a moment. I don't think that was my mother's hair."

Campbell wanted to believe her—and anything that took those shadows of fear from her eyes was well worth evaluating further—but he also didn't want her to develop false hope. "Why?"

"I think that package this morning was meant to scare me, nothing more."

"That's an awfully calculated risk."

"Think about it, though. That was a pretty significant hank of hair. And my mother died twenty-five years ago. Wouldn't it have aged somehow? I don't know how to explain it, but I just don't think it would look quite as shiny and new as what was in the box."

Forensics wasn't his area but Campbell figured she might have a decent point.

"And further, while I'd be hard-pressed to remember anything about my mother's viewing and funeral, I know my father would have noticed if a large piece of her hair was missing. Or it certainly would have been addressed by the funeral home."

"So you think it was a ploy to scare you?"

"I do. I'd like to get the sample tested all the same but I find it hard to believe it's really my mother's hair."

Campbell turned the thought over in his mind. The box of hair had been sick and twisted, but it would also be a thoroughly effective way to scare someone and throw them off of the real problem.

In fact, it *had* thrown them off the real problem, tying up the security team for a few hours and off the bigger task at hand which was securing the house.

"You really think she was the victim of an accident?"

"I've got no reason to think otherwise."

"I hope you're right."

"For the moment, let's assume I am right. And if I'm not, then we'll deal with that bridge when we come to it."

They'd discussed her mother in small snatches of conversation, but this was the first where he didn't hear that ages-old pain layered underneath her voice. Instead, her pragmatism was refreshing and he couldn't hold back the surge of pride at her ability to keep her focus.

Especially in the midst of a chilling personal attack.

"I'm also glowing because despite the current situation I find myself in, I love the first day of the Paris trip and thinking about what's to come. I think that's what's so upsetting about all this."

"The break in rhythm?"

"That and the fact that there is so much work that goes into this week, it's fun to sit back and relax and take the time to enjoy all the effort. And some jerk's messing with that and taking away all the joy."

"You're certainly not afraid of hard work."

"Why should I be? We all have gifts. I can't think of anything more boring or unfulfilling than sitting around waiting for something to be handed to me instead of using those gifts."

The earnest expression that filled her face simply shattered him. Here was a woman who could have anything in the world she wanted, yet she'd chosen a life that provided her with fascinating challenges that stretched her mind and tested her abilities.

"I take pride in a job well done and I enjoy the collaboration with others. And right now, someone is trying to take it all away from me."

"We're going to get him, Abby. I know we are."

"I believe you." She reached over and laid a hand on his arm. "I really do."

He saw the trust in her gaze and knew he wouldn't let her down. No matter what, he'd find the person responsible.

He'd done the same for Sarah and had gotten her justice.

There was no way he'd allow Abby to settle for anything less.

Kensington Steele paced her office, staring over T-Bone's prodigious shoulder midway through every crossing. "Why is this guy so hard to find?"

"We're doing our best."

"I know you are. Which is why I'm getting more and more concerned. There are none better than you and my brother. And this jerk's making things awfully difficult."

"Challenging," T-Bone muttered through gritted teeth as he pounded in a few commands on his laptop. "That's all it is. Challenging."

"Sorry. Challenging."

Since she couldn't understand a bit of the endless strings of code that flew over the man's screen, she resumed her pacing and headed for the inlaid bookcases that filled the far wall of her office.

A family portrait taken in the South of France the year before her parents were killed sat in a place of honor, framed in ornate leaded glass.

She remembered that day as if it had happened only the week before. They'd laughed like loons on that trip, teasing each other, swimming all day like a school of fish and playing endless rounds of games each night on the boat. That was also the first year she'd kicked Liam's ass at poker, earning a deep smile of pride from her father.

The image of her and her family in the photo summed up the last time she was truly innocent as a human being.

And now her brother and one of her best friends were in the middle of something that was decidedly *not* innocent.

"You get Campbell's email earlier?"

T-Bone never looked up but he was totally in tune with the conversation. "The photo of the hair? Sick bastard."

"That's the one. Abby doesn't think it's real."

"Why not?" T-Bone looked up from the screen, his focus fully on her. "It's sick either way, but who does something like that?"

"Someone trying to drag interest off of the main event." She resumed her pacing and came to stand next to one of the few people who'd ever penetrated the inner workings of the Steele family. "You find anything in Abby's secretary's computer?"

"Not yet. But I did find some interesting things in her personal email."

"You got in?"

The look of disgust on his face had her lifting her hands. "Sorry. Sorry. I should have known."

"Then you also know I do not make it a habit to go rooting through others' personal emails unless forced, but this is worth taking a look at."

"What is it?"

"Look first and tell me what you see."

T-Bone minimized the window that displayed the endless lines of scrolling computer code and pulled up a well-known free email provider.

She leaned more fully forward. "What am I supposed to see?"

"You tell me."

"T. Come on, enough with the riddles. There's nothing there other than two statements telling her that her credit cards are due."

"That's my point. It's the woman's personal email, yet there's not a single email in or out of it."

"People are known to file or delete what they don't need."

"Right. So look at this." He flipped to the sent folder, but it was totally empty. "Nothing."

Kensington wanted to believe there was something there, but a small voice kept rationalizing the woman's behavior. Stef Nichols was an administrative assistant, for heaven's sake. She knew how to keep things on track and presumably how to streamline her life. "I'm not buying this as proof, T. Maybe she's neat. She may just want to keep her personal files clutter-free. I realize most of the world's population are email hoarders, but it's not a crime not to be one."

"Then how do you explain this?"

T-Bone flipped to one more email client, this one a clear portal into the McBane Communications server. "She's got work email out the wazoo."

The urge to argue rose up, but she knew the argument was weak. "Because it's her job. You can't treat your work email like your personal email."

One lone eyebrow rose over the penetrating depths of his dark eyes. "Aren't you the one always saying there are no coincidences?"

"Yeah."

"So why does the woman have every email she's ever received since, oh—" T-Bone did a quick re-sort of the main folder "—the last six years, including an endless barrage of messages that contain the daily lunch special at Lucky Frankie's Sub Shop, but she's got nothing in her personal email?"

"I don't know."

"Well, I do. It smells funny. More to the point, it smells like a deliberate deletion of any and all record of her relationship with whoever it is we're looking for.

Now all I need to do is look at how often she logged into it from the office and see what traces I can find on her machine."

"Abby already authorized the access but I'll call her and let her know what you've found and what you're going to do."

Kensington pulled out her cell phone and dialed Abby's number. As she waited for her friend to answer, her gaze drifted once more to the image of her family.

Innocence lost.

Just like Abby's trusted assistant, Stef.

"I'm still not quite sure this is what T-Bone meant when he suggested you pay your neighbors a visit."

Abby stared over the rooftop from her home to the ones on either side. Fresh air whipped around her and the bright light of day caught the strands, coloring them a rich shade of chocolate-brown.

The fresh air felt good after the forced confines of first the plane and later the house and it was nice to be outside.

What he couldn't quite get comfortable with was the calculating, oh-so-slightly maniacal gleam that seemed to have settled itself in Abby's eyes. "What else did he mean? We need to get inside and look around."

"We can still contact their security companies. I've probably underestimated the speed which Dave can get through to the bigwigs."

"They'll stump him faster than the Bullet train."

"It's worth a try, Abby. You should be concentrating on what's coming in a few hours and not planning a con into your neighbors' house."

"You know as well as I do the security firm that represents this home won't share a blessed word if they think they're being accused of not providing best-in-class service. Come on, Campbell. We need to get in and look around and we can't wait. We need another clue to find our ghost."

"You're awfully chipper about this."

She turned toward him, a broad smile covering her face. "I'm excited we finally have something *we* can take action on instead of sitting still under some puppet master's strings."

"We're making progress and T-Bone should have some news any minute on Stef's email."

"I know." She brushed off the monumental streak of embarrassment she felt at digging through her assistant's email, even though she was well within her rights to have a search of anything that was done on McBane property and through their technology systems.

Still, it bothered her and she'd almost called off the search altogether as it felt like such a violation.

Of course, it wouldn't feel like a violation when it definitively cleared Stef's name from consideration.

"So come on. Back to all that progress. Let's go."

"You sure you're ready?"

"I'm more than ready. The last few days have been like sitting in the middle of the street, naked, with everyone watching and no way to find my clothes."

She knew the moment the word *naked* hit his thought processes because she saw that sloe-eyed look come over Campbell's face as his blue eyes turned a deep shade of indigo. With the sweetest voice she could muster, she widened her own eyes. "What is it? You look upset."

"Never use the word *naked* around a man."

She added a saucy wink to the grin she couldn't hold back as they descended toward to the first floor. "All part of my diabolical plot."

"Which is?"

"You'll be thinking of my naked body instead of how much you'd rather not be traipsing through my neighbors' house."

Since the comment shut him up, Abby figured her plan had real merit. She was also comforted by the exceedingly legitimate setup they'd concocted for the discussion with her neighbors, Etienne and Celine.

Campbell might be the security expert, but it was common knowledge in technology fields that the best hacking consisted of advance planning that had nothing to do with technology and everything to do with human behavior. Identifying the proper levers to pull—and working through a realistic con—were essential to a successful hack.

So she'd gone to work on as many realistic levers she could think of and when she'd run them past Campbell, he'd nodded approvingly before adding a few stellar touches that made their whole fishing expedition sing.

They'd concocted a vague story about needing to understand the layouts underneath the roofs in this part of the city because she needed to quickly add some technology to her home for the board meeting. As a lie went, it wasn't completely farfetched. Old cities and old buildings within those cities often had architectural similarities that could be leveraged when identifying a solution to a technology problem.

Despite the reasonable nature of the argument, they both knew full well that in the end, you crafted the right solution for the building you were in and that was the end of it.

She could only hope her broad smile and the too-short formfitting skirt she'd changed into did the trick.

Especially since her intel suggested the Dufresnes' majordomo was a man still in his looking years.

Abby collected her "props" in the hallway—the small leather folder that contained her meeting agenda as a means to look official and a bottle of a vintage Bordeaux that regularly sold for a couple thousand a bottle as a neighborly peace offering. With one last look at Campbell for good luck, she pointed toward the door. "Let's go."

As they crossed next door, the bustling activity of the Sixteenth arrondissement hummed with life around them.

"Aside from your impressive body which I am now imagining naked, I'm also rather impressed you can lie through your teeth in French."

She enjoyed the light flush that flooded her chest at his comment before turning toward him with a breezy smile. "I learned young and did plenty of lying with it to get out of homework at my oh-so-French private school."

"And here I thought you were the proverbial good girl. Am I now to understand you might have a few less than saintlike urges underneath that pristine exterior?"

Just like with the naked comment, she couldn't quite hold back the urge to bait him. The air around both of them had been charged since their kiss in the kitchen—hell, it had been charged from the moment they'd met—and Abby was rapidly growing tired of resisting the dance.

She wanted this man and there were fewer and fewer reasons to stay away.

Pushing thoughts of what might still be between them, she kept up the breezy tone as they walked up the Dufresnes' front steps. "You have no idea, Mr. Steele."

Campbell's hand snaked out toward her waist as he pulled her close. "Try me."

Triumph blossomed in her veins at his touch, while a good old-fashioned dose of feminine surprise gripped her. And here she thought she had the upper hand.

It was encouraging to know Campbell had more than a few moves of his own.

"You're a fascinating woman." His lips pressed to her ear before he released her to climb the front stoop of the house.

"Thank you." Abby let out a small discreet cough, willing her racing pulse to slow before she lifted the large brass knocker on the front door.

She could do this. Correction, McBane.

They could do this.

After she dropped the brass knocker, Campbell turned toward her, his conversational tone a far cry from the sexual innuendo of the past few moments. "Why'd you pick this house? It's a fifty-fifty chance."

"Not really. This one was the second one hit."

"Meaning?"

"In the event our con man practiced on the first house, he likely got it right with this one."

"I stand corrected."

"Corrected of what?"

"*Fascinating* is far too tame a word for you. So is *interesting, captivating, enchanting, charming* and *tantalizing*."

"Aren't you quite the thesaurus?" Abby heard the thud of footsteps on the other side of the door, but couldn't hold back her curiosity. "What would you call me, then?"

"Besides infuriating, headstrong and opinionated?"

He neatly sideswiped her swat with the leather folder. "That's just mean and undignified."

"Of which you are neither. No, my dear. You're something else entirely."

"What's that?"

He leaned over and pressed his lips to her ear. A light shiver gripped her shoulders as his tongue lightly traced the shell. "You're enthralling. Absolutely, utterly enthralling."

The majordomo chose that moment to open the door and Campbell had already straightened to his full height, his movements so smooth and immediate she'd never have known he'd even leaned into her if she hadn't felt his tempting presence for herself.

"*Mademoiselle.* What is the purpose of your call?"

Abby launched into rapid French, her gaze never leaving the majordomo as she waved her leather file folder and the wine for emphasis.

Even so, a small nerve ticked in the back of her mind.

Campbell Steele was really too smart for his own good. And he'd definitely evened the score since she'd mentioned the word *naked.*

The majordomo turned and gestured with a hand over his shoulder that they should follow and she mentally added goofy to Campbell's list of attributes when he wiggled his eyebrows.

Which also had a small giggle erupting in her throat that she diligently coughed back.

Damn the man and his wiggling eyebrows and come-hither eyes and big smile and broad shoulders. And damn his ability to make her forget everything but the insane desire to crawl into his arms.

Since the majordomo deposited them in a small parlor off the front hallway, Abby tried to focus on the lushly appointed room and off the distractions of her hormones.

"I only caught about four words in that entire exchange, but from your tone I got haughty frustration, near-weepy desperation and a strange sort of embarrassment."

She turned toward Campbell in relief. "Excellent. That was my goal."

"Intimidate him, get him to take pity on you and flash the expensive wine to back up you are who you say you are and he'd be a fool to ignore your needs."

"Bingo."

"Well played."

"We're not upstairs yet."

Before he could reply, the sound of clicking heels and muted voices echoed from outside the door. Abby stood as the diplomat's new trophy wife, Celine, came into the room. Her smile was reserved yet welcoming and Abby got the quick sense the woman was sharper than she might have originally given her credit for.

She'd do well to keep that in mind.

After their brief introduction, Abby once again launched into a virtual torrent of words, willing the woman to understand her desperation as she laid it on thick.

The upcoming board meeting scheduled to start the next day that had serious implications for her company.

Before that had even sunk in, she moved straight into the desperate need to run a line into her house for a vague set of technology needs—Abby made sure she threw in words like algorithm, satellite optimization and a few vague references to McBane's stock price—as the woman's bright eyes went from attentive to glazed over.

She then went in for the kill by pointing at Campbell and venting her frustration with her very sexy yet lackadaisical tech guy who couldn't seem to figure out what was needed.

Celine perked up at the reference to the "sexy tech guy," her gaze roving appreciatively over Campbell. It took every ounce of Abby's self-control not to laugh at the young woman's blatantly carnal look but was rewarded for her restraint when Celine graciously took the bottle of wine and gestured for them to head on up the main stairs and "do what they needed to do."

Three stories later, she and Campbell roamed the top floor hallway. The layout was different from her home, but the same architectural style was in evidence as they started on the first room at the top of the stairs. They'd been given directions to the attic, but a quick look in each room ensured they wouldn't miss anything.

"She bought it." His voice was low but Abby didn't miss the respect she heard underneath the words as he opened a closet.

"I laid it on pretty thick, but it was my last argument that seemed to do the trick."

They walked on to the next room, Campbell's gaze following the lines of the ceiling. "Which was?"

"I told her my tech guy was sexy yet clueless and couldn't seem to figure anything out. She watched your ass the entire walk out of the room."

His next words were strangled as they moved on to yet another room. "I feel so cheap and used."

"Well, we all make sacrifices."

"Right." He rubbed at his neck, the light flush there giving away his discomfort before he tossed an accusing gaze toward her. "What were yours?"

"I made sure that wine bottle was level with my cleavage the entire time I talked with the majordomo."

Campbell grabbed her arm and pulled her back into the hallway and on to the next room. "Well, well, aren't we a couple of cheap operatives."

"If we find what we're looking for, you won't see me complain."

They made it to the last door and, as described, the access to the attic was at the south end of the room. As Campbell pulled open the door, Abby's pulse kicked up another notch.

It wasn't until that moment—faced with the possibility the end of this ordeal might soon be put behind her—that she allowed a sense of relief to fill her.

If they could just find whatever the intruder left behind, they could get some sort of ID on it, Campbell could electronically fingerprint their ghost and she could go back to living her life.

Without Campbell Steele in it.

If that thought gave her a moment's pause, she pushed it away. This wasn't about Campbell or even her inconvenient attraction to him.

This was about getting her life back.

"Abby?"

She glanced up into that face that had become both a source of comfort and increasing anxiety before taking his outstretched hand.

"Be careful on these steps. They're narrow and steep."

They climbed to the top, both of them carefully planting their feet, before they crossed the threshold to a large attic that ran almost the entire length of the house.

They'd barely cleared the landing when Campbell came to a hard stop in front of her, his gaze directed toward the top of the far wall, in the darkest part of the attic. "Well, I'll be damned."

"What is it?"

"T-Bone had it right, after all. See that?" He pointed toward a small black spot, high on the wall, before reaching for her hand and dragging her toward it.

As she got closer, the small black piece registered with the force of a battering ram.

"I don't believe it." She exhaled the words on a heavy whisper as the bottom fell out of her stomach.

"What is it?"

"That's mine. Ours." She shook her head. "It's a McBane prototype. We've been working on it for three years. I wrote the damn patent on it myself."

Chapter 11

"You did what?"

If his words sounded half as inane as he felt Campbell wouldn't have been surprised.

Abby was being spied on with a McBane device? And her own damn prototype to boot.

"It's my invention. My patent." Abby dropped her hands to her waist and bent over as if trying to catch her breath. "I do not believe this."

Campbell pulled out his phone and snapped a few pictures. "Tell me what we're up against, will you?"

The words snapped her back to attention and she stood to her full height as she began to list off the capabilities of the device. "Assuming he hasn't made any modifications to it, it's a remote server interface that doesn't require actual connection with the server."

"You can tap in remotely? From anywhere?"

"You've got to be in a specific range, but basically. Yes."

Campbell thought of every spy movie he'd seen in the past five years and the proverbial "server room scene" where the white hats went to key into the secured technology.

And she'd figured out a way to do it remotely.

"Does it work?"

"Sometimes. Depends on the firewalls. The range."

"Are we in range here?"

Her grim expression told him all he needed to know. "This is more than close enough to tap in."

He shook his head, unable to believe what she was saying. "So you've created a bug? Only instead of listening to conversations, you're spying on technology. Is that what you're telling me?"

"It's not that simple, Campbell."

"Well, it's not that freaking complicated, either. Is McBane responsible for crafting a technological device that can spy on other equipment?"

"Yes."

"How could you do this, Abby?"

"It was a business decision and it was an outcome of one of our government contracts."

"So you were well paid to create subterfuge via high-tech gadgets." He ran distracted fingers through his hair, tugging on the ends. "This is bad. Even for the government."

Her gaze was bleak as she stared at him. "You know as well as I do technological advances are the way of the world. And it's got a number of uses beyond the nefarious place you've leaped to."

"It's not right."

"What do you think this is, Campbell? A game? Satellite technology isn't just used to power your damn cell phone. It runs every major military initiative in the world and there are times when we're not only the good guys, we're the only guys in the game."

All the warmth leached from his body at her ready acquiescence and defense of her choices.

He'd trusted her. Had been adamant about protecting her. And to find this?

Whatever belief he'd carried for her vanished, his faith in her right along with it. Without warning, he heard her comments from the day before, echoing in the back of his mind.

"I'm not sure you're right about the good guys."

"You don't agree?"

"Let's just say my experiences have clearly been different than yours."

"Come now, Abby. You have to have had a few experiences that reinforce good choices."

"I have. I just don't think good always triumphs. I think there are a lot of bad people in this world who come out on top, over and over again."

It broke his heart to think she was one of them.

Abby ignored the bleak expression that rode Campbell's face. She wouldn't think of that now.

Wouldn't think of the disappointment that filled his gaze or the very high wall that had materialized between them despite the fact they still stood less than a foot apart.

No, instead she had to focus on one simple fact. Where she'd been looking for a singular threat tied solely to her, the fact this technology had gone missing indicated something else.

The nameless, faceless threat was about McBane and its technology.

Another thought followed on its heels.

All of their technology developments went through strict protocols and management yet she didn't even know this device was missing. How could it have escaped the research and development team that the device had vanished?

Until the answer jingled loud and clear in the back of her mind.

Stef.

Abby moved forward and lifted the device from the wall. Assuming it was running as designed, moving it wouldn't trigger any awareness on the part of the person who'd put it there.

It would only register if the device was made inactive.

"Can we destroy it?"

"Not if you don't want to tip your hand." Abby refused to look at Campbell, instead, she tucked the small piece—no larger than a domino—into the slim pocket of her skirt. "Let's go."

"So if we can't destroy it, that means it's still transmitting information."

"Yes." She accidentally moved into his space as she reached for the leather notebook she'd set on an abandoned chair. The move was unintended, but the moment their bodies came into contact she felt the heat that still arced between them. It traveled the length of her body, coalescing in her stomach in a hard tight ball.

Whatever she'd accepted, even anticipated, on the walk over—that she would like to take things with Campbell to the next level—vanished as if it had never been.

And from the look in his eyes, all he wanted was to get away from her as fast as he could possibly move.

* * *

Campbell stared at the innocuous-enough-looking device as he barked out orders to T-Bone. The man had him on speaker and he could hear his sister's voice in the background.

"She did what?"

Campbell relayed the full story to Kensington, placing particular emphasis on McBane's new technological developments.

"Okay." Kenzi's sigh drifted through the phone and he heard her flip it off of speaker, the tinny echo vanishing as her voice snapped through the connection. "I need you to stop speaking geek for a minute and explain what really has you upset."

"She's created spy technology, Kensington. Your sweet innocent friend has created a device that can remotely monitor technology infrastructure and use that to the remote party's advantage."

"Do you not have the skill to do that to any computer system in the world?"

His sister's question caught him up short and he stumbled for a moment as he tried to come up with an answer.

"I'm serious, Campbell. Isn't that something you can do? I realize it takes time, but you're fully capable of penetrating a computer system that doesn't belong to you."

"Yes."

"How often do you do that?"

"Not nearly as often as you seem to think I do." Campbell knew his youthful escapades had left his entire family with the illusion he got his kicks off of running through systems that weren't his, but nothing could be further from the truth.

Yes, he hacked when he needed to complete a job, but that was it.

"What's your point?"

"Just because you can do something doesn't mean you do it. Talk to her and tell her your concerns. There may be a very valid reason they've designed this technology."

The mad that had carried him back to Abby's house on a self-righteous cloud vanished. "I thought I was the reasonable one."

"You are. You're just too deep in this to see the forest for the trees."

"Gee. Thanks."

"You're welcome. And one more thing." He waited without saying anything further. "Nothing is black-and-white. You know that."

"Of course. If things were black-and-white we wouldn't have jobs."

"Well said, my brother. Well said."

They said their goodbyes and Campbell shoved his phone back in his pocket, his sister's calm, rational thoughts a subtle irritation under the skin. Even if they were also a deep source of his pride and love for her.

Kensington knew people. She understood what made them tick and she had a clever way of presenting two sides of an argument so you were forced to think through your own personal, pigheaded viewpoints.

Had he been too hard on Abby?

The memory of her pale skin and grim features as they stood in her neighbors' attic suggested he had been.

Abby tried to focus on the caterer's words but had to ask the woman to repeat herself three times. She wished she could excuse her malaise on the woman's rapid French, but Abby knew full well the responsibility lay elsewhere.

The caterer had waylaid her the moment she and

Campbell had arrived back from what Abby had mentally dubbed an apocalyptic disaster and all she wanted to do was escape.

After a quick confirmation that cocktails and hors d'oeuvres would be served at seven with dinner at nine, Abby gave the instruction to call her if anything was needed but that she trusted them implicitly to put the meal together.

And then she fled to the study and resumed her preparations for the evening, willing Campbell Steele from her thoughts.

Tonight would kick off a highly productive week in which she'd continue to prove to her board how she was leading McBane Communications into the twenty-first century and beyond.

She had spent months planning and preparing, crafting her annual business plan and five- and ten-year forecasts.

She had developed a week of presentations that would inspire and motivate her team.

She was going to kick ass.

And she'd ignore Campbell—*Stubborn Idiot*—Steele and his judge and jury attitude and focus on the job at hand.

Her gaze drifted to the small device that was at the root of their disagreement.

Had she crossed a line?

The self-righteous anger that had carried her back to the house and up to her study faltered a bit as she turned his concerns over in her mind.

The development of the server device hadn't been simply to spy on other technologies. It had several practical reasons for being the biggest of which was enabling some key communications between their existing pool of satellites.

She wasn't a thief and she hadn't built her business to steal from others or create tools that effectively did the same.

But she wasn't silly enough not to realize that even tools created for one purpose could be abused for another.

"Hey." The single word, along with the knock at her door, pulled Abby from her thoughts.

"I'm surprised to see you."

"Yeah, I guess you probably are."

Campbell leaned against the door and Abby fought the immediate leap of her hormones as she took in his long rangy form. Jeans covered his slim hips and his T-shirt bulged slightly over his biceps as he crossed his arms.

Not for the first time she wondered how she could possibly have such a completely inconvenient attraction to someone.

Especially someone she was so mad at she could spit.

She knew it was petty, but she refused to initiate the conversation. He'd come to see her for a reason and she'd leave it up to him to tell her why.

If he'd expressed his disapproval with her business choice she'd have been more than willing to discuss his objections. What she couldn't accept was the way he'd judged her actions, leaving her no room to make her case.

He pushed off the door and crossed to her desk, taking the chair opposite her. "Can I have a few minutes?"

"Of course."

"You caught me off guard earlier."

"It wasn't a picnic for me, Campbell. The fact this device—" she grabbed the remote piece for emphasis "—was tacked up next door in my neighbors' home means a hell of a lot of things. None of which required me to stand beneath your oh-so-judicious stare as you treated me like a common criminal."

"No, it didn't."

His ready acquiescence took some of the wind from her sails and she dropped the server device back on the desk. "It was never designed to be a technological bug."

"What was it designed for?"

"It has several uses, but its eventual ability to allow us to communicate between satellites will be invaluable."

"I see."

"And yes, I fully realize if it were accessible to less upstanding individuals, it could be programmed to do some damage. But it's not easy. Especially not as we continue to engineer it. I never designed, nor did I take on the development of a project that would effectively steal data."

Campbell's contrite gaze drifted to the device, his visage turning thoughtful as he stared at it. "So this had to be programmed in order to read your systems?"

"Of course. You don't just plug it in and like magic see into another server. The devices need to be programmed to each other. Deliberately."

"Which means for the device to be of any use, our ghost needed to find a way to program it to monitor your systems."

"Sure, but—"

"And since there's no way it's just been sitting at your neighbors', it might have more details on our ghost and the devices he used to program it?"

"Well, yeah. I mean…yes."

The simplicity of the solution—a trap to catch the one who set it—was almost too delicious. Even with the knowledge they were a step closer to catching their ghost, she also knew they were more than a few steps closer to catching Stef.

"I've turned this over and over in my mind and I can't help but believe Stef is involved."

"Have you contacted her?"

"I haven't heard from her yet today which is odd, but not completely unexpected. She works so hard I often tell her to come in a bit later when I'm out of town."

"The security team can still send someone to her home."

Abby knew it was the best choice and conceded. "I'll authorize the team to make the visit to her home. I'll also alert the security team at McBane to snag her when she gets in."

Campbell picked up the device and turned it over in his hands. "I'm sorry."

"It's not your fault."

"No, but it doesn't change the fact that I'm sorry this has happened. You've trusted Stef and it appears as if that trust was misplaced."

Abby heard the remorse and empathy in his tone and couldn't hold back the thoughts that had dogged her since speculation had first turned toward Stef. "I just keep asking myself if there's something I could have done differently. Some way I've acted that made her feel as if she could or should do this to me."

"We never know people's true motives, no matter how well we know them."

"Do you really believe that?"

"I'd prefer to believe we can be better than we are, but how often does that happen? If you really look at it, how often do people make choices in reaction to the actions of someone they love?"

Did he mean Sarah and her misguided teenage actions at the dissolution of her parents' marriage? Or was there something else?

"Not everyone does that."

"No, sometimes they just avoid any hints of love and commitment so there's no chance of getting hurt."

Whatever she'd expected when Campbell had arrived in her office, a conversation about love and loss and the lack of emotional growth wasn't it. Yet now that she was confronted with the matter, she had to wonder if she'd behaved that way.

If the real reason she was alone was to avoid the pain of some imagined future betrayal by a loved one.

"I'll let you get back to your prep. I would like to do a briefing at five in the dining room. One last session with the security team before your guests arrive."

"Of course."

Abby waited until he reached the door before calling out to him. "Campbell?"

"Yeah."

"I'm still mad at you."

"You've got a right to be."

Campbell gritted his teeth as David's right-hand man, Simon, ran his lascivious gaze over Abby's bare shoulders.

Again.

The urge to reach up and slam the man face-first into the dining room table was strong, but Campbell kept quiet. This was Abby's meeting and he'd already behaved like a raging ass once today. It would do him no good to get caught behaving that way a second time.

She wore a peach gown that made her look like some

Greek goddess. Her hair was caught up in a sweep of ringlets which had the incredible effect of leaving her neck exposed. The dress then gathered at the base of her neck, leaving her shoulders bare. Of course, the view that all of them were begging to see just once more was the low-cut back that bared the subtle arch of her spine before her skin disappeared below the cut of the gown.

She was breathtaking.

And obviously still not over their earlier argument based on the fact that she'd barely spared him a glance since the beginning of the meeting.

Oh, she was cordial and professional, as she'd been to the rest of the team, but that was the extent of their contact.

"Again, I must stress how imperative it is that our guests don't know you all are here. You need to be unobtrusive and avoid contact with the crowd. If the person responsible is here, and we believe he likely is, we can't risk him fleeing into the wind."

"We're going to keep you safe."

Abby shot Simon a dull smile and Campbell had the momentary satisfaction to see her stare down her nose at the pompous ass. "Let me repeat my point. You've been hired by me. And I'm telling you I don't want my guests to know you're here. So either stay out of sight or leave now."

The reprimand had its desired effect and Simon backed down, especially after a particularly firm glance from David.

Campbell had to hand it to Abby. The woman knew what she wanted and she didn't tolerate those who didn't agree.

Which only reinforced his poor move over the hidden server device.

He should have given her the benefit of the doubt. Should have allowed her to explain.

"That'll be all. You may set up in the third-floor parlor or stick to the surveillance vans you've got parked down the street. I've also made sure there is more than enough food so feel free to head down to the kitchen and help yourselves."

Campbell remained in his seat despite Simon's pointed glare and waited until he and Abby were alone.

"That went well."

"Oh, bite me. It went horribly and you know it."

"They're programmed for the hunt and you've effectively tied their paws."

"Simon's a jerk of the first water."

"Simon's a jock with too much testosterone who's trying to impress you. He'll get over it."

She shot him a sideways glance at the testosterone comment before focusing on the underlying issue. "We simply can't risk whomever's responsible finding out they're here. We've done everything possible to keep their presence undetectable. I won't have all that effort wasted."

"You look beautiful."

The words were out before he could stop them and after they were out, Campbell found he didn't want to.

She was beautiful.

And he'd be damned if he'd hold the thought back any longer.

"Thank you."

Campbell got up and walked around the long table to where she sat on the other side. Anticipation quivered off her skin when he reached out to run a finger over the smooth skin of her exposed shoulder. "Promise me you'll be careful."

"I promise."

"I mean it, Abby." The urgent words rose up from his chest as a wash of fear coated his throat. "You can't take any chances."

She reached up and laid a hand over his. With tender motions, she rubbed the pad of her thumb over his knuckles. Need ratcheted through him with the force of cannon fire as desire flooded his system with an ardent fury.

Bending down he pressed his lips against her ear. "I want you."

He felt her light shiver underneath his fingers before she tightened her hand over his. "Now's not the time."

"Later."

"Yes." She nodded, the move nearly imperceptible. "Later."

Campbell stepped back and allowed her to stand, helping her from the ornate dining room chair.

They didn't touch again, but he felt the heat of her skin long after she'd departed from the room.

Lucas tied his bow tie into a faultless knot, each side a perfect mirror of the other. The tie conveyed a muted elegance that said he was a member of a rarified circle.

That he belonged.

That he mattered.

He shot one final glance in the mirror, satisfied he looked as he should, then resumed a place in front of his computer in the sitting room of his suite.

He'd monitored Abby's movements on and off throughout the day, watching when she logged on and what files she opened and changed, the others that she opened and discarded. Although he'd spent months coding and recoding the small device until it was ready for his use, he'd still not figured a way to make it work on cell phones, but he was hell-bent to try to figure it out.

Stef had secured four prototypes for him and he had two left.

Had he been too hasty in getting rid of her?

Although he rarely second-guessed himself, she had been an incredible asset to him. Add on her blind devotion and Lucas had to wonder if perhaps he'd been a bit quick to jump the gun on her execution.

That said…he raked his gaze over the small billfold that held the remaining two devices and knew they'd put him closer than ever to his goal. Stef Nichols was baggage and he ran the very real risk she'd flee once she discovered what he'd actually had planned for her boss.

No.

It was better this way.

Satisfied after reconsidering his decision—a sign of his agile mind and ability to fully assess his actions—he picked up the server devices and locked them in the small safe in his room.

While they surely held very little interest to anyone who might happen upon them, there was no reason to leave them lying about. When the maid came in for turndown service, all she'd see was the obsessively neat room of a man who traveled for a living.

His personal things sat in perfect order in the bathroom and his clothing hung in neat rows in his closet as his mother had taught him.

Just like your father.

Like a man who knew how to care properly for the things he'd earned.

Like a man who commanded respect from all who

dealt with him, from the fiercest business adversary to the man who shined his shoes.

Like a man who owned the world.

Chapter 12

Campbell read the brief text on his phone—NEED TO SEE YOU—and went into action. He worked his way across the ballroom, his sights on Abby. As he walked the periphery, he mentally catalogued his evaluations.

For the past hour, he'd mingled with her guests and subtly dropped clues he and Abby were an item.

To a person, everyone was friendly. And to a person, everyone's gaze had turned speculative when he mentioned the fact they were dating.

Campbell filed it all away, cataloguing responses into one of three categories.

Gossipy interest. Disappointment she was off the market. Or opportunistic calculation at what her new relationship—especially one she was comfortable enough with to bring to the event—meant relative to her position at McBane.

One guy had even gone so far as to ask Campbell when the two of them were planning on having kids.

His gaze roamed over Abby, deep in conversation with one of her guests—Martin, Campbell remembered—and the comment about a baby took hold deep in his mind. The image of her long slender form transformed in his mind as he imagined her heavy with pregnancy and the image stopped him in his tracks.

Where had that come from?

"Darling." She waved him over and he pasted on a smile, relegating the image in his mind to some deeply buried place where he wouldn't see it again.

She linked his hand with hers before turning in and pressing a hand against his chest. His heart leaped at the contact and he saw the briefest question glow in the chocolate-brown of her eyes before she composed herself, totally focused on the moment at hand.

"I'd like to introduce you to Martin."

They chatted in that politely inane way that fueled dinner parties the world over and it took Campbell longer than he'd have preferred to get her alone, especially when two new people drifted into their conversation circle even before Martin left.

"I'm terribly sorry to do this." Campbell finally cut through the polite chitchat, especially after Carina from the New York office made a production about how she was convinced they'd met before. Campbell would have sworn they hadn't, but he wasn't all that interested to stick around and swap stories to find out if he had it wrong. "I need to make a quick call for work."

Abby's gaze stayed bright on his but he felt the subtle tightening of her hand on his forearm. "I hope everything's all right, sweetheart. I was looking forward to introducing you to everyone this evening."

"I'll only be gone a few minutes." He kept his tone upbeat and his smile broad. "Let me just make a quick call and I'll be back in a bit."

"Don't be long."

His body tightened on the subtle breathy notes of her voice and he had the fleeting thought that he wished she wasn't quite so good at the charade. Even as his mind knew they were putting on an act, his body was more than willing to play an active role.

Campbell met the wry glance of the third man in their circle. He didn't know the guy's name, but recognized the quick smile of supportive brotherhood that spoke volumes.

Women.

He couldn't say what it was in the guy's stare that put him on edge, but he let it go in the buzzing of what was no doubt a second text from David asking him where the hell he was.

"I'll be back shortly." Campbell pressed a quick kiss to her forehead, then took off for the door. He turned at the last minute before vanishing down the hall and couldn't shake the inconvenient attraction that threatened to scramble every last one of his brain cells.

He stopped for the briefest of moments, willing her to turn and look at him, but she'd resumed her conversation with her guests.

When had he become so damned fanciful?

Shaking it off, Campbell took the stairs two at a time and knocked at the door before slipping inside. David and his team waited for him, each and every one at rigid attention.

"Quite the party."

"She does know how to entertain." Campbell launched into a quick briefing of what he'd assessed so far before David waved a hand to shut him down. "What's going on?"

"We got some intel on Stef Nichols."

A raw chill ran the length of his spine and Campbell knew the information wasn't good.

"She was found about an hour ago, dead in her apartment."

"Not by accident, I assume?"

"No. Her neck was broken. Time of death was estimated last night around midnight."

Campbell waited for the full report even as the implications of the woman's death swirled in his mind.

He needed to tell Abby. But did he dare tell her now? She was a good actress and had been more than convincing in the role of dewy-eyed lover, but she was already upset about Stef's possible involvement.

Could he really put the entire evening at risk by telling her now? By confirming the incontrovertible proof of the woman's involvement with the very worst of news?

"Has anything been found on her electronics?"

Simon stepped in and shook his head. "The cops won't share it. We have a fair amount of pull, but a dead woman sort of trumps our authority and we weren't given access to them."

Campbell heard the implied "yet" in Simon's voice and knew it wouldn't be that easy. "Let me see what I can do on that front."

Although the House of Steele didn't have much more pull with the NYPD than David's firm did, he'd worked enough projects for them that he had developed a sizeable network of contacts. One of them should at least be able to tell him what the security team hadn't yet found out.

Especially if there was anything on the electronics and if he could get into them and dig a bit more deeply.

"The cops want to talk to Abby as soon as possible." David handed him a message he'd scribbled on a notepad. Campbell didn't recognize the name of the detective, but he did recognize the precinct number and mentally catalogued a few of the people he knew there.

"Can you hold them off?"

"Not for long. I explained she wasn't available and got the tersely worded explanation that she needs to make herself available."

"Stall them."

"I'll do my best."

"She needs to get through this evening. We've come too far and we're too close to getting a bead on this guy. Tonight's essential and if the guy is here, she needs the time to work the room and get a sense if anything seems off. There's no way the knowledge that Stef is dead isn't going to mess her up and pull her off her rhythm."

"I understand."

Abby smiled and nodded at the assembled crowd as happy conversation swirled around her. The first guest had arrived promptly at seven and she hadn't stopped smiling since.

Or evaluating each and every person who'd walked through her front door.

Three people had popped as slightly off, but she'd managed to eliminate one of them when she realized his wife and new baby had been home from the hospital a total of three days. Despite her encouragement he leave and fly home, he ran through the typical song and dance about the importance of work, how they had a nanny and that his mother-in-law had descended for a month-long stay. She'd nodded politely throughout but knew she could remove him from the list of suspects.

What she couldn't quite remove was the image of a husband and baby that exploded in her mind with surprising force. Or the fact that the person she saw as sharing the journey of parenthood with her was Campbell.

"This is quite the party."

Abby willed the thought—and the traitorous heat that suffused her body with pleasure—as Lucas Brown drifted back to talk to her.

He was the newest member of her board, his financial firm in London having come on her radar two years prior when they'd managed a capital expansion in Europe. He had a ready understanding of business and she'd always appreciated his thoughts on McBane's growth opportunities. When a seat on the board had opened up, one of her advisors had suggested Lucas and he'd been a match from the start.

She estimated he was about three or four years older than herself. He had an appealing look to him, with a fit body more than evident underneath his power suit and warm brown eyes that always filled with a ready smile. She'd liked him from the first and thought he brought a youthful perspective to the board that was often missing from some of the other members. Where they had the wisdom of experience on their side, he had the aggressive, entrepreneurial focus of youth and it created a nice balance.

"So Campbell's a new addition to your life."

She heard the question and pasted on a demure smile that wasn't all that hard to conjure up. "Yes."

"The two of you are quite the subject of conversation. What does he do?"

Abby walked through the agreed-to script on how they met and Campbell's role as a software developer for the financial industry before she thought to censor herself. Saying Campbell was an expert in financial markets wasn't going to go over Lucas's head as it would with most and his attention perked up immediately.

"Who does he work for?"

"He works rather independently most of the time." She made a mental note to share that tidbit with Campbell before she added a bright smile with what she hoped was a vague, dreamy gaze. "I can't say I've spent all that much time asking him about his work."

"The joys of new love."

"Yes."

"Even when you get left at the party all by yourself."

Abby kept up the good-natured attitude but couldn't shake the subtle awareness that Lucas had paid rather close attention to her and Campbell's exchange before he'd left the room. "He's a busy man. Since I've left more than one party on more than one occasion I can hardly complain."

Abby saw Lucas's gaze shift to a point behind her and turned to see Campbell striding across the ballroom. "Speak of the devil."

Campbell extended a hand, his smile bright and convivial even as she saw the tension that bracketed his eyes in tight lines. She made the brief introductions before Lucas started in with a jolt. "I understand from Abby you work in software for the financial industry."

She took heart at Campbell's light squeeze to her hand even if she couldn't shake the underlying feeling something was wrong.

And then she could only admire his acting skills as Campbell launched into a mind-numbing description of his "work." The man might not work in the financial industry, but you'd never know that from his ready description of complex technologies and evolving solutions in the field.

The heavy bell announcing dinner had their conversation ending and Abby excused them both to Lucas with the claim that she needed to speak to the event staff. Since her hand stayed firmly wrapped around his, Campbell added a good-natured wink to their departure and promised further discussion with Lucas over dinner.

Abby dragged him with her into the kitchen, unwilling to say anything until she knew for certain they were out of earshot of her guests.

"Did you just tell him anything that wasn't true?" Abby kept her voice low so as not to be overheard but she couldn't completely eradicate the panicky urgency that gripped her throat as they huddled in a small butler's area that held several rows of wine racks.

"Of course not."

"But you don't work in financial software."

"Sure I do."

"You what?"

"I work across many fields. You don't think I'd make up a job I didn't know how to do, do you?"

Abby clamped her mouth shut, convinced the gaping hole made her look like a gasping fish. "Well, I'm—"

"I know what I'm doing and I know how to talk tech."

"I guess you do."

The same tension lines she'd noticed in the ballroom were once more in evidence and she couldn't stop herself from reaching a hand up to settle against his jaw. "Is everything okay?"

"Sure."

"What did David want?"

Campbell glanced around them and pointed toward

a small group of caterers that stood along the far wall. "Nothing that can't wait a bit."

"Later, then?"

"Later."

Before she could even think to say anything further, Campbell took full advantage of their private moment to lean in and press his lips against hers. The light taste of the wine served during the cocktail hour still lingered on his tongue and she marveled at the sensuous blend of taste and the warm, masculine scent that filled her nose as she opened for him, tangling her tongue with his.

Campbell.

A light sigh rose up in her throat as she wrapped her arms around his neck and pulled him closer for their kiss. Whether it was the fact she had more than twenty people awaiting her arrival or the delicious smells wafting from the kitchen or the simple joy of once again being in his arms, Abby didn't really care.

She simply hung on and rode the moment.

Dark, sensuous needs exploded on her tongue as he made love to her with his mouth. His powerful body caged hers as he plundered, each moment sweeter than the one before. He pressed his lips against hers, their mingled breaths a testament to the deep need that pulsed between them.

"Abby."

She pulled herself from the brink of madness—and the increasingly insistent demands of her body that ruthlessly whispered she needed to drag him to her room—and let the quiet moment settle in her bones. "Hmm?"

"We need to get back to dinner."

"Right. Dinner."

"You okay?"

"Hmm."

He released his hold on her and stepped back. She felt the light touch of his fingers as he skimmed one down the side of her face. "You're so beautiful."

The delightful hum that filled her veins grew heavier at the lovely compliment. "Thank you."

"You ready to go back to the party?"

"Do we have to?"

"Unfortunately, yes."

"Then yes, I'm ready."

"And are you now convinced I can hold my own in a conversation with your guests?"

She smiled at the sweet notes of his voice. "I was convinced before. And while I'm quite sure kissing is not a way to convince me further I'm also not going to argue with your methods. Not one bit."

He leaned in and nipped a quick kiss along her jaw. "That was just for fun and to see if I could ruffle your very beautiful feathers."

"I see. And what do you think?"

His smile spread and she saw the distinct notes of "cat with canary feathers" painting that lush mouth. "I think I'm going to enjoy making love to you tonight."

Lucas pulled the slim tablet from his inside coat pocket and punched in his password as the various guests assembled for dinner. The mini-tablet fit his exact specifications and he was more than satisfied with how the incremental modifications he'd programmed had made the small device invaluable.

Which was why he never let it out of his sight.

He tapped in a few commands, pleased when he saw the various screens that indicated he was inside McBane's technology systems. Even more delicious, he knew he was inside the system with Abby's log-in.

There was nowhere he couldn't go.

He reviewed the data for a few more minutes—little had changed since the last time he'd checked, which made sense since she'd been in the ballroom the entire time—before closing out of the program.

He was so close.

So it was with no small measure of surprise that he saw Campbell Steele's interest as he and Abby walked through the doors at the opposite end of the dining room.

The image of Abby's face as he'd made his parting pronouncement—*I'm going to enjoy making love to you tonight*—kept Campbell vivid company as the tedious dinner conversation hummed around him.

Her lush brown eyes had widened in tandem with the rich swell of her just-kissed lips and he'd nearly dragged her right back into his arms or, even better, up the back stairs that led out of the kitchen.

The fantasy took shape in his mind before he remembered he had to share the news of Stef's death.

Or her murder, he silently amended to himself.

He knew Abby believed in Stef's loyalty—knew she'd fought the increasing evidence stacking up against the woman point by point—and it pained him to think of the additional pain Abby would suffer when she learned the news.

Poor choices and lost lives.

Just like Sarah.

The image of the girl he'd loved before he'd even fully understood the emotion reached up and grabbed him by the throat, squeezing with tight fingers.

This wasn't the same. *He* wasn't the same.

He had the power to do something now.

But the sickening fear someone had set his sights on Abby left a raw hole in the pit of his stomach.

"How are you enjoying Paris, Campbell?"

"I'm sorry?"

Campbell gave up the circling thoughts that didn't want to settle and turned to the woman next to him. She was nice enough—and had already introduced herself and her company with a description so detailed he'd briefly contemplated a nap—but he knew full well the role he played.

The fact this woman and all her counterparts at the event were blessedly oblivious to the underlying problems was something to be pleased about.

And while the overt purpose they were all gathered together in Abby's home was different from the myriad of events he'd attended throughout his life, the constant posturing, posing and jockeying for position was the same.

With wealth and position came the distinct desire to maintain it.

Campbell knew he didn't have the best attitude about his upbringing or the more social aspects of his life and he knew he'd have to get over that crappy outlook since entertaining was such a significant part of Abby's life.

The thought caught him off guard and he cleared his throat on the rich piece of filet mignon that attempted to turn to dust in his mouth.

"Are you all right?" Abby settled a hand on his thigh, her face full of concern as she turned to focus on him.

"Fine." He waved a hand as he reached for his glass of water. "Good."

Fine? Good?

To borrow one of his grandfather's most favorite phrases, *not bloody likely.*

Try completely and utterly bewildered, off-kilter and undeniably disoriented instead.

He laid a hand over hers, the moment of panic flashing into a hard jolt of need as she ran her fingers in a light caress over his thigh before she removed her hand and placed it back in her own lap.

Where he thought he'd won Round One in the kitchen, she'd clearly owned Round Two and Campbell was forced to manage both his rampaging thoughts and his traitorous body.

Rounds Three, Four and Five, too, his conscience whispered, if the raging kick to the head he was currently experiencing was any indication.

He reached for his water glass and tried desperately to gather his incoherent thoughts into something he could digest. On swift feet, one thought rose up from the rest.

When the hell had he started thinking in terms of such permanence with Abby?

They were going to figure out who was harming her and then he had to move on to the next thing. A new assignment.

One that didn't involve her.

That was all this could be.

And if—no, when—they made love, it would be as two consenting adults who wanted each other.

Not as two consenting adults who were moving their relationship to the next level of permanence and a lasting commitment to each other.

The wholly unsettling thoughts had him desperate for a new topic of conversation and he latched on to the one thing guaranteed to trip a new trigger in his brain.

Technology.

"Lucas. If I may be nosy, when I walked in I noticed

you had a rather sleek tablet in your hands. I don't think I've seen it before. Is it new to the market?"

The man's ready frown caught Campbell off guard as a heavy flush crept up Lucas's neck. In his experience, a fellow tech-geek was as eager to share his toys as most men were to show off a brand-new TV or a hot new girlfriend.

Which made Lucas's stammer and clear annoyance that much more curious.

"I'm afraid I can't do that. It's a new proprietary prototype my company has built."

"Of course. I understand. My apologies."

Lucas nodded, but the deep flush hadn't quite left his cheeks. And what had started as innocuous conversation in their section of the table had rapidly garnered everyone's attention up and down the length of the room.

Abby broke the noticeable silence with a light clearing of her throat. "I'm so pleased you all could join us. I know most everyone knows each other, but we'll be finishing up the evening in the library with a selection of desserts and after-dinner drinks. You'll have an opportunity to sit next to someone new and get further acquainted."

The conversation murmurs resumed and the caterers busied themselves with pouring more glasses of wine around the table. The flush had receded from Lucas's face, but the man hadn't managed to erase the hard glint that flashed in his eyes.

Although the urge to bait the man further was strong, Campbell avoided all talk of technology and instead kept his comments to an upcoming soccer match that had been the subject of eager speculation among those at dinner.

And made a mental note to look a bit more deeply into the background of Lucas Brown.

Chapter 13

Abby closed the door behind the catering staff and pressed her head against the leaded glass that framed the front entryway. "Are they all gone?"

"Security's still upstairs."

"Everyone besides them?"

"Yes." Campbell ran a hand down the smooth column of her back. "They're all gone."

"I thought they'd never leave."

"You're a good hostess."

"Clearly too good a hostess." She lifted her head and offered up a small smile. "Remind me next year not to serve such good liquor."

The thought of next year—and the idea he'd be around to remind her of it—stilled them both and he saw the edges of her smile quaver at the realization of what she'd said.

And then he thought of the news that awaited her and reached for her hand. "I need to tell you something."

"Oh, no."

"I'm afraid so." Campbell squeezed her hand before pulling her toward a small sitting room that sat off the main hallway. "It's not good news."

"Stef?"

"Yes."

A hard sob caught in her throat as she dragged a hand to her mouth. "Tell me. Now."

"She was found earlier today."

"Earlier? How long ago?"

"Security told me before dinner. She was found late morning New York time."

Whatever he expected, the virago who turned on him at the entryway to the sitting room wasn't it. "How dare you keep that from me?"

"Abby—"

"No! Do not try to placate me."

"I'm not placating you." He pointed toward a chair. "Sit down and I'll tell you what happened."

She ignored the directive to sit and stood with fists clenched in the center of the room. "You had no right to keep this from me."

He didn't miss the trembling that gripped her bare shoulders or how frail she seemed standing in the center of the room. "What would have been better? Telling you while you're in the middle of entertaining? Have every one of your guests see you like this?"

"I wouldn't have acted like *this*. I'd have held it together."

"Like you are right now?"

Where he'd seen self-righteous anger and a heavy dose of grief, her face changed into pure rage. "You have no right. This woman is dead and no matter what you think of her, she's dead because of me!"

"She's dead because of herself."

Even as the words spilled from his lips, Campbell knew each word was like a bullet and every single one had landed in the vicinity of Abby's heart.

"She's dead because she trusted the wrong man. She's dead because she betrayed you for money or love or who knows what sort of incentive he promised her that she believed enough to get herself killed."

"Campbell—"

"No!" The words came out on a harsh breath, his patience fully overridden by his anger and concern for her safety. "Be sad because she was a dupe. Be sad because her life is snuffed out, but you will not be sad because she is suffering the consequences of betraying your trust."

Abby wrapped her arms around herself and willed the bone-deep cold to subside.

Stef was dead? Murdered?

The words scratched her throat, but she kept her gaze steady on Campbell's. "Tell me about it."

"Please. Sit down."

She did as he asked, her hands folded in her lap as he recounted the awful details.

The intrusion into her apartment that showed no signs of forced entry. The unnatural angle Stef was found in. Even the puzzling news of the woman's personal emails and the lack of any evident communication with anyone.

"I should have seen it. Should have done something."

"If you'd seen it you would have done something."

"Why is this happening? If we're correct and Stef was used, this has been going on for some time. We worked together for almost three years, Campbell, and she's been a part of the company for more than six. That's a long time and I never knew there was a problem."

"People can hide their true selves."

Abby tried to process that, mentally flipping through any number of scenarios to try to make sense of the situation, but ended up discarding each and every one.

"Look. She and I were never close and that's on me and my reticence to get close to any of my coworkers. But we worked in close quarters. Late hours. I knew her comings and goings. Hell, I had to authorize her vacations. If someone seduced her, it had to take time."

"Planning."

"Yes. An inordinate amount of planning. She only started talking about a boyfriend a few months ago, but for her to be turned against me so completely? That took time. Add on the fact that the prototype has been missing for a while and this was well planned."

"Patient," Campbell added. "Think about it from his point of view. The lonely secretary, vulnerable to seduction by an outside force. The slow migration to get her to believe him over you, a woman she'd worked with for years. The even slower migration to get her to start thieving inside McBane."

"What could he possibly have told her to play her like that? I get the lonely part and the flattery at having a new, likely worldly boyfriend. But the theft? That wasn't her personality."

"He dangled something that had her dancing to his strings."

The image of Stef as a puppet only made the sorrow deeper, somehow.

"What can someone possibly want with me?" Before he could answer she had another. "The level of detail. The methodical planning. This goes beyond even basic corporate espionage. He wants something from me and I have no earthly clue what it could possibly be."

Campbell dropped to a crouch in front of her. "We're going to find out, Abby, and we're going to stop him. I promise you." He grasped her hands in his own, the warmth of his broad palms providing comfort even as she wondered if the horror would ever be over.

"How do you know that?"

"Because we will. We're determined and we're on to him and we're both too stubborn to lose."

She wanted to believe him—truly wanted to believe everything would work out—but any way she looked at it they were at a disadvantage.

"Years, Campbell. He's been at this for years and we're trying to catch up to him with less than a week's worth of effort. We can't beat him."

His hands tightened around hers. "Don't talk like that. I know you don't mean it. You can't." Without waiting for her to reply, he pressed on. "I've been working on a reverse-engineer of the server chip. That should give us a sense of who's responsible. Give us a signal to narrow in on."

She listened to Campbell's words but had no idea what he'd actually said.

Stef was gone.

Her company had been breached.

And the person responsible had likely spent the evening in her home, eating her food, drinking her liquor and having convivial conversation all the while smirking behind her back.

"Look—" Campbell broke off and she didn't miss the distinct discomfort that stiffened his shoulders. "There's one more thing you need to do and then I think it's time to get some rest."

"What thing?"

"The police want to talk to you."

"Of course they do." She stood up and reached for his hand. "And after the conversation with the police?"

"Rest. I think that'd be best."

She knew without him saying anything else the promise of making love had vanished.

"David's got a link set up in the study. It's not routed through your systems at all so it should be secure from prying eyes. You can video chat with the police from there."

"Let's go then and get it over with."

Lucas slammed from one end of his hotel room to the other, the Scotch in his glass sloshing with every step. He was so close.

So damned close.

The image of Campbell Steele, those sharp, assessing eyes staring him down across the dining room table, filled his mind's eye. The man's questions, like a damned investigation, yet phrased as if it were the simplest matter in the world.

One guy to another.

You shouldn't have used the device in his presence.

The small voice rose up to taunt him, crooning like an angry lover in his ear.

He'd silenced the voice the day he made his first kill and in one evening it had come roaring back.

He wouldn't let it rule him.

He wouldn't listen.

Even as it screamed inside his head, taunting and teasing like a manic child.

Idiot.

Useless dolt.

Unworthy wanker.

No!

He'd lived his life under its influence for many long, lonely years and once he'd grown strong enough had vowed it would never control him again.

The kills had always calmed the voice in the past, so why didn't the news of Stef's death do anything but make the voice louder?

Why couldn't he *calm down?*

Steele.

With shaking hands Lucas brought the Scotch to his lips, drinking the liquor like a dying man desperate for water.

It was Steele. The boyfriend. The one who'd surprised his hit man in New York during Abby's evening out on the town. The same one who'd arrived in Abby's office a few days ago with no advance warning for Stef.

It was *him*.

Steele had changed the balance of things, just as the plan was nearing completion. Even as he loathed the need to change his carefully ordered campaign at this late a date, Lucas knew the truth.

The man needed to be eliminated.

It was the only course of action before he could put the final piece of his plan in place. Before he could make sure Abby understood exactly who he was and what he intended to do to her.

Lucas knew he'd promised the pleasure of ultimately removing Steele to another but he was changing the game.

The situation had altered, shifting to an entirely new playing field and he was flexible enough and powerful enough to change with it.

With shaking hands he poured another glass of Scotch, then dialed the man who had just arrived in Paris.

Abby let her gaze roam over the rooftops that made up her neighborhood as she stared at the city. Pale curtains fluttered in the evening breeze floating through her window and the hum of Paris could be heard through the window.

Normally the sounds of the city comforted her, but tonight all it did was make her feel lonely.

Stef was dead. Her business and possibly even her own life were threatened.

And the man she was coming to care for deeply had kissed her on the head and sent her to her room after the call with the police.

Tears stung the backs of her eyes and Abby brushed them away, unwilling to give in to them. If only she could brush away the fear that echoed through every fiber of her body as easily.

The sound of footsteps down on the street drew her attention and she watched Simon, David's right-hand man, stomp down the street toward an unmarked luxury car. The vehicle fit in with the other cars on the street, but the brawny, well-muscled security man wasn't quite as hard to ignore.

She watched him move, intrigued by his athletic grace, even as she wondered why she felt nothing for the man other than a passive interest in his rather attractive features. He'd given her more than a few appreciative stares earlier during the briefing. Had even gone so far as to suggest she should consider having him on her personal detail for the duration of her meetings before getting the eye from David.

Wouldn't he be just as good? An itch to be scratched

was just that—a normal, healthy urge that did a body good to satisfy.

And without warning, those tears were back in full force, falling before she had a chance to brush them away.

Damn Campbell Steele.

She didn't want to simply scratch an itch or exercise a few healthy urges.

She wanted him.

Wanted to share her body with him, breathing the same air, wrapped up so tightly in each other there was no room to let anything else in.

Not either of their pasts, nor whatever unimaginable things awaited them in the future.

The light knock on her door broke through her thoughts. "Who is it?"

"Abby. Let me in."

She dashed at the tears, torn between elation that he'd somehow sensed her thoughts and frustration he'd find her crying.

She hadn't bothered to lock her door, but rather than just call out and allow him to let himself in, she opened it and stood on the opposite side of the threshold. "It's late, Campbell."

"I know."

The urge to posture and make up some flippant excuse was strong but she was tired and, more than anything, she was disappointed he'd left her alone. "And you've made it abundantly clear you're interested in sleeping alone tonight."

"I'm not sure what gave you that idea but nothing could be further from the truth."

"Did you come here to convince me of that?"

She didn't miss the stiffening of his shoulders as his hands balled into fists at his side. "No."

"Then why are you here?"

"Because I can't stay away."

Those hands flexed once more, like a last-ditch effort to restrain himself, before he walked through the door, pulled her into his arms and kicked the door closed with a foot. She briefly registered that he reached back and flipped the lock before his mouth came down on hers.

Abby wrapped her arms around his neck and mumbled against his lips, "Took you long enough."

She felt the traces of a smile against her lips before he plundered. Abby thought the kisses they'd shared up to now had prepared her for the full onslaught of his lovemaking, but quickly realized nothing could be further from the truth.

He absolutely devoured her.

And she went willingly.

Campbell ran his hands over her lithe form, the thin silk nightgown bunching in his fingers as he sought flesh. She was amazing—warm, willing and so damned sexy he couldn't see straight for wanting her.

Couldn't think over the insatiable need to make her his own.

Campbell knew this way lay madness, but he was fast coming to accept that the path without her wasn't a picnic, either. And then he simply gave up any attempt at rational thought and allowed himself the time to enjoy the woman in his arms.

Their lips met and merged, tongues clashing in an erotic ballet that satisfied even as it left him desperate for more. Their breaths mingled with each kiss and he filled his hands with her as he walked them toward the bed.

Her hands gripped his waist and she gathered the hem of his T-shirt in her hands before lifting it up and over his head. He broke contact with her—the brief moments without his hands on her an agony—as she slid the shirt over his head.

The moment he was free of the shirt Abby pressed her lips to his chest, her tongue tracing an erotic path around one nipple before moving lower to trail a wet row of kisses to his belly button.

"I want to see you," he whispered against her temple as he pulled her in for another kiss. In movements that mimicked hers, he fisted handfuls of silk at her waist, dragging the nightgown over her head and tossing it. He abstractly noticed how the silk seemed to float toward the ground before the need to look at her consumed him completely.

A sharp intake of breath stuck in his chest as he gazed on her perfect form for the first time. High, tight breasts with lush, pointed nipples. Slim hips and a flat stomach that begged for his touch. Long, slender legs that he already pictured wrapped around his waist as he drove into her, their bodies matched in rhythm.

Enchanted, he pressed his hands to the heavy weight of her breasts, running his thumbs over her nipples. He was rewarded with a soft moan as her head fell back, those gorgeous eyes lidding to half-mast. Despite his body's urgent demands, hard and unyielding against the fly of his jeans, he kept up the gentle assault on her breasts, overwhelmed by the beauty of her response.

Without warning, her hands snaked forward to the snap of his jeans and before he even fully registered her movements, she had her hand under the waistband of his underwear, her hand fisting him with tight, controlled movements.

Stars swam before his eyes and he fought to maintain some measure of control when all he wanted to do was drop to the bed and bury himself into her. "Abby."

"Hmm?"

"You're amazing."

Her smile was full of secrets and feminine power before she leaned up to nip a kiss on his chin. "Right back at ya, sexy."

With gentle movements he removed her hands from his jeans. Her pout was unmistakable, but he only smiled when that same small moue turned to a smile of delight as he lifted her off her feet and carried her to the large four-poster bed that dominated the far wall of her bedroom.

He laid her across the bed, following her down and covering her body with his. She dropped one leg so he was nestled between her thighs and he felt the wild heat of her through his jeans. Desperate to feel some of that heat for himself, he reached between them and slipped a hand beneath the thin silk of her panties.

His body hardened even further at the slick evidence of her need and he pressed a finger to those hot folds, then another. The low moan that greeted his actions had him increasing the pressure and her body responded with a liquid wave of heat that had his own primal satisfaction roaring in his chest.

Had he ever seen a woman more magnificent in the throes of her pleasure? Or one more beautiful?

Her orgasm crested and he captured her hard cries with his mouth, their tongues merging in rhythm with her body's response. Although he was nearly mindless for her, Campbell kept up the relentless assault, willing her to wring every last drop from her release.

When he felt her body go lax, he shifted, rolling to the side and gathering her in his arms.

"Did you truly think you were going to stay in your room tonight?"

Abby's words—and the wry tone with which they were delivered—caught him off guard and a hard laugh welled in his throat before he could think to stop it.

Had he ever felt so good?

Or had he ever simply enjoyed a woman's company more?

"My intentions were noble."

"Well, consider me thrilled you got over that." She smiled up at him and laid a hand against his cheek. "I'm glad you're here."

"I'm glad I'm here."

The haze of passion was still more than evident in the dark discs of her pupils, wide in those delicious brown eyes, but it was rapidly pairing with something else.

Renewed desire.

"Campbell." She whispered his name.

"Yes?"

"You're wearing too much."

Before he could confirm or deny the sentiment her hands returned to the open button of his jeans and made quick work of the zipper. Her efficient movements were somewhat stunted by the thick denim and he couldn't miss her frown of frustration.

"Let me."

With some efficient movements of his own, he had his jeans and briefs down in one coordinated motion, then rejoined her on the bed.

"Smooth moves, Steele."

"I've got a few more where those came from." He

bent his head, recapturing her mouth once more before murmuring against her lips, "But wait."

"What?"

"Now who's the overdressed one?"

He reached for her waist, hooking his fingers in the tiny panties that still rode her hips and dragged them down her spectacular legs. As she lay fully exposed to his gaze, Campbell had to stop a moment and simply look his fill.

"What?"

"You're so beautiful. Inside and out."

A light flush worked its way over her body, the delicate pink adding to her already-glowing visage.

Without breaking eye contact, he leaned forward and kissed her.

The last kiss he'd give her before he fully made her his own. And as she maintained his gaze, he knew she sensed the same.

Nothing would be the same. But they were both committed to making it better.

"Campbell." Her voice was whisper-soft in his ear.

"Yes?"

"Make love to me."

He looked his fill one last time before fully giving in to the increasing demands of his body.

She was a goddess.

And in that moment she was his.

Abby felt the air shift around them. What had been fun and lighthearted morphed into something deeper. More intense.

And altogether more profound than anything she'd ever expected to experience.

She wanted this man in a way that defied logic and reason.

His large body covered hers and she once again opened herself to him, amazed at how well they fit together. The hard length of him pressed at her core and she was nearly ready to assure him she was on the pill—a medical assist that ensured she stayed regular—when he lifted off of her to snag his jeans.

The moment was surprisingly tender as he made quick work of the small foil packet and returned to her, a warm smile on his face. "I have to admit I'm suddenly very relieved I packed those."

"We have a work-around."

"We'll worry about that later." He pressed his lips to hers. "Now. What was that you requested? Something about making love to you until your toes curled."

"Is that editorializing?"

"Consider it going above and beyond in full commitment to my duties."

"Who am I to suggest you shouldn't give it your all?"

And then he proceeded to do just that.

The light banter faded away as they found their rhythm, the tension in their bodies spiraling as they pushed each other, sending one another to the brink... and beyond.

Abby knew the moment he was nearing his release—felt it in the tightening of his lower back and the increased pressure of his thrusts. She felt herself following, her own orgasm coming fast on the heels of the one he'd given her only moments before.

"Abby!"

Her name had never sounded sweeter and she clung to him as he poured himself into her.

And as she followed him into the abyss, Abby knew she'd never felt more protected in her life.

Chapter 14

Abby lay curled in the cocoon of Campbell's arms, her body limp and sated. The house was quiet around them, everyone having settled for the night. If she hadn't known David and his team had taken up residence on the guest floor, she'd have thought she and Campbell the only people in all of Paris.

Their explosive lovemaking was a revelation.

She'd known their attraction was more intense than anything she'd ever experienced, but even she couldn't have imagined how that would translate into the physical.

How one man could be so gentle yet so fierce. So thoughtful yet able to laugh and smile with ease. So incredibly bright, yet deeply sensitive, as well.

He was a protector. A warrior. And a man unlike any other.

Her conscience rose up in quick admonition she not

make more out of sex than she should, yet even as she gave in to the thought, she readily discarded it.

Something had changed between them and it was more than simply giving in to a physical urge.

If she were really honest, sex—though outstanding—was simply the culmination of what had been building since that first moment in her office. From the first, she'd been drawn to him and every moment in his company only made her want to curl up and settle in more deeply.

Uncover more layers to this fascinating man and—even more surprising—share the things in her own life she normally kept to herself.

His fingers roamed over her skin as he traced lazy circles over her flesh and she wondered how she could feel so calm—so at peace—while in the midst of her entire world melting down.

"What do you know about Lucas Brown?"

Campbell's question penetrated her delightful haze and she turned to stare at his face, now drawn in solemn lines. "You can't seriously be asking me about my meetings right now?"

"The question's been in the back of my mind and I meant to ask you earlier then forgot."

"Clearly I did something wrong."

"You did nothing wrong. Not one—" he pressed a kiss to her exposed ear "—single—" then to her cheek "—thing—" then to her lips. She turned in his arms, falling into the kiss as the moment quickly took them over.

How could it be so easy? She marveled as his hands roamed over her body, igniting sparks wherever he touched. She reached between them, her hands closing around the hard length of him when his hand stilled her and he groaned against her mouth.

"Abby." He nipped at her lips again. "We have to talk."

She gave him one long, thorough stroke for good measure before settling in beside him. "Thanks for the buzzkill."

"It pains me more than it does you, believe me."

"It'd better." She shifted to sit up but he pulled her back into his arms, tickling the sensitive skin over her ribs for good measure.

When she finally caught her breath, she turned to stare at him. "So why do you ask about Lucas?"

"He struck me as curious tonight."

"Curious how? Every time I looked at him he was the life of the party. He's bright and articulate and one of the better conversationalists among my lovely, albeit slightly boring, board of directors." Campbell rolled his eyes at that description and she recalled a conversation she'd overheard between him and the woman who had sat on his other side during dinner.

If she hadn't been mistaken, Campbell was seriously considering suicide by butter knife.

"I think you're giving them too much credit by calling them boring."

She swatted lightly at his arm. "All I'm saying is that Lucas is a good guy. *And* he has a personality."

"I can respect he livens up the room, but something struck me as off."

She couldn't hold back the surprise at Campbell's assessment, even as she trusted his instincts too much to dismiss it out of hand. "Not only is he one of the best board members I have, he's been a huge champion of my business."

"How so?"

"He helped us secure some financing a few years ago as well as putting in a good word for us with many of Europe's finest investors."

Campbell propped himself up on one elbow, his eyes alighting at her explanation. "Don't you find *that* curious?"

"Why would I? It's been a major boon to have such a well-placed champion. When his name was suggested to me for our open board position last year I jumped at the chance to get him."

She didn't miss the skepticism that painted Campbell's face or the hard play of muscles as his arms tightened around her. "Spill it. It's more than you simply having reservations about him. You obviously don't like him."

"I don't know him, but something about him trips my senses. You saw our exchange at dinner."

"What was that about, anyway? I missed the beginning and all of a sudden the entire table was staring at the two of you."

"I asked him about a small tablet I noticed he was using."

The thought briefly flitted through her mind that perhaps those weird moments at dinner were some sort of cultural difference, but ultimately discarded it. "I'm not seeing what upset him."

"My point exactly. I know gadgets and I know gadget guys. And he looked like I'd punched him in the face while insulting his grandmother."

Abby struggled to sit up. "Do you think there's something to it?"

"I think it's worth paying attention to him tomorrow. Keep an eye on him and see what he does with that tablet."

"If he's anything like you, he treats it as an appendage." She couldn't hold back the smile as she allowed her hand to drift lower beneath the covers. "A rather favored appendage."

"If you're implying—" His sharp intake of breath let her know he knew *exactly* what she was implying.

"If the shoe fits."

"Oh, baby, last time I checked, my gadgets didn't respond nearly as favorably to external stimulation."

She leaned down and pressed a kiss to his neck before working her way lower across the expanse of his chest. "Perhaps you just don't give them proper—" she blew lightly over the path of kisses she'd trailed with her tongue, satisfied to see the light shiver that gripped his skin "—care and attention."

"Why don't you show me how it's done?"

"It'd be my pleasure."

Abby's words echoed in his mind the next morning as Campbell ran another set of diagnostics against the server device. She'd gone downstairs to meet with the caterers and set up the dining room for her presentation, kissing him on her way out with the promise she'd pay particular attention to Lucas Brown.

He had every intention of joining her but wanted to get through another layer of tests before heading down to breakfast. He knew he was close on the diagnostics—like the last few pieces of a puzzle that just needed to be properly aligned with the whole—and wanted to make the best use of his morning.

He hummed along with his work, mentally cursing under his breath when a line of code he'd thought particularly inventive missed the mark, then went back to solving the puzzle.

And all the while, Abby wasn't far from his thoughts. The memory of their heated lovemaking would keep him company for many years to come, but it was more than that.

He couldn't get the image of waking up with her out of his mind.

She fit.

No, he amended to himself, *they* fit.

They fit incredibly well if last night was any indication.

And the more time he spent with her, the more he wanted to fit with her. Permanently.

The thought was as exciting as it was unexpected, but the more he tried it on for size, the more comfortable the fit.

Campbell left the thoughts humming in the back of his mind like lines of code and turned once more to his computer. After reading the results of his latest adjustments he modified and made a few more. And nodded with grim certainty. As he'd suspected, the system had been probed last night, the honeypots he'd set up blazing with evidence of a repeated breach.

The sound of the front doorbell echoed through the house, just as he got lost in the lines of code that ensured he was getting close to an answer.

"It's a good day," he muttered to himself as he tapped in a few more commands. "A very good day to catch a ghost."

Kensington read the email from her brother on her phone and decided to put her insomnia to good use. Slipping from bed, she padded down to her office and logged in to one of several databases they had special license to access.

Campbell had reservations about several of Abby's guests, one he'd prioritized to the top. If the guy had a record, she'd find it.

Hell, if he'd ever kicked a puppy or punched his grandmother, she'd find it.

She was just that good.

The familiar screen flashed on her secure system and she typed in her credentials, then went to work inputting various search queries and navigating several interesting threads.

The work was often slow, but she found it endlessly fascinating to see how one line of inquiry could lead to another which could lead to another that held the answers she was looking for.

In the meantime, she played a bit of technology archaeology and fancied herself a female Indiana Jones.

The light knock on her door was a surprise and she glanced up to see her sister, Rowan, highlighted in the doorway. "What happened to going to bed after we polished off that bottle of wine?"

"I couldn't sleep."

"Big surprise." Ro's eyebrows shot up over that liquid blue gaze the Steele siblings were so renowned for before stepping into the room. Her short brown hair the color of rich mocha—normally spiky on a good day—stuck straight up at odd angles.

"Sorry if I woke you."

"Nah. My body clock's a mess."

"Hong Kong, Rome and Chicago in one week will do that to a person."

"I take solace that I will sleep well, when I do eventually sleep, secure in the knowledge I caught the bastard." Rowan snorted before running a hand through the spikes. "Antiquities dealer my ass. Common street thief with a well-heeled network of scholars feeding him leads is more like it."

"Spoken like a woman with a deep and abiding passion for museums and the artifacts they make available to the masses."

"You know me so well." Rowan stood up and crossed around to Kensington's side of the desk. "What are you working on?"

"Someone's got Campbell's feelers up and I'm checking him out."

"You get anything yet?"

"Nope, not yet, but I just started."

Rowan covered a small yawn. "I've got faith in you. If there's something to find, you'll find it."

"Thanks for the vote of confidence."

"What's the case about?"

Kensington caught her sister up before letting loose with the concerns she'd hesitated voicing to Campbell, especially since Abby's assistant had ended up murdered.

Whoever was responsible wasn't messing around and her brother and one of her closest friends were smack in the middle of it.

"He's falling for her."

"That's great!" Whatever sleep deprivation Rowan might be feeling vanished at the evidence her brother had a new girlfriend. "It's about time he got serious about someone."

"Make sure you don't say that in front of him. Those are fighting words."

"They're truthful words. He's a good guy and his heart's about three sizes too big for his chest. He deserves the best."

"Well, Abby McBane's the best, but he's sitting on a world of hurt he's never really dealt with."

"Sarah?"

"Yep." Kensington nodded, the lingering sadness of how their childhood friend died one of the life experiences they all carried with them.

And one of the experiences that had contributed to what they'd built with House of Steele.

"Does Abby know about Sarah?"

"I never told her." Kensington wondered now if that had been shortsighted, but Sarah's death—and Campbell's subsequent grief—had always been a private matter.

Of course, that was before she saw the heat that blazed like a forest fire between the two of them.

"They'll figure it out."

"I hope so, Rowan. I really hope so."

"I'll let you get back to what you're doing. If you don't see me for a few days, just send up food and water intermittently."

Kensington couldn't hold back the smile. Where most youngest children fussed for the independence, Rowan had always been more than willing to let all of them pamper her. It was one of her more charming traits, because she did it with such grace and aplomb. "I'll make sure you don't starve."

"That's a relief." Rowan dropped a kiss on her head. "Try to get some sleep."

"I will."

"Yep. That's your standard answer, but you never do."

Rowan's words still echoed in her ear several hours later as the sun rose over Manhattan. She was nowhere near finding any information for Campbell and that alone was troubling.

Everyone had a record because everyone had a past. So where the hell did Lucas Brown come from?

* * *

Abby knew she'd missed what had to be very obvious clues from Stef, but no matter how she looked at it, she couldn't find anything amiss with Lucas.

The morning had gone well and he'd contributed significantly to the discussion on McBane's continued global expansion as well as how they were going to source investment beyond the next five years. He also had a lot to say on some debt restructuring that showcased considerable strategic thought and raw intelligence.

What could Campbell possibly have seen?

She did keep an eye out for any use of the handheld device Campbell was so concerned about but other than a slim tablet he kept propped in front of him throughout the meeting—one that didn't fit Campbell's description—Lucas used no other technology as they spent the morning working.

Abby ducked into the kitchen after they broke for lunch to check on the caterers and provide directions for the meal service when Simon came barreling through the swinging door.

"Simon. I asked you not to come down here."

"There are enough people in this house one more won't matter." He kept a bright smile on his face but she sensed the petulance underneath his tone.

"I'm not all that interested in whether or not you agree with me. I've asked you to stay out of sight."

"How are we supposed to keep an eye on you?"

"Oh, I don't know. How about with the surveillance equipment you've set up all over my home? I swear, a fly can't land anywhere on the first floor without you guys knowing about it."

"You hired us to be thorough."

"I also hired a team I thought respected my wishes. Now please get out of here before my guests see you."

Simon looked about to argue once more, but turned on his heel and marched back through the swinging door.

Straight into ten of her board members lingering in the back hallway, taking various calls or talking in small conversation areas.

Abby saw Lucas among the group, his phone pressed to his ear as he gave instructions to someone in German. His focus never wavered from his call and she offered up a silent prayer that everyone was too busy to register Simon's disgruntled features and disappearance up the back steps of the house.

"What's the matter, darling?" Campbell came into the hallway from the opposite direction, so he missed Simon's departure. What he didn't miss was Lucas's presence in the hallway. With an ardor she knew wasn't even remotely fake, he leaned in and pressed his lips to hers, lingering extra long while his hands reached for her, linking their fingers.

"Campbell," she snapped. "These are my colleagues."

He made a little show of pretending to tease her before dragging her back into the kitchen. They took the butler's wine pantry again, away from the prying eyes and busy footsteps of the catering staff.

"What was that about?"

"Just hamming it up for the crowd."

"Consider yourself hammed and stop coming on to me in front of these people. I'm supposed to be their fearless leader."

"So be their fearless leader who's got a sexy new boyfriend." He glanced over his shoulder in the direction of the hallway. "What just happened out there? You looked like you'd gone three rounds with a grizzly when I walked up."

"Simon." His name was out before she could think to censor herself.

"What the hell?"

"It's nothing." Her hand on his arm did little to cool the anger flooding his cheeks but it did have the effect of keeping him put in the kitchen. "He came down here sick of being cooped up on the third floor and I asked him to return there as quickly as possible."

"He's a hothead and he deliberately defied your wishes."

"I know."

"I'll have David get him off this assignment."

"Don't. The board meetings finish tomorrow and then we move into a smaller set of meetings. He's already entrenched. I'll talk to David about it at the next break."

Campbell looked ready to protest but she quickly cut him off. "You figure out anything with the prototype?"

"I'm this close—" He held up two fingers, no more than a quarter-inch between them. "And I should have a few answers by later this afternoon at the latest."

"You get anything on our friend?"

"No."

"Anything jingle on anyone else?"

"No." As the word came out—full of angst and a good layer of disappointment—Abby caught herself. "Goodness, what is wrong with me? It's like I'm hoping we find someone."

"No, it's not. You've accepted there's an issue. There's a difference."

"It still doesn't feel right."

He placed a finger under her chin and lifted gently until her gaze was level with his. "Nothing about this feels right, Abby. That's what we're working toward. It's what we're going to figure out."

She knew he was right. Knew the continued lack of information or confirmation on an assailant was only prolonging what was already a stressful situation.

"I'm glad you're here."

Campbell bent down and pressed his forehead to hers. "I'm glad I'm here, too."

She felt his comfort—knew he was there for her—and knew that support made all the difference.

"Now. On to more important matters."

"More important?"

"Do you have time for a quickie?"

Her mouth dropped as she pulled back but he kept a firm grip around her waist. "You did not just ask me that!"

"I sure did." His grin was broad and cocky and she couldn't hold back the answering smile, even as she tried for mock sternness.

"You don't even look remotely contrite."

"Why should I look contrite? I had the best night of my life last night and I'm anxious to repeat the experience."

Lucas waved off the other attendees, gesturing he'd be in shortly, pleased when the hallway emptied of everyone. His call had provided an excellent cover and he stayed on the line, contributing every so often to remain engaged, asking questions of his staff to get them to run through an entirely new set of answers.

The best part was he could let it run as long as he needed, so long as he kept up a steady stream of questions his underlings had to scramble to get answers to.

The big man who didn't look like he belonged had

fled up the back servant's stairs after his words with Abby. He'd already sensed there was something else going on in the house and this confirmed it.

On swift feet, Lucas took the stairs two at a time, the inane voices in his ear rambling on about investment yields in the Pacific Rim and expectations for the Euro. He could have cared less—he already had all the information, anyway—but he made simple sounds of agreement, encouraging them to continue.

The staircase ran to all the floors and he had a sense the second floor had no one so he kept going to the third.

And confirmed his hunch the moment he heard voices when he hit the top of the landing.

With a quick flick of his finger, he disconnected the call, unwilling to risk the slightest bit of noise echoing from his phone. He was the boss so he could do whatever he pleased, but if questioned directly he could simply say his call disconnected and he was seeking a better vantage point to pick up cell service.

Raised voices streamed out of a door down the hall and Lucas could make out the edges of a body as it paced back and forth.

"She requested we stay up here."

"Are we security or lackeys?"

"We're hired guns and we do what we're told."

"You've had a bug up your ass about Steele from the jump. That's the real problem and if you can't get it together, Agent Green, I'll have you reassigned."

Lucas heard the faint clinking of plates from two floors below, signaling the start of lunch. As he didn't want to be missed, he descended back down the stairs, but now with all the confirmation he needed.

Security sat two floors above them, keeping an eye on the proceedings and ensuring Abby's safety. Along with

Steele, there were enough eyes and ears in the place to make sure he wouldn't be able to touch her.

Lucas hit the back hallway and lifted his phone to his ear in the event he needed to playact about his call, but no one came.

He slipped back into the dining room just as the meals were placed before each board member and thought about the new details.

And plotted out how he'd incorporate this new intel into his plans.

Chapter 15

Abby removed her jacket and settled it on the back of the small chair she kept in front of the writing desk in her room. She'd hang it up later—she was well able to care for her own things—but for the moment she just wanted a few minutes to think about the day.

The meetings had gone well—incredibly well considering everything that had led up to them. The board was open to her ideas and listened when she offered up solutions to their various business needs.

If only she weren't dealing with a hidden assailant, how much more productive might she have been?

If only...

She'd learned long ago not to worry about the things she couldn't change. Even if you oftentimes wanted to.

The night spread out beneath her once more as she looked out her bedroom window. The second night of the week in Paris was always an open evening and her European assistant had arranged for various options for the guests, ranging from show tickets to dinner reservations to spa appointments if the individual was so inclined.

For her part, she was just thrilled to have some quiet.

The light knock on the door thrilled her even more thoroughly and she called out a soft, "Come in."

Campbell came up behind her, wrapping his arms around her waist as they both looked out into the night. "Good day?"

"Productive." He nuzzled her neck, pressing a line of kisses along her collarbone. Abby tilted her head, allowing him better access as the slow waves of pleasure swamped her senses.

Everything was more sensitive—more heightened—when she was with him.

Although she couldn't argue with the delicious response he pulled so effortlessly with his lips, she also couldn't hide her eagerness to put the current danger behind them so they could focus on the future. She turned in his arms. "Did you find anything?"

He pressed a quick kiss to her forehead before wrapping his arms around her waist and pulling her against him. "I'm so close. I had a breakthrough earlier this afternoon and nearly had the signature right there, but it's proving elusive. I've got another program running."

"Can I interest you in some dinner, then?"

"You want to go out?"

"David's already arranged for security detail with car service for my meetings later this week since I do have a few in the city before I leave. We'll get one of his guys to drive us and keep an eye on us from a distance."

She saw the briefest hesitation in his eyes, but pressed her case. "We'll be fine. That's why we have support from others. Why I hired them."

"I know." His arms tightened around her. "I know."

"Come on. We'll have some wine and cheese and put all this behind us. And when we come home, your tests may even be completed and we'll be another step closer to ending this."

He agreed to go along with her dinner plans but as they climbed into the sleek gray luxury car fifteen minutes later, Abby still saw the tension lines that bracketed Campbell's mouth.

And for the briefest of moments, she wondered if she was making the right decision.

The Eiffel Tower rose proudly in the distance as he and Abby enjoyed a small table near the window of the restaurant she selected. *Bistro,* he amended to himself. The lushly decorated place would qualify, with black-and-white parquet floors, colorful old French advertising posters lining the walls and a generally welcome air full of baked bread and active conversation.

She'd wanted to sit outside but he'd drawn the line at being fully out in the open and requested inside by the windows as a compromise.

Paul, one of David's agents, had impressed Campbell thoroughly, doing a sweep of the restaurant before he left them to their evening with a solid nod.

With the excellent company and confirmed safety of the location, he settled in and tried to make the most of his evening out in Paris with a beautiful woman.

They drifted through conversation, various topics drawing them in before taking them down a new path. Things they'd both experienced in childhood. Funny or odd experiences each had had as an adult. And a funny series of stories about international travel and working with others whose cultural background and upbringing was different.

"You really dropped the sushi?" Campbell took a sip of his wine and eyed Abby's smiling face over the rim of his glass.

"All over. I was intending to welcome my guests and my very American high heels snagged in the carpet and I tripped and fell flat."

"You're lucky you didn't get hurt."

"Oh, my pride suffered enough for the both of us."

Campbell didn't miss the sweet pink that lit up her cheeks and realized she was a woman of contrasts. Where the world saw a competent businesswoman— and she *was* that—she was so much more.

He'd observed her behavior the past few days and saw a woman full of intriguing contrasts.

She lived a life of privilege, yet she was unfailingly kind to the staff, thanking them for their hard work and recognizing their help in putting on the event in her home.

She hated having the security team in her home, but she'd ensured they were well-fed and given ample room in the house to give them both space and personal time.

And probably most telling of all, despite the clear evidence Stef had betrayed her, Abby had already made personal calls to deal with the arrangements for the woman's funeral.

She reached for her glass and took a sip. "It's nice to talk about these things."

Campbell pulled himself from the warm thoughts of her. "Oh?"

"I often downplay them on dates. For some reason, a woman who has traveled the world isn't all that interesting as a dinner companion."

"Well, I don't know who you're dining with but they've clearly not seen what I see." He reached out and laid a hand over hers. She turned her hand palm up so they met in the center of the table. "Which is obviously to my advantage or you'd be sitting this very moment with some banker named Chuck or some stuffy Wall Street analyst named Pierre."

"I dated a Pierre once."

"And I actually dated a Chuck." At her bark of laughter, he added, "Her name was Charlotte, but that had been her nickname since she was a kid."

When her laughter subsided, Abby's gaze roamed toward the windows, staring at Paris's most famous landmark, before turning back to him. "Yet here we are."

"Here we are."

"It's easy, isn't it?"

Was it?

Even as the question rose up in his mind Campbell knew the truth. It wasn't simply easy to be with her, it was becoming increasingly *necessary.*

"You matter, Abby." Her fingers squeezed his in a flirtatious gesture that went straight to his groin.

"So do you, Campbell. What do you say we get out of here?"

The immediate shift in tone—from congenial conversation to lush needs that could only be sated together—had him waving down their waiter. Within minutes, he'd made quick work of their check with a few hastily thrown bills that offered a generous tip for their waiter's expediency and was escorting Abby to the exit.

Campbell waved in the direction of the gray vehicle parked a short ways down the sidewalk as he and Abby stepped in front of the bistro. Paul flashed his lights in confirmation he'd seen them as he pulled out of the space. Abby linked her fingers with his and laid her head on his shoulder as he pulled her close.

Paul pulled up to the entrance and Campbell reached for the door just as a loud noise lit up the night. The briefest of moments passed—no more than a second or two—but Campbell thought it an eternity as his mind tried to process what was happening.

Screams echoed from the people sitting at the bistro's outdoor table and Campbell leaped on Abby, pulling her to the ground as the sound of gunshots registered.

"Get down!" Paul screamed from the car and Campbell abstractly heard his car door open as he emerged to face the threat.

The ringing of bullets stopped, the last striking metal and causing the car to quiver on its tires.

The car…the car…

Campbell leaped up, dragging Abby with him. "He's hit the car. Come on."

"Paul! Paul!" Abby screamed their guard's name and Campbell heard himself doing the same through the ringing in his ears. The patrons from the outside tables began streaming past them and as Campbell dragged Abby determinedly toward him, they both turned to see Paul lying beside the car, blood rapidly pooling around his head.

"Paul!"

"Abby!" Campbell dragged on her arm when she tried to go back. "Abby!"

She struggled in his arms and he just kept moving backward, willing her to understand. "The car. The gunman hit the car."

She continued to struggle as he pulled her onward and then there were no words as the world exploded around them.

* * *

Abby felt Campbell's strong arms around her—heard the endless screams and sobbing and abstractly realized they came from her—just as a huge cloud of fire exploded before her eyes.

The instinct to cower pulsed through her body as she and Campbell both bent over to shield themselves from the blast. The odor of oil and gas and a horrible burning smell filled her nose and flooded her mouth with taste.

The sidewalk brushed her cheek and Abby realized she and Campbell were both prone on their sides. She struggled to sit up as he did the same, pulling her close.

"What happened?"

"I don't know."

"Paul." A sob rose up in her throat, hard and swift, at the evidence their guard had gotten caught in the crossfire.

"Who did this?" The question rose up in her mind, followed by a cacophony of others.

How did this happen?

Why had they targeted an innocent man?

Why? Why? Why?

Questions without answers.

Sirens echoed in the distance and within moments Abby saw the lights that ensured help was on the way.

Three hours later, Abby leaned her head back against the sofa in the living room and let the tears fall. The police had been kind yet firm and promised a return visit the next day.

She'd already sent out the emails canceling the next day's meetings. Had explained there had been a serious accident involving an employee acting on company time and she needed to attend to the needs of his family.

David's team was visibly shaken and Abby knew they'd already increased their efforts, calling in additional staff and instituting patrols of the perimeter of her home. She and Campbell had also updated the police on the situation with her business.

Which had prompted the promise of a return visit.

Campbell slipped into the room and crossed to the small liquor table she had set up on the far side. She watched, as if outside of herself, as he poured two fingers of bourbon for both of them, then came to sit beside her with the two leaded crystal glasses.

She took the one he offered, sniffing the liquor before setting it aside.

"Take a sip. It'll warm you up."

"Nothing will warm me up." She turned toward him and saw the lines of tension that bracketed his mouth. Knew she had to have similar lines creasing her own face. "Nothing can change this awful, awful thing. Or the fact that I insisted we come here."

The words were freeing as they finally took shape and form and Abby set her glass down, unwilling to numb the guilt with liquor.

She was responsible for Paul's death. Further, she was responsible for putting her entire board in danger. And she could add Stef's death, as well, even as she knew Campbell wouldn't listen to that in her litany of charges.

The only saving grace was that all of the restaurant's patrons had escaped unharmed.

She didn't know what she'd do if she had the blood of innocent bystanders on her conscience, as well.

"Nothing will warm me, Campbell."

He reached for her but she pulled back, standing instead to pace the room. She saw the hurt that flashed in his eyes and wanted to erase it, but couldn't bring forward the proper emotion to do so.

"Don't push me away, Abby."

"I didn't listen to you. You said I should cancel this until we found out who did it but I didn't listen."

"This isn't your fault."

"Of course it is." The urge to rant and rail rose up in her throat, yet all that came out was a quiet voice that couldn't be silenced. "It's all my fault."

He moved behind her and she stepped away from him once more. "I need to go up."

"Let me come with you." He stretched out a hand before pulling it back. "Let me hold you. Nothing more. Just let me hold you."

She wanted that, Abby knew, more than she could ever say. But she'd gone into this alone, unwilling to take anyone's counsel.

And now she needed to face the consequences alone, as well.

The night sounds of the Bois de Boulogne drifted around him as Lucas opened his flask and took another drag of his Scotch. The liquor burned a light path to his stomach but it couldn't divert his rampaging thoughts.

Couldn't make it quiet.

Why wouldn't the voice stop?

He'd taken action, securing yet another kill along the way, but nothing worked. Nothing quieted that damned voice that whispered in his ear and taunted him.

Undeserving. Unworthy. Unloveable.

The voice rose up out of the woods behind him as the hit man Lucas had hired came into view. "Nice meeting place. I like the atmosphere. And the group of addicts

I just passed will ensure even if we're overheard, we're not going to be disturbed."

The smile was broad—jovial even—and Lucas knew the killing had calmed the hit man even as it had given him a high. A soaring height bigger than the one the addicts down the path were searching for yet would never find.

Lucas observed him just as he had at their first—and only—meeting.

Slim form, nondescriptive face, expensive shoes that looked like loafers but were in reality designed for speed, with rubber soles that made no noise when he walked.

The man's reputation was unprecedented, but he'd grown increasingly tedious.

Even as he'd proven highly effective.

"Ms. McBane's home is on the other side of this park."

"Avenue Foch. I did my homework." The man's dark eyes glinted in the moonlight, a mix of avarice and anticipation.

"Indeed."

"I've told you that you can't touch her. She's for me."

"I can take care of the boyfriend."

"I'm coming to think of him as mine, as well."

That anticipation flared once more in those predator's eyes before the hit man tamped down on it, silencing whatever emotions—or lack thereof—fueled him.

"I've done what you asked."

"And there will be more jobs. But I've changed my mind on Abigail and the man she's sharing her time with."

"Suit yourself."

"You don't agree?" The words were out before Lucas could censor them.

Traitorous words that allowed an opponent to think him weak. That he'd be willing to reverse his position.

"I never enjoy giving up prey."

"Neither do I."

"Yet you were more than content to allow me to do your dirty work. First your girlfriend, then the driver earlier tonight. Tell me, what's changed your mind?" The man shifted on the balls of his feet and Lucas had the disorienting sense the man had moved closer, even though that couldn't be quite right.

Could it?

"You get a taste for it? She piss you off enough to make this personal." Shift…shift…shift. A gun flashed from his waistband.

Lucas followed the man's eyes yet still had that disturbing sensation the man was moving closer. "Or was it the fella? New boyfriend in the mix. Changes the rules. Maybe you've got a little thing for the woman and don't like him horning in?"

At the idea he'd want Abby in that way, the increasing discomfort crashed through Lucas with the speed of a bomb blast. He leaped on the small man, dragging him to the ground.

Lucas reached for the man's neck, the urge to squeeze the very breath from him the only thing that would bring him peace.

The only thing that would quiet the voice.

The hit man was spry and Lucas knew immediately he'd underestimated his foe. Underestimated the powerful strength in that slim body and those careful hands.

The ground was hard beneath them as they rolled, crashing into a small copse of flowers as they struggled against each other. Lucas had the physical advantage but the hit man had years and years of brutality and sheer stubborn will on his side.

A heavy fist to the stomach knocked Lucas's breath but it was in that moment, as his free hand went to his stomach, that he remembered the small syringe he'd prepared in his vest.

It had been impulse, really, that quick purchase when he'd entered the park, but now knew the advance planning would be his saving grace.

He'd learned a long time ago not much beat a well-placed dose of heroin. Especially not when it held twice the limit most humans could reasonably consume.

Regaining his feet, Lucas hunched over as if to attack, bull-style, but the move was intended to shield the work of his hands. The hit man moved back, deflecting the blow Lucas telegraphed with his stumbling steps, but he wasn't fast enough to see the lethal flight of one lone hand gripped tight around a syringe.

Lucas plunged the needle the moment he found open flesh—a thin thigh as it attempted to connect with his stomach—and depressed the plunger with one swift thrust.

He then moved out of the way to enjoy his handiwork.

Campbell tugged at the ends of his hair with frustrated fingers, the glow of his computer screen taunting him as a clock somewhere in the house rang in 1:00 a.m.

He'd spent the late hours alternating between anger at Abby and anger at the stubborn set of codes he couldn't seem to crack.

How the hell had this guy made himself so damned elusive?

He'd already rerouted all of Abby's data so it appeared as if the device still had access to her systems, even though all it could pull was a dummy interface, but no matter how hard he tried he couldn't get the codes right on the reverse engineering part of the equation.

The closer he got, however, the more convinced he was he could trace the user.

An image flashed in his mind once more of Lucas Brown and his strange reaction to questions on his tech device but even that seemed a bit flimsy under the circumstances.

Especially since Kensington still hadn't turned up a thing on the guy. Everything he was purported to be— namely the well-respected owner and head partner of a major European private equity firm—was all she could find.

He slammed the lid of his laptop down and pulled away from the desk. A large glass of whiskey might go a long way toward helping his mood—it couldn't hurt—and he needed some time away from the endless string of code.

Maybe some liquid relief would free his mind to look at the problem a different way.

Again, Campbell thought ruefully, it couldn't hurt.

He stalked down the hall to the small sitting room that sat at the end of his wing. The room boasted a beautiful view of the city and a few minutes of fresh air at the windows along with his drink should go a long way toward clearing his head.

Until he saw Abby standing at the window, her hair rippling against her temple in the light evening breeze.

She still wore the outfit she'd worn to dinner—a slim pencil skirt and silk blouse tucked in at the waist. Her heels were long gone but she hadn't changed into something more comfortable.

Or clean.

He could still see the scuff marks that ran along the side of the fawn-colored skirt from where he'd pressed her to the ground outside the restaurant. "You haven't changed."

"Haven't I?" She turned from the window, her gaze distracted and unfocused.

"What are you looking at?"

"Nothing. Everything."

He tried his question again. "Why haven't you changed yet?"

"I will. It seems..." Her hand floated into the air. "I guess it just feels that if I change, it means I've accepted what happened. It means I've accepted that Paul died."

He felt the tug of her sad, sad eyes and couldn't resist walking toward her. "No, Abby. It doesn't. He's still going to be gone, long after you change. Long after you leave here. Long after we catch who's doing this."

"I just keep seeing it and no matter how many times I do, I can't believe it happened. One minute we're wrapped up in each other, that sexual hum between us practically dragging us from the restaurant, and the next the car's exploding in flames." She dropped her head in her hands as her face crumpled. "Paul's lying in a pool of blood next to the burning car."

"Abby." Her earlier resistance be damned, he closed the distance and pulled her into his arms, pressing his lips to her temple as he crooned nonsense words. "Shh. It'll be all right. Shh."

"It's not all right. And it won't be. So many dead. Gone."

"That's not you. Why can't you see that?" He stepped back and held her slim, quivering shoulders in his hands. "Why can't you understand that?"

The grief that rode her eyes receded, replaced with a

hard, burning anger he'd never seen before as she shook off his embrace. "My entire life I've avoided entanglements. Avoided caring about people or sharing my life with them. That was the way to sadness and grief and I wanted no part of it. Yet here I am."

She whirled back to stare at the window, looking at something only she knew, but her voice drifted over toward him. "It found me. Grief and sadness and hurt found me, anyway. Only now I have the blood of innocents on my hands."

He refused to let her take the blame.

Refused to allow her to think she owned the actions of others or that her own actions were somehow responsible. Before he could argue with her, she flung his imagined words back at him.

"You claim I didn't do this. That Stef made her own choices. That Paul was a trained operative."

"Yes."

"None of it changes the fact that they would still be alive if they weren't a part of my life."

"You can't think like that. Can't assume you have responsibility for others."

"Like you, Campbell?"

He heard the question. Heard the soft, probing undertones. "What do you mean, like me?"

"Sarah. That poor sweet girl who lost her life a lifetime ago. Are you over her? Are you over thinking you have any responsibility for that?"

"It's not the same."

"No?" She turned from the window. "It's exactly the same. You were barely sixteen years old. How could you have done anything to change that?"

"You know nothing about it."

"No? I know it haunts you. You admitted as much to

me. Admitted it was the act that drove you to what you do. Can you honestly stand there and tell me it doesn't drive you still?"

The urge to deny it was strong on his lips but Campbell held back, certain in the knowledge Abby was right.

He had let Sarah's death and the subsequent loss of his parents define that time in his life.

And he continued to allow it to define his adult choices. Who he let get close and the majority who he kept at a distance, or more likely, pushed away.

With that knowledge came more. He wanted Abby in his life. Wanted to pull her close and never let her go. "Don't push me away, Abby. Please."

He wanted her to come willingly—wanted her to take what he offered and give it back to him in return—but he couldn't stay away. Couldn't stand there and *not* touch her.

"Campbell."

"Let's take it, Abby. Reach for it and take it with open arms."

And then she was in his arms and there were no words. No more conversation. Only the two of them and what they shared.

"Yes." She whispered the words against his lips.

If her rejection earlier had left him ice-cold, the heat arcing between them had him thinking of the hottest summer days. The air around them sizzled and even the cool breeze floating in through the window could do nothing to dim what passion generated between them.

How had he lived without this woman?

Or had he never found anyone else because no one else was Abby?

The events of the past days flashed through his mind on a loop as he touched her.

The competent businesswoman. The beautiful society woman. The fearless leader.

All were a part of her—and parts she played—but none of them came close to the thoughtful woman who lived with a world of hope in her heart, even as she hid herself from the world.

And he wanted all of them. All the things that made Abby the amazing, incredible woman she was.

A fresh swirl of air blew across his hair as he bent his head and for the briefest of moments he stilled and simply stared at her, breathing her in.

The heat of her skin highlighted the delicate scent that defined her. Her pulse throbbed at her throat, passion evident in the heavy beats under that delicate band of skin. A light sigh escaped her lips as a small smile spread across those lush lips.

And in that moment, Campbell knew he loved.

The vague, faceless woman of his dreams was real and tangible in his arms.

And she was better than he'd ever imagined.

Secure in the knowledge of his feelings, he painted kisses over her lips, down her cheek then into the concave dip of her collarbone. He flicked his tongue lightly against her flesh, satisfied when her breath caught in her throat just before she tightened her grip on his waist.

Another light breeze wafted over them and he wanted to take it in—wanted to feel it blowing across them as he stripped her—and turned her so she faced the window, his body at her back. He was already hard and aching for her, the heavy thrust of her butt against his groin the most exquisite torture. He settled a hand against her stomach, pulling her back so that soft cushion could press more intimately against him and used his other hand to work the small pearl buttons of her blouse.

One by one, the buttons slipped from their holds and he used his pinky to caress the flesh that spilled over the cups of her lace bra before moving lower to flick one hardened nipple.

Abby's moan encouraged him on and he kept up the contact unwilling to relent for the slightest moment.

He wanted to brand her. To scorch his need for her so deeply into her skin there'd never be room for another. A long soft moan drifted up to him, floating on the air just as he slipped the last button free.

And just as he turned her so her breasts were flush with his chest, the loud, shrieking burst of the house alarm went off without warning.

Long, low screams of the alarm echoed through his ears as Campbell dragged her away from the window.

"What's that?"

"The garage. The cars." Her eyes were wide in her face, the passion that had filled them vanished with the silence.

"Someone's in the house."

Chapter 16

Abby gathered her shirt as she followed behind Campbell's retreating form. The combination of his long legs and the fact he still wore shoes gave him the advantage and she took off after him, stopping briefly in the hallway.

A dim memory of leaving a pair of running shoes proved correct and she dragged them out of the hall closet, slipping them on before shifting to focus on her open blouse.

Heavy action flooded the stairs and David and his men descended, guns in hand, and Abby had the briefest moment of panic.

"We need you secured, Abby."

"Campbell!"

David blocked her way. "You're the job. Back in the room." He gestured for one of his guys to escort her back to the study and Abby had the briefest urge to race away before she tamped it down.

She'd follow where they told her to go and would rationally figure out a course of action.

Until the man in front crumpled like a rag doll as his body fell to the ground, blocking the rest of them. Gunfire still echoed around the small landing as heavy footsteps thudded back down the stairs toward the first floor.

"Man down!" David screamed the order as he and his men dealt with their fallen comrade, then followed in the direction of the gunfire.

Whatever limited acquiescence she had to staying put vanished at the two thoughts that clanged through her mind.

Campbell's safety and her unwillingness to sit alone in her house, unarmed, not knowing who might await her.

Another gunshot echoed from the direction of the garage and she raced toward it. Carnage greeted her as she stepped over the threshold as another of David's men lay on the ground. She saw the retreating form of another as he raced down the street in pursuit.

And then she caught sight of Campbell, reassurance flooding her veins that he was unharmed.

"Let's go."

Campbell's voice echoed in her ear as he dragged her toward a small two-seater. "You have the keys?"

"They're in the car."

She abstractly noticed one of the other cars was missing. "Why's there an empty space here?"

"Shooter took it."

"Who was it? Did you see him? You know my executives. Was it Lucas?"

Campbell pushed her toward the passenger seat before running around to the driver's door. "I don't know. All

I got the moment I stepped into the garage was a hail of gunfire so I stayed down while I looked for something to go after him with."

Once they were both in, he turned to her. "I don't suppose I can convince you to stay here?"

"No way."

"He's gone."

"I'm not sitting here alone and I'm not letting you face him alone. This is about me and I'm going to see it to the end. Besides, he's got a car which means he's got keys and access to the house. I'm not staying here."

"All right." His face was grim, yet resigned, and she offered up a quick prayer of thanks his stubborn streak didn't pick that moment to argue.

Instead, he gunned the engine and drove them into the Paris night.

Lucas wove in and out of traffic around the Sixteenth arrondissement. He kept a clear eye on the large SUV that pursued him, thrilled that the idiot security team had selected the largest vehicle in Abby's fleet.

Muscle men.

He scoffed at their ridiculous decision but also knew it gave him a decided advantage. Not only could he slip through traffic far easier, but there was no way he'd miss them in and among the various cars filling the streets.

And bless Paris, the city was wide-awake, irrespective—or in deference to—the late hour.

Which gave him an idea.

The apartment he'd prepared wasn't that far away. He'd lead them down the Champs-Élysées, past the Arc and lose them from there. He could abandon the car at the first moment and slip into the night undetected.

He didn't think he'd been recognized but couldn't risk

going back to the hotel and a quick tap of reassurance on his inside front pocket ensured he had the only thing of value he needed, anyway.

As if it mattered.

When this was all over, he'd have what he wanted as well as all the status that would confer with it. He could gather his things then.

Lucas glanced in the rearview mirror, pleased to see the bulky SUV had fallen farther behind. It would only take a few more minutes and he'd be well rid of them.

And then he would go make sure his trap was well-baited.

"Do you see him?" Campbell wove in and out of traffic as Abby kept a steady focus on the cars in front of them.

"No, but I know we passed David and that damn SUV. I hate that car."

"Simon probably picked it," Campbell muttered as he wove around another car. "And I suspect David's sentiments match yours right now."

"There!" She pointed, then shook her head. "Well, maybe it's him. Why the hell are all my cars black?"

He couldn't hold back the quick grin at that one. She'd been a rather intrepid passenger and he realized she'd also provided a pair of eyes he desperately needed as he navigated the crowded streets.

"He's headed for the Arc. See."

Campbell caught sight of the tail of the black sedan and sped up as soon as he realized he had a hole.

"Campbell! Look. He turned off."

Campbell saw where she pointed and cursed. He was so far left it was going to be hard to get all the way right.

"Go down another block. We'll cut him off."

"He's going to get bottlenecked in there." A sudden opening had him zipping across several lanes and taking the right Abby had pointed out. "And now that he's slowed down we'll close the gap. This car is small and it's got zip."

He knew that was more than true. It had given them the advantage against the SUV the security team had chosen and had even allowed them to gain ground on the larger sedan.

"Stop!"

The words were no sooner out of Abby's mouth than Campbell saw what had her issuing the command. The car they'd been following had been abandoned, the door hanging open and the interior lights bright. He saw the driver fleeing on foot down the street and pulled to a hard stop a few feet down.

"What are you doing?"

"Following him."

She had her belt off and was reaching for the door handle. "Can you at least lock this one? I'd prefer to avoid the insurance paperwork on two cars."

He leaned over and grabbed her arm, dragging her back for a quick kiss. Whatever they lost in time he knew was well worth the moment. "I love you. You know that?"

Her smile dimmed as she went totally still. "Really?"

"Yep. Now let's get this bastard so we can get on with it."

She allowed herself the briefest of moments—barely a second or two—to savor his words.

He loved her.

And with unerring certainty she knew she loved him in return.

Abby was all speed and motion as she leaped out of

the car and raced around to his side. In deference to her request, he alarmed the car as he shoved the keys in his pocket.

"Go! I'll keep up and I've got running shoes on. You're tall and you're easy to keep sight of."

"There are too many people." He grabbed her hand. "Come on, I'm not letting you go."

Another wave of happiness assailed her at his words, completely at odds with their situation. She followed behind him as they dodged people who streamed up and down the avenue. The man they were pursuing—was it Lucas?—had a good head of steam but he was as delayed as they were by the throngs of people and slowly Campbell and Abby narrowed the gap.

"You see him?" She gasped behind him but never lost her ability to keep pace, despite her shorter legs.

"Yep."

"Where?"

"Look toward the Arc. He's about a street away."

"He's going to have to veer off!" He saw what she meant as they got a few feet farther. "There's a traffic circle around the Arc. He'll have to take a side street that spokes off."

But which one?

Campbell tried to keep his focus on his quarry but the foot traffic had grown heavier, tourists and city dwellers alike out enjoying the late evening.

Where was he?

"There!" Abby pointed and Campbell followed the direction, the two of them off in further pursuit.

A huge cry went up ahead of them as their guy obviously knocked over a few people. Campbell pulled Abby to the far side of the sidewalk, determined to avoid the aftereffects, namely a heap of people lying on the sidewalk trying to figure out who might be hurt and what had just happened.

"Back that way."

"Where?"

Her hand tightened in his. "I think he's backtracking to the car."

Campbell could only hope Abby was right as he took another turn. His chest began to tighten with the exertion and he knew she had to be getting winded. As soon as he saw a clear stretch ahead of them he turned his head for a quick check to see how she was doing. "You okay?"

"Keep going."

He fought through the burn and kept up the pace. What he couldn't account for was his inability to see the man they pursued.

"You see him?"

"No. Where'd he go?" Her voice rose behind him.

"I don't know. He was just there."

He slowed their progress, moving into a steady jog as they doubled back toward the street where they'd parked.

"He was running as long as we were," her heavy pants assailed him. "He can't have gotten to the car yet."

Campbell came to a full halt as he scanned the street. "Where the hell'd he go?"

"I don't know."

The heavy blow that slammed into his head prevented any response. Dimly, as he fell to the ground, Campbell heard Abby screaming.

Chapter 17

Abby stared at the well-appointed apartment and knew, without the slightest doubt, that it was lined in some way that made it soundproof.

"No one will hear you." Lucas Brown stared at her from across the room. He stood behind a built-in bar mixing a drink in a martini shaker, looking for all the world as if he were entertaining.

"Figured."

His eyebrows lifted at her comment but he didn't reply, instead just kept shaking his cocktail as a thick sheen of cold water formed on the metal.

"Comfortable?"

Restraints held her hands pinned to the arms of a dining- room chair. "Delightful."

"I'd suggest you appreciate what you have as I can make things a whole lot less delightful."

"Since I'm sure that's already on your agenda why don't you dispense with the formalities."

He shrugged as he poured his cocktail. "Not yet."

"You know we're on to you. The theft of the device. Your fake relationship with Stef. The hit on Paul."

He shook his head as he crossed to take a chair opposite. Despite the fact he'd also restrained her legs to the chair, Lucas sat a fair distance away from her.

As if she were distasteful to him.

He'd done something to her in the street that caused her to black out so he'd had to have touched her then. Despite that, she knew, without a doubt, that he hadn't enjoyed it, nor was he interested in repeating the experience anytime soon.

Curious.

Where she'd originally feared rape and death, she could at least cross one worry off her list.

And why did that make her want to laugh out loud?

"A smirk, Abby? Really?"

"Consider it a recognition of the absurdities of life."

He shrugged and she saw something familiar in the gesture, even as she couldn't place it. "Suit yourself."

"Oh, I will." She hesitated a moment. "Won't you tell me anything?"

"Soon enough." He lifted his glass to her in toast. "Soon enough."

Campbell rubbed the back of his neck as David drove him to the house. Abby had long since vanished and panic had taken counterpoint to the hard throbbing in his head with the vicious fists of a bass drummer.

Where was she?

He knew he needed to stay calm and think through it.

Lucas Brown had been the one jingling his chain all

along and he'd already had David dispatch a team to the man's hotel. They didn't expect to find Lucas—if he were, in fact, responsible—but maybe something would turn up in his room.

The moment they reached the house, Campbell raced for his room and the makeshift office he'd set up.

And saw his buzzing phone where it danced on the top of the desk.

"Kenzi—" His sister's name came out on a harsh sob he couldn't hold back. "They've got her."

"They who?" Kensington's normally calm tone rose several notches. "Who, Campbell?"

"That's what we don't know. We couldn't see him, damn it." The worst sort of frustration rode him.

That Abby could be gone and he had no idea where was as painful as it was impossible to believe.

"It's Lucas Brown."

"How do you know that? Are you sure?"

"I have it right here. Listen to me."

He listened to Kensington recount the specifics. How the man had been born Lucas McBane Brown.

How there had been several notations on file in the McBane security archives about a woman and her son who'd tried repeatedly to get entrance to visit Abby's father on his business trips to the London office.

Each and every one was denied.

And then a rather large financial payment made to the same woman two years after Abby was born that had ended the visitation attempts.

"It was a blip, Campbell. A well-buried blip. The only reason I even thought to look at it was that I kept asking myself what a powerful man like Abby's father might have had in his closet."

"You found it."

"Fat lot of good it's done."

"Actually, it's done more than a lot of good." Campbell felt the phone vibrate in his hands and removed the screen to look at it.

And went still when he saw what came up.

"Kenzi. I'm going to transfer you to David. The two of you can run point on Brown's company. I know where she is."

"How?"

"My ghost just took form."

"What the hell are you talking about? Enough with the geek talk."

He didn't have the strength to smile, but he did take comfort from his sister's reaction. "No geek here. I cracked the device. The one Lucas stole from Abby."

"Yes?"

"I can find him. He's using a wireless device to manage the tracker and I've reversed it."

"You found him."

"Gotta go."

"Campbell! You can't go in there alone."

"Work it out with David."

Campbell disconnected on the shouts of his sister.

Abby jerked her head back, the lazy edges of sleep clearing at the pain in her neck.

Had she actually slept?

Early morning light crept through the window and she knew she hadn't been here all that long. Even so, her arms had gone numb and her legs felt like lead weights in the chair.

Campbell.

He was foremost in her thoughts, the only driving thought whether or not he was okay.

The thought was swiftly followed by another. Where was Lucas?

She sat still and tried to listen for any sounds—that subtle evidence that another person was in the same place as you.

The soft creak of the hardwoods down the hall confirmed he was there and she took an easy breath.

At least he hadn't gone after Campbell.

It still didn't explain his game. What did Lucas want with her? Or them? Whatever it was, the evidence that his feelings were personal were mounting.

"You're awake."

"Hard to sleep tied up."

"You'll get used to it."

"You think I'm going to be here awhile."

He flicked a glance at her as he folded the cuffs of his fresh shirt. "Good plans take time to execute."

"There's a plan?"

At the mention of a "plan" her mind briefly latched on to the Joker in one of the Batman movies and his gleeful taunts that there were no plans.

"Of course there's a plan. I'm a strategic leader in my field. I know how to plan and execute. A well-planned strategy trumps flash each and every time."

"How long have you been working this one?"

"About twenty-five years."

"What?" She did some rapid math in her head. "But you're not more than thirty-five."

"In November, as a matter of fact."

"So how is it possible you've been planning to kidnap me since I was five?"

"Ten was when the idea of vengeance first took root in my mind."

At his use of the word *vengeance* any hope this wasn't personal fled.

"Most ten-year-old boys are interested in footballs and trains."

He reached for the tie that hung around his neck and began tying a Windsor knot. "Let's just say I was advanced for my age."

Diabolical more like but she held the thought. He was finally opening up and it would do her no good to bait him to the degree he refused to say anything.

He crossed to the mirror that hung on a wall near the apartment's entry. "Your innocence is charming."

"Innocent of what?"

She saw his gaze flick to her in the reflection of the mirror, but still had no idea what this was all about.

"Didn't you ever wonder about your father? His youthful escapades."

"Not really."

"Well, my dear sister." Lucas crossed the room, his gaze never wavering from hers as he placed one deliberate foot in front of the other. "The result of his escapades have thought about you."

Her brother?

Shock layered over disbelief layered over a strange sense of happiness.

A brother.

His flat cold stare froze any semblance of joy, but even so, Abby couldn't dismiss the way several pieces fit into place. The vague familiarity in his movements. Their easy camaraderie. An overall level of comfort with him she'd had from the start, even as there were no overtones of anything sexual in the least.

"Why didn't you tell me?"

"There was nothing to tell."

"Lucas! Of course there was." The hard glint in his eyes caught her up short and she was forced to acknowledge there was no welcoming look in his gaze.

No happy reunion or even any interest in one. "What did he do to you?"

"Nothing. He did absolutely nothing."

She fought to find the right words to penetrate the cold. "Surely you can't think I'd do the same."

"It's too late to find out."

When the door slammed behind him, Abby knew it was true.

Whatever forces had shaped him—her father's clear dismissal of the boy's existence at the top of the list— were too well embedded to be changed.

She glanced down at her tied arms and knew her first hopeless moments.

How would anyone ever find her? Or even know to look for her here?

"You can't go barreling in there like the freaking cavalry."

David's words were a strict warning and Campbell had gotten sick of listening to the man's "recommended restraint."

He wanted Abby back and he had no interest in delaying that goal for any reason.

"You don't know how he's got it armed, Campbell. We need to watch and observe. She's alive."

"How do you know that?" His voice was quiet, the words lodged tightly in his chest.

"She's valuable to him. He hasn't gone through all this effort to waste it now."

Campbell heard the underlying message. *Or kill Abby yet.*

Damn it, he wasn't going to go there.

Was. Not. Going. There.

"You know the device is calibrated properly?"

"Of course."

"You sure?"

Campbell brushed off the skepticism and recognized David's questions for what they were. An effort to be well prepared so they could get in and get Abby without anyone getting hurt.

David had lost men, too. Good people who'd followed him into battle and Campbell tried to keep that thought in mind as he and the security lead mapped out their next steps.

Campbell walked him through the program he'd written. The final fix had been simple, but the program itself was rather complex, using a mixture of GPS data, individual phone fingerprinting and a little overlay he fondly thought of as his gray hat special.

He might have started his hacking career as a black hat and might now wave the proud flag of the white hat, but he'd learned through the years his very best strategies used a mixture of both phases of his profession.

The little fingerprint he'd put on Lucas was just that.

Right now, he was picking up a signature of each and every device the man went anywhere near.

"See this." Campbell pointed to a three-dimensional map on David's workstation.

"Yep."

"He's centered at this address which Simon already confirmed is a high-rise apartment."

"So you can tell what building but not which apartment."

"My sister's working through that now, combing ownership records, but right. We don't have the exact apartment yet."

"No video surveillance?" Simon probed.

Campbell had to hand it to the man, he'd come online, more than ready to help in the fight to bring Abby back. "Bastard's worked his way around the video. It magically disappears each and every time he gets near the building."

"And no one's noticed? These systems are designed to manage outages and report them as problems."

"Not when you give the system a happy little program to keep it occupied." Campbell tapped on the screen once more. "He knows what the hell he's doing. He's really, really good."

"And yet you've scented him down like a bloodhound." David turned to slap him on the back. "We're going to get her."

"I know."

But every minute they were apart Campbell wanted to rip something apart. He just prayed Lucas had enough control to keep her unharmed.

Abby shifted in her chair, fighting the near-nauseating need to use the bathroom, and considered her options once more.

Lucas's use of the shaker the previous night—as well as the ready supply of liquor bottles on the sidebar—would make an adequate-enough weapon.

She had to be let loose first.

The lock sounded and she turned as the object of her calculations walked in. "And how was your morning?"

"I'm nearly floating."

"Hmm?"

"Bathroom, Lucas. Can I use one?"

His gaze was skeptical, but she knew she had him on that one. Mother Nature always won.

She'd nearly congratulated herself when her world went vertical. She felt his hand through the slats at her back as he dragged the chair—and her—down the hall to the bathroom.

He positioned her at the open door, then stood behind her and undid the restraints.

"There's nothing in that one so just go and keep it quick."

She stumbled as he tilted the chair, shoving her through the door. Nearly her entire body had fallen asleep and pain rushed through her limbs with all the finesse of nails driving into her skin.

Abby stumbled to the toilet and relieved herself, considering the room. He hadn't joked—the room was bare. Even the toilet paper sat by itself on the back of the toilet. She briefly considered lifting the toilet tank lid and using it as a weapon but couldn't remove it. The seat was glued down, too.

Damn.

Frustration rose up to mix with sheer exhaustion.

She had to get out of here.

With a resigned sigh, she prayed Campbell would have some way of knowing where she was and knocked on the door.

She might as well learn as much as she could in the meantime.

Lucas made quick work of retying her, then dragged her back the way they'd come.

Without warning, an unexpected wash of tears hit her. Where she'd have expected them as a result of the exhaustion, she had to admit they came from another source.

Now that she knew why she saw similarities, when she looked at Lucas she saw her father.

The same well-framed jaw. The same sweep of how that jaw descended into his chin. The same arc of his cheekbone.

"Tears, Abby?"

"I see my dad. I've never noticed it before, yet I've always felt there was something familiar about you, but there it was as you bent over me to drag the chair.

The quiet look she received in return—the sheer emptiness in his gaze—showered ice pellets over her spine.

He might look like her father but there was none of the associated warmth. And there certainly wasn't any love or affection.

"Lucas. Why are you doing this?"

"Because I'm going to win."

"Win?" She shook her head, willing there to be something—*anything*—inside his mind she could appeal to. "What's there to win?"

"My legacy."

He resettled her chair in the corner, then took his steps to put the distance between them.

"You can have it. You always could have had it. I'd have been more than willing to share."

"I want what's mine."

The reality of his sickness rose up to choke her, threatening another layer of tears. "What if I just give it to you?"

"Nope. You need to lose everything. That's the only way my plan will work."

Plans…back to the plans.

"And what is your plan?"

"Those satellites you're deploying next month?"

"Yes?"

"I'm going to sabotage their launch, indicating the damage you've done to them in various cost-cutting measures."

"No, Lucas."

"You'll be nowhere to be found because you'll be right here, tied up nice and tight. And then I'll swoop in and buy up the company. You know, with all my experience on the board I've got the exact credentials to bring the company back from the brink of financial disaster." His gaze floated to the window and it was in that moment— why it had even taken her this long, Abby didn't know— that she accepted he was lost to her.

The brother she'd never known would never be hers.

"No doorman," David grumbled as he scanned the ornate lobby. "Who the hell builds an apartment like this and leaves off a doorman?"

Campbell glanced down at his phone, the lights on the face indicating the man he'd tracked was in the building. "A landlord who's catering to a more average clientele while assuring them, and himself, they've got the height of security wired in to keep them safe."

"Tenants sleep soundly, thinking of the foolproof cameras in their lobby."

"Yep, and we know different." Campbell saw Simon through the front door of the building, his gaze pointed up the front of the midsize high rise as he strapped on rappelling equipment. Two other men stood on the roof, ready to drop his rope and pull him up.

Simon shot them a thumbs-up before his body began to ascend.

Kensington had come up with the purchase details and they'd narrowed Lucas's apartment down to three possibilities. Since all three faced the front of the building, Simon would rappel up the side, out of view from any of the three possibilities and do some external spying until he found the right one.

Voices echoed in the matched earpieces Campbell and David wore and he heard Simon confirm he was ready to begin climbing.

Campbell and David took the stairs to the third floor as Simon's voice echoed in their ear. When they heard him confirm the third floor wasn't it, they kept going toward six.

The image of getting to Abby filled his mind like a mantra—a prayer—the need to hold her a living, breathing need inside of him.

What if he got there too late?

Again another denial went up which meant they were headed to twelve.

Campbell picked up his steps, taking them two at a time on a renewed burst of speed as David's heavy booted footsteps clattered behind him.

As he approached the door to the twelfth floor, Campbell heard the scream echo through his earpiece along with the rail of gunfire.

David screamed his name from behind, demanding he halt, but Campbell ignored it as he dragged open the stairwell door and raced for the sounds of battle.

Abby struggled to duck and knew she had nowhere to go but down. With hard bursts of her feet, she pushed on the chair, desperate to make herself topple over to ensure she was out of the line of fire.

The gun in Lucas's hand had been a shock, but the sight of Simon outside the windows even more so. She saw him in the briefest moment before Lucas made out the threat and screamed as loudly as she could to alert him to the danger.

She screamed once more as Lucas fired on the man, dangling in a harness, but it must have given Simon enough warning because he pushed himself off the window just before it shattered.

The force of her feet had her own momentum shifting and she fell to the side with a hard thud. It was only when she looked up that she saw the apartment door slam open, Campbell barreling through it, his face a mask of determination.

"Campbell!"

His gaze alighted on hers and in it she saw relief as well as a bone-deep anger that was glacial in its intensity. Then she watched as he turned that stare on Lucas.

And then everything happened at once.

Abby screamed that Lucas had a gun a split second before David lifted his weapon to fire. Simon's momentum on the swinging harness carried him back through the opening, sending more glass flying into the room and crashing to the floor.

In the midst of it all, Campbell charged forward without stopping, straight into Lucas. The force of his body was enough to propel Lucas off his feet.

Campbell never stopped, just pushed forward until Lucas was scrabbling for purchase on anything, desperate to keep himself upright as Campbell pushed him inexorably toward the window.

On a final push, Campbell's momentum took the man over and everything went silent as Lucas's screams faded as he fell.

Abby stared at him—this man that she loved—and saw the mirror image of his warrior ancestors in his stance.

"Abby." Campbell was by her side, dragging on the chair so she could sit upright. His hands ran over her arms, tugging on the tight knots, his gaze roaming everywhere at once.

"Campbell. It's all right. I'm all right."

"I can get them." David pushed Campbell to the side before he flipped open a switchblade and made quick work of the knots. He'd barely sliced the last knot around her ankle before Campbell was dragging her into his arms.

His hands were everywhere as he scanned her for injuries. "Are you okay?"

"I'm fine. It's okay."

She finally stilled him by taking his face in her hands. "I'm fine. Really. Fine." She glanced at the window. "Are you okay?"

"You're safe."

"I mean it. Are you all right?"

"All I saw was you. Lying there and he had the gun pointed at you."

The brief moments assaulted her senses and she knew she'd see them for years to come. "It was pointed at you. I was so scared."

"I had to keep you safe. And the only way to do that was to charge him."

"My stubborn hardheaded man."

He bent his head and pressed a kiss to her lips. It was brief but it held a lifetime of promise. When they finally came up for air, he winked at her. "Good to know it's useful for something."

She laughed at that as she pulled his head down for one more kiss before stepping back and dropping her hands to her hips. "I've had twelve hours to think about this and I love you."

"I love you, too."

"I know and I'm kind of mad at you for it."

"For being in love with me? Or for me being in love with you?"

The fear of the past several hours vanished at the reality that she would get to tell him. Would hear him tell her he loved her in return, again and again.

"For telling me first and giving me no way to tell you back."

His smile spread—the one that promised their bright shiny future was theirs for the taking—and he wrapped his arms around her waist. "Tell me now, baby."

"I'll tell you every day. I love you, Campbell Steele."

"I love you, too, Abigail McBane."

"Forever." She whispered the promise against his lips and let it unfurl in her heart.

Epilogue

Abby sat in the living room of the Upper East Side brownstone that also acted as the main conference room for House of Steele. Kensington had a bottle of champagne chilling on the sideboard and Abby didn't miss the anticipatory glances Campbell kept shooting toward the door.

"Have you met our grandfather?" Rowan reached for a square of cheese off the large tray Kensington had placed in the center of the table.

"Yes, but it's been years and I'm quite sure he won't remember me."

"Of course I remember you." A deep voice, thick with the sounds of Britain, echoed off the wall as Alexander Steele marched into the conference room behind his wife.

"Mr. Steele." Abby stood and took comfort from Campbell's hand which sat on her lower back.

"Come here."

He barked the order with such force she didn't dare disobey and stepped forward, skirting the edge of the conference table.

"It's lovely to see you again, Mr. Steele." She nodded to Campbell's grandmother, Penelope, who looked resigned to her husband's antics. "Mrs. Steele."

"So you've snared my grandson." Alexander Steele's words were frank as he continued to stare her in the eye, that rheumy blue gaze still as sharp as ever.

"Um, well…" She broke off at the mischievous smile that rode his features. It was a smile she knew well and whatever anxiety she'd felt waiting for the arrival of Campbell's grandparents fled on swift wings. "Well, yes."

"Good for you. Smart girl. I always knew it. Always suspected you two would make a fine match."

Penelope waved her husband off. "Don't listen to him. He has no idea what he's talking about."

"Not true, Penny!" Alexander bellowed. "Not true. I told you about these two years ago. That time Abby came and you dragged her through Harrods for three days. I said it to you then."

Penelope's gaze turned speculative before she turned back to her husband. "So you did."

Campbell leaned forward and kissed his grandmother before turning to shake his grandfather's hand. "I wasn't aware fortune-teller was in your job description."

"I can see what's in front of my own eyes. That's not fortune-telling, that's being observant."

Truth be told, Abby thought the man had a rather valid point.

"But Abby and I didn't meet on her visit to London all those years ago."

"I knew, anyway."

Campbell winked at her before turning back to his grandfather. "Just like you know everything."

"Everything worth knowing."

Campbell helped his grandparents to their seats as Kensington took care of the champagne. Despite Alexander's formidable presence, Abby observed Campbell's gentle care of his aging grandparents and felt another tick mark go up in the "reasons she loved him" column.

As if she needed another.

Kensington filled the glasses and Rowan passed them around and it was only when everyone had a flute in hand that Alexander stood up once more.

Lifting his glass he turned to Abby and Campbell. "There's never been a day since my grandchildren arrived that I haven't thanked God for them. But I'd be remiss in not saying I'd have always loved to have more."

Alexander extended his glass toward her and Abby touched her flute lightly to his. "To my new granddaughter. I had to wait a bit longer for you, but I've no doubt you'll be well worth the wait."

The happy sound of clinking glasses and laughing conversation filled the room as Abby leaned forward to kiss Alexander.

And when he patted her on the back and told her he expected she'd give his grandson hell and make him enjoy each and every minute of it, Abby knew she'd found her family.

For years she'd drifted, alone in the world.

But it was Campbell Steele who had brought her home.

* * * * *

Will House of Steele continue to expand?
Find out in THE LONDON DECEPTION,
where Rowan Steele puts her skills to use,
just as her past returns to haunt her....

REQUEST YOUR FREE BOOKS!

2 FREE NOVELS PLUS 2 FREE GIFTS!

⊞ HARLEQUIN®

ROMANTIC suspense

Sparked by danger, fueled by passion

YES! Please send me 2 FREE Harlequin® Romantic Suspense novels and my 2 FREE gifts (gifts are worth about $10). After receiving them, if I don't wish to receive any more books, I can return the shipping statement marked "cancel." If I don't cancel, I will receive 4 brand-new novels every month and be billed just $4.74 per book in the U.S. or $5.24 per book in Canada. That's a savings of at least 14% off the cover price! It's quite a bargain! Shipping and handling is just 50¢ per book in the U.S. and 75¢ per book in Canada.* I understand that accepting the 2 free books and gifts places me under no obligation to buy anything. I can always return a shipment and cancel at any time. Even if I never buy another book, the two free books and gifts are mine to keep forever.

240/340 HDN F45N

Name	(PLEASE PRINT)	
Address		Apt. #
City	State/Prov.	Zip/Postal Code

Signature (if under 18, a parent or guardian must sign)

Mail to the **Harlequin® Reader Service:**

IN U.S.A.: P.O. Box 1867, Buffalo, NY 14240-1867
IN CANADA: P.O. Box 609, Fort Erie, Ontario L2A 5X3

Want to try two free books from another line?
Call 1-800-873-8635 or visit www.ReaderService.com.

* Terms and prices subject to change without notice. Prices do not include applicable taxes. Sales tax applicable in N.Y. Canadian residents will be charged applicable taxes. Offer not valid in Quebec. This offer is limited to one order per household. Not valid for current subscribers to Harlequin Romantic Suspense books. All orders subject to credit approval. Credit or debit balances in a customer's account(s) may be offset by any other outstanding balance owed by or to the customer. Please allow 4 to 6 weeks for delivery. Offer available while quantities last.

Your Privacy—The Harlequin® Reader Service is committed to protecting your privacy. Our Privacy Policy is available online at www.ReaderService.com or upon request from the Harlequin Reader Service.

We make a portion of our mailing list available to reputable third parties that offer products we believe may interest you. If you prefer that we not exchange your name with third parties, or if you wish to clarify or modify your communication preferences, please visit us at www.ReaderService.com/consumerschoice or write to us at Harlequin Reader Service Preference Service, P.O. Box 9062, Buffalo, NY 14269. Include your complete name and address.

SPECIAL EXCERPT FROM

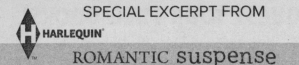

HARLEQUIN®

ROMANTIC suspense

No one believes Nev's disturbing dreams are coming true. But when her life is threatened, Detective Ty Gadney risks it all—including his heart—to find the truth.

Read on for a sneak peek of

COPPER LAKE ENCOUNTER

by Marilyn Pappano, coming August 2013 from Harlequin Romantic Suspense.

He saw her car before it turned into the lot. By the time she'd parked a few spaces down from his, he was there, opening the door, helping her out. Her coffee-with-cream eyes were filled with concern, and she looked graver than he'd ever seen her.

"I'm not going to like this, am I?"

He shook his head. With his hand barely touching her upper arm, they walked across the parking lot and right up to the open door. Her jaw tightened, her mouth forming a thin line, as she looked inside, her gaze locking for a moment on each note. It was hard to say which one disturbed her most. It was the stick figure that bothered Ty, the idea of taking something so simple and innocent as a child's drawing and turning it into a threat. From the tension radiating through her, he would guess it was the knife in the pillow that got to her.

"The crime-scene techs are on their way over," Kiki said. "Does anything appear to be missing?"

Nev shook her head. "The only thing I have of any value is my laptop, and it's in the room safe."

"Do you think this was done by the same boys who sprayed shaving cream on my car last night?" Nev asked, her demeanor calm, her voice quiet with just the littlest bit of a quaver.

"No." Kiki was blunt, as usual. "Gavin and Kevin Holigan are twelve and thirteen. They probably can't spell that well, and besides, this isn't their style."

"Do you have any problems at home in Atlanta?"

Nev smiled wryly. "No. I live with my mother, grandmother and sister. I work at home. I go to church every Sunday and Wednesday. I don't have any enemies there. I don't inspire that kind of passion, Detective."

Those self-doubts again. Ty didn't doubt she believed that. She had no clue what kind of passion she could inspire. He wanted nothing more than an opportunity to show her.

He needed nothing more than to keep her safe.

**Don't miss
COPPER LAKE ENCOUNTER
by Marilyn Pappano,
available August 2013 from
Harlequin Romantic Suspense.**

SADDLE UP AND READ 'EM!

Looking for another great Western read? Check out this August read from the SUSPENSE category!

TAKING AIM by Elle James
Covert Cowboys, Inc.
From Harlequin Intrigue

*Look for this great Western read AND MORE
available wherever books are sold or visit*
www.Harlequin.com/Westerns